AN EAR FOR TROUBLE

RIVERBEND K-9S: BOOK 2

K.T. LEE

VERTICAL LINE PUBLISHING, LLC

K.T. Lee

www.ktleeauthor.com

Publisher's Note: This work of fiction is a product of the writer's overactive imagination. It is not intended to be a factual representation of events, people, locales, businesses, government agencies, or wildlife biology. Names are used fictitiously and any resemblance to actual people, living or dead, is completely coincidental. Resemblance to the writer's dogs, past and present, however, is almost guaranteed.

An Ear for Trouble/ K.T. Lee - 1st ed.

Paperback ISBN: 978-1-947870-21-5

Hardback ISBN: 978-1-947870-22-2

Cover Design by Rachel Lawston

For my family

PROLOGUE

FBI Special Agent Finn Cooper cleared a path through the dense Nepalese jungle. Sedona, his yellow Labrador retriever, followed close behind. Light rain masked the noise of their footsteps, but occasionally, Finn heard the tap of his K-9 partner's wagging tail against the wet leaves. Tonight, they were searching for something deadlier than the tigers Sedona had been trained to detect; they were looking for the two-legged mammals who trapped, sold, and killed endangered species for profit. The FBI believed the animal traffickers were responsible for the death of a local man. Thanks to a tip from the man's family, Finn had spent the past several weeks in Nepal, building trust with a small but passionate local crew. Tonight, with his help, they'd find the poachers' campsite amidst the dense vegetation of the Nepalese national park. At worst, they'd stop this group. At best, they'd finally figure out who was paying for the whole operation.

Finn spotted a barely visible flash of metal. He swore, quickly disabling the wire snare. It was designed to catch wild animals, often injuring them or trapping them until the person who set it returned. If they returned. Unfortunately, the snares were much harder to find than they were to purchase and set. Finn stuffed the now-disabled snare into his backpack, sure as Sedona on a scent that the wire meant he was on the right track.

While the FBI generally focused on problems stateside, the illegally captured and killed animals were being monetized in the United States. Finn had quickly discovered from his new allies that the trades they'd intercepted were coming from this national park. He considered it his duty to stop the citizens of his country from causing any more ecological damage. If he could find the group of poachers tonight, the FBI could finally do more than stem the bleeding by confiscating their wares.

Behind him, Sedona barked. Finn froze. It was unusual for his well-trained partner to bark while on duty. She often moved more silently than he. Slowly, Finn took a careful step. Eyes sweeping the path ahead, he spotted the danger and unwound another snare that would have hit him at knee level. He ground his teeth, pushing back a growl of frustration. Focused on untangling the metal wire, he didn't notice the well-camouflaged trap at his feet. Before he realized what was happening, he heard a snap, felt a sharp pain in his leg, and went down. Hard.

CHAPTER 1

*E*lise Butler poured herself a cup of coffee with less than a minute to spare before her 6:00 a.m. meeting. She shuffled over to the kitchen table and sat in front of her laptop to start her virtual meeting with the Riverbend Animal Conservation Center. She was still wearing her fuzzy slippers and comfy pajama pants, but they were paired with a professional top since it would be a video call. Her friends balked at her schedule, but she'd always been an early bird. Still, she made some allowances for comfort when it was dark o'clock, morning person or not.

Elise's laptop made a cheerful sound and her computer connected to her regular meeting with Kai Torres and Heath Green, the head zookeeper and director of the Riverbend Animal Conservation Center, respectively. Today, they'd also invited Dr. Oliver, the Center's long-serving veterinarian, to talk about the clouded leopard breeding program. The Center's expertise in breeding endangered animals was well known within the animal conservation community, and Dr. Oliver was the Species Survival Plan coordinator for clouded leopards in the United States.

Less well known in the zoo community were the Center's

recent financial problems, which, after a few weeks of combing through their financial records, were even worse than Elise had expected. Located half an hour from her sister Zoey's new home in Riverbend, Indiana, the Riverbend Animal Conservation Center was a recent addition to the World Wildlife Trust's list of partner members. Given the Center's proximity to her sister, Elise had eagerly volunteered to help complete their official financial assessment and provide support as needed. As the WWT's key finance contact, a business visit was virtually guaranteed. Elise travelled frequently for work and had become skilled at squeezing in a visit to a friend or her sister whenever she could.

Elise checked the time and took her first sip of coffee. It was unusual for Kai to be late for their calls, so he must have a good reason. While she waited, she pulled up her latest projections for the Riverbend Animal Conservation Center's expenses and deposits. The Center's finances were, in short, a mess. Their previous accountant was the cousin of the niece of a friend hired by Heath after he'd been selected to lead the facility. Elise had found this out (without asking) from Heath's administrative assistant, Freya Griffin, who had also worked for the previous three directors. Once Elise realized how dire their financial situation was, she'd quietly offered to help the RACC sort out their financial challenges beyond the WWT's usual level of support. The RACC had accepted Elise's help, albeit grudgingly, once it became clear that proving that they were financially stable enough to care for their animals long-term would be a condition of their membership.

After some initial awkwardness, the Center had largely been receptive to Elise's sometimes-critical feedback on their budgeting strategies. And, thanks to the Riverbend gossip tree, Elise had heard from Zoey, who heard from the local coffee shop owner, who heard from the owner of her favorite pub, that the Riverbend Animal Conservation Center employees were happy with her work. Freya occasionally complained to the proprietor of the local pub that the WWT was bringing in big-city ideas when they just needed to realize that one plus one didn't equal three, but she didn't seem to have a problem with Elise personally. And even if Elise hadn't heard the feedback from Zoey, Kai's friendly demeanor and willingness to collaborate had made it clear enough. They shared an easy camaraderie, even though their working relationship had been entirely remote. Kai's support had made slogging through Riverbend's financial plan a little less exhausting. Despite the financial hurdles they would need to overcome, the Riverbend Animal Conservation Center had recently welcomed two clouded leopard cubs. They were now a few months old and completely adorable. She wasn't sure how anyone could look at the cubs and not feel at least a little hopeful.

Elise considered her still-empty virtual meeting room and tapped her fingers on the kitchen table she'd refurbished with her sister. Something must have come up. With her cursor hovering over the "End Meeting" button, Kai's face finally appeared on the screen. He was alone in the zoo's conference room. Even before he even spoke, it was clear something was wrong. While Kai wore his usual khakis and his well-loved coffee mug was in its normal place on the conference table, his short black hair was messy and his face was drawn, unusual for the affable zookeeper. "Good morning, Elise. How are you?"

"Forget about me, Kai. Is everything okay?" After all of their work together, Elise considered Kai a friend, and as a friend, the only right thing to do was to pry. As soon as reasonably possible.

Kai closed his eyes. "Dr. Oliver won't be making it to our meeting today. He's gone. Missing. We've reported it to the police, but even his family has no idea where he went. He's not taking calls, he's not home. No one knows where he is. I've already spoken to the sheriff." He ran a hand through his hair, only further mussing it. "Heath is busy dealing with all of it. So, he won't be here either."

"Oh, Kai, of course. I wouldn't expect it. I'm so sorry. You don't need to meet with me right now."

"It's okay." Kai rubbed his temples. "I needed to catch you up. You may need to run interference with your management at the WWT if this all blows up. Heath is running around like a chicken with his head cut off telling everyone here to stay calm."

"That's a horribly unoriginal idiom for a zookeeper, Kai," Elise pointed out, trying to break the tension. She could spot a vein throbbing in his forehead even with the low resolution of the video.

Kai sighed. "You're right. Maybe we'll go with a frightened rhino? But that assumes Heath is destructive. Really, he's amped up and trying to find out if anyone knows where Dr. Oliver could be. Even Freya can't get him back to regular stress levels. But that may be because she's leaving the office to sneak cigarettes behind the construction site, even though she told us all she was quitting."

"You should ask her if she wants your help," Elise said, with a mischievous smile. "That went over really well for me when I asked if she needed my help sorting invoices."

Kai snorted. "Not likely. I know better than to suggest she's not keeping up. She is a force of nature, and like all forces of nature, you want her working for you, not against you."

Elise reached for her coffee mug, tapping her fuzzy slipper against the ground. "Do what you have to do to manage your stressed-out rhino/chicken. And to get your force of nature focusing her energy in the right places." Elise took another drink of coffee. "All kidding aside, let me know if I can help. Is there a search party or anything?"

"In a place like Riverbend? Oh yeah. The sheriff is looking. He's got connections with handlers from the Riverbend K-9 Academy who have offered their assistance as well, for whatever good it will do. The last anyone heard, Olly was headed home. They found his car near some running trails, so we think he might have been going out for a run. No one wants to overreact, but normally, he is super dependable. It's so out of character for him to fall off the map. Something happened, I just know it."

Elise stilled her foot, then started tapping her fingers on the kitchen table. "Okay, you keep tabs on the search party. If we don't hear anything soon, I can get someone else in our network on deck to help with the day-to-day. We can probably get support from a vet we work with in the Indy area, Dr. Veronica Perry."

"Okay. Yeah. That'd be good." Kai cleared his throat. "She's been here before. Anyway, hopefully this is nothing. I'm sure Dr. Oliver will turn up. I'm sorry to burden you with this. It's probably nothing. I mean, I hope it's nothing. I'd love to call you this afternoon and tell you everything has been blown totally out of proportion. Best case scenario for sure." Kai took a long drink from his sky-blue travel mug, emblazoned with RACC's old logo. She almost teased him about the missing "R" from the logo, long worn away from use, but it didn't seem like the right time.

Elise wished she could give something beyond video-chat-based platitudes, but even the wonders of technology had their limitations. "I almost hate to ask, but is everything else okay?"

Kai winced. "No." His shoulders dropped and he stared at his coffee mug. "We lost Atma, one of our clouded leopard cubs. Yesterday. Before Olly went missing, he sent an email letting me know our cub had died unexpectedly. It was the last I heard from him. I thought we could talk about it this morning, but..." Elise's heart ached at the extra layer of pain in Kai's voice. Yes, his job provided an income, but his work was a labor of love. Kai was one of the many keepers who got to know their animals, even naming them something meaningful from their native countries. Atma's name originated from Nepal, one of several countries in Southeast Asia their clouded leopards called home. "Between you and me,

I'm worried his disappearance has something to do with Atma's death. Olly works so hard and was even helping me hand-raise the cubs."

"Was there something wrong with them? Why did they need to be hand-raised?" Elise tipped her head.

"It's what's considered best practice right now for clouded leopard breeding programs. It means it's harder for us not to get attached. Olly was as proud as any dad I've ever seen when our mama, Daxa, had babies." He looked to the ceiling. "I just hope he didn't go do something risky because he was upset."

"Did Dr. Oliver say what happened to the cub? It wasn't mom leopard, was it?" Elise cringed. As much as she didn't want to ask the question, WWT would need to word the release carefully, so as not to upset the animal lovers in the community. The fact was that no matter how cute the clouded leopards were, they were still wild animals.

Kai shook his head. "No, they could see each other but were physically separated. Oliver's notes in the system said there was no sign of injury. He suspected a bacterial infection but was light on other details. He sent a short email explaining that he'd completed extra cleaning, sent the cub out for further testing and that he would add more information later. He said he'd be back today, but then he disappeared."

Elise felt a headache forming. No wonder Dr. Oliver had gone for a run to work off the stress. And unfortunately for Elise's equation-driven brain, her next thought went straight to the financial impact of the loss. The Riverbend Animal Conservation Center had taken out a loan to build an extension onto the zoo, including an updated clouded leopard habitat that was nearly finished. Heath had proudly shown off RACC's five-year plan, explaining that the extra space would increase the number of people coming to the Center, and therefore increase donations. It was admirably ambitious, but not a great time to be taking that kind of financial risk. However, Heath's decision had been championed by the cousin of a niece of a friend prior to the Center's partnering with the World Wildlife Trust. The new space, at least, had been designed by Kai, who had been assured (incorrectly) that it was well within the financial capacity of the Center. At least his skill had contributed to creating best-practice facilities that would stand the test of time. As long as Elise could keep RACC afloat long enough to pay for it. She closed her eyes. They'd make the numbers work. Somehow.

"Okay. Good. I mean, it's not good. It's obviously bad. But, it could be worse." Elise stared into her now-empty coffee cup. Today was going to take a refill. Or two. Regardless of past decisions and current chaos, it was her job to help keep the Conservation Center running well into the future. As insensitive as it might sound, the more practical side of her felt some measure of relief that their leopard had had multiple cubs. At least one remained to help expand the clouded leopard population and bring in people to visit. The less they had to worry about money, the more animals could be helped by their work. It was as simple as that. However, Kai's worry for his friend and grief for the cub was more important than her overdeveloped sense of responsibility for all of the Center's financial problems. She refocused on Kai. "I'm so sorry, friend. I mean, teammate."

Kai gave her a rueful smile. "No worries, Elise. I'm glad to call you a friend too. And thank you. It's been a tough week. I'll feel better when I know Dr. Oliver is safe and sound. I can't remember when I last got a full night's sleep. For the past few months, it was for the more exciting reason that we had new zoo babies and now...well, I shouldn't be bothering you with my worries. My landlord probably thinks I've been out partying every night."

Elise chuckled. "Ah yes, the glamorous life of a zookeeper. You might shock your landlord if you tell them how much cleaning is involved."

Kai's eyes got a little of the twinkle back. "Thurston is pretty hard to shock."

"Wait, the mayor is your landlord?"

Kai grinned. "I forget you have family here. As your sister may have mentioned, Thurston is also the proprietor of Bridges, the best and only pub in Riverbend. He's also on the board of directors of RACC, so I suspect he cut me a deal on my apartment above Bridges."

"Small world. But hey, knowing the locals in Riverbend at least makes me look like I know what I'm talking about." Elise took a sip from her mug, then shook her head when she realized it was still empty. "You know, I've been meaning to come visit to meet everyone. Now seems like a good time."

"You want to come in the middle of all of this?" Kai waved his hand at the imaginary chaos. "We're short-staffed and you'll likely get roped into cleaning out animal habitats. Of even the large animals." His brown eyes lit up with challenge.

Elise raised an eyebrow. "I'm not afraid of a little dirty work. Let me send an email to Director Kim to see if I can come help you all out for a while, at least until things settle down. Frankly, after what you've been through, coming out to organize your books and help out around the Center sounds downright easy. I mean, it's first thing in the morning and your problems are elephant-sized already. Honestly, Kai, what else could go wrong?"

CHAPTER 2

*E*lise spent the rest of her morning in back-to-back virtual meetings with World Wildlife Trust partners scattered throughout the U.S. She didn't pay as much attention as she should, subtly checking her email and phone for updates from the Riverbend Animal Conservation Center. After her call with Kai, the other tasks of the day seemed less urgent. Elise connected a few partners interested in swapping porcupines and helped one animal rescue center advocate for themselves when they had been overcharged by a vendor. A firmly worded email from Elise with the World Wildlife Trust's attorney copied motivated the vendor to fix the error but left her thoroughly annoyed by how quickly she'd solved a problem the small not-for-profit had been fighting for months. But, then, that was why the WWT existed. They didn't own their partners, instead serving as a hub for collaboration. The various zoos, aquariums, and rescue centers all pitched in to fund a common resource pool where they could come for help, including when they needed the muscle of a knowledgeable lawyer for an hour or two per year.

Like with the porcupines, the WWT also acted as a third party to facilitate animal trades between zoos. This helped to maintain a genetically diverse captive population while staying away from any actions that would encourage animal trafficking. It wasn't usually as simple as swapping animals, though; the trades themselves could get quite complex. The WWT also ensured all animals involved in the trades would be well cared for and had a plan for where they would live out their lives. Elise's team made it a point to know the people on the ground, not just on the phone. She checked her email again, but there were no more updates. The Riverbend Animal Conservation Center was past due for a visit even without the soap opera-level drama of the morning. When Elise finally got a break between meetings, she sent a detailed update to her boss and offered to visit if needed.

Elise checked her watch and stepped away to take a walk so she could get through the next few hours of sitting at her kitchen table without her legs completely falling asleep or her activity tracker shaming her into moving. While she normally preferred tactile crafts to relax, there wasn't exactly time for it this morning. She'd been outside for what felt like only a few minutes when her phone buzzed with an urgent meeting request from the director of the WWT, Carmen Kim. In person. Downtown. In less than an hour.

Elise sprinted back to her apartment, fluffed her hair in the mirror, and changed into a skirt suit. She locked the door and pushed against it for one final check before digging to make sure her car keys were in her purse. She'd had a break-in a few months ago, and still hadn't completely recovered her faith in people. Granted, the break-in was part of a novel-worthy plot to explode a battery farm, and the burglars weren't there to hurt her, but she'd still gotten a sprained wrist and more than one sleepless night out of the ordeal. Elise shuddered to think of what could have been. She'd been taking self-defense classes to help her rebuild her confidence, but there was something invasive and personal about a break-in that would take a little more time to shake. She'd love to live in a close-knit town like Zoey, but her job required travel, and travel required an airport.

Elise plugged the address for the World Wildlife Trust offices into her GPS and quickly glanced at the time. She was going to have to hustle *and* get lucky with parking and traffic in downtown Denver. After a tense drive, watching her GPS's predicted arrival time creep up one minute at a time, Elise broke into the closest thing to a jog that was possible in heels on her trip from the parking garage to the offices. Moments later, she stood outside Dr. Kim's office, fanning herself to cool her face and trying to slow her breathing from the unexpectedly athletic trip. The wait in the silent area outside of Dr. Kim's closed door was implausibly harder than the drive. Elise ran a hand through her long, wavy brown hair, probably worsening the frizz she'd created in the car. Oh well. A soft, natural look was in style, wasn't it?

Dr. Kim opened the door and gave her a warm smile, but Elise wasn't fooled by her petite stature or welcoming personality. If ever there was a human embodiment of, "Do no harm but take no bull," it was Carmen Kim. With no small amount of curiosity about why Carmen wanted to meet with her on short notice, Elise joined the director of the World Wildlife Trust in her office. Dr. Kim was dressed in a classy blouse and tailored trousers, her sleek, black hair pulled back in a neat ponytail. She wore chunky ceramic beaded jewelry that clicked softly when she moved.

Dr. Kim gestured to her guest chair. "Please, have a seat. How are you doing, Elise?"

"Fine, Dr. Kim," Elise said, still a little out of breath. She technically reported to Dr. Kim, but most of their conversations came in the form of update presentations or emails, rather than face-to-face meetings. Her boss had a full schedule with plenty of travel and didn't usually give her much one-on-one attention, so their relationship had a more formal air than Elise normally had with her colleagues. Particularly when she'd been summoned at a moment's notice. She fidgeted in her seat. "I'm sorry, but did I do something wrong?"

"No, no, not at all. And, please, Carmen is fine." Her hazel eyes sparkled with intelligence. "I had a free moment on my calendar and wanted to talk about the email you sent."

"Kai said that sort of thing happens to cubs sometimes. And we're not sure that Dr. Oliver is...well, we think he's missing. And probably upset by the news. He'll turn up, I'm sure." Elise furrowed her eyebrows. "I don't have to go to Riverbend. It's just that Kai seemed stressed about the cub's death and I've been meaning to go anyway. Full disclosure, my sister lives in Riverbend and I would definitely tie in a visit with her on this trip. I can keep working on the numbers remotely — I just have a personal interest. That is to say, I don't want to see them fail."

Dr. Kim gave her a sympathetic smile. "They're doing better than they were, thanks in no small part to your personal interest in the facility's success. And I didn't call you in to talk about the cub, although the death is extremely sad. I think you know Heath Green, the director of the Riverbend Animal Conservation Center? He called me personally after you sent the email. The local sheriff believes, based on the evidence they found this morning, that Dr. Oliver passed away during a run yesterday evening. Heath is still holding out hope, and he wanted me to keep the faith too, if I heard the news." Her eyes were gentle. "I think Heath unintentionally made the case to send someone a little more objective to help at the Center. I'm so sorry to be the one to break the news to you, Elise. Did you know Dr. Oliver well?"

"Not as much as I would have liked, but from what I knew of him, he seemed really nice. Kai talked about him on our calls, and I spoke to him on occasion." Elise exhaled with a whoosh. "Still, that's awful. I should send a card to his family. Or flowers. Are we doing that? Can I help?"

Dr. Kim waved her concerns away. "Yes, we will handle all of that, but I'm afraid we just started getting the Riverbend facility on the right track. We have some major donors with an interest in the clouded leopard program asking for updates. Riverbend is the most successful of any of our leopard breeding programs. The death of the SSP coordinator and a cub in the same week is obviously concerning. We've very nearly secured funds to support a clouded leopard habitat restoration project in Bhutan, and Riverbend's program had been bringing it the right kind of attention. I've fielded several questions about the clouded leopard project this month alone. How would you feel about staying for a while to make sure they're really back on their feet? It's unconventional, but you're the kind of Swiss Army knife employee they need. Goodness, with your background, you could probably run the place if you wanted to."

"Oh wow. That's kind of you to say." Elise considered the unexpected and appealing offer to spend more time on the ground with one of their partners. She'd started her career at a big city accounting firm, but she'd always been passionate about helping animals, even majoring in wildlife biology in college and interning at zoos. However, after she lost her parents in college, she added an accounting major to her college program. After she graduated, finance had seemed like the more predictable and stable career path. She counted herself lucky that she'd escaped the drab cubicle walls of her old accounting job and re-careered herself into a position that married her two passions with the World Wildlife Trust. Elise straightened. "Of course, I'm happy to help. If that's what the WWT wants. I can still do some finance work remotely if you need me to. This will just redirect my work to help fund one of our most important projects. Yeah. That makes sense."

"Great. I'll let the Riverbend facility know." Carmen reshuffled papers on her desk.

Elise scrunched her nose. "Is the Riverbend facility going to be happy someone from the mothership is descending upon them? Especially after losing their veterinarian? I mean, it wasn't something violent, but their veterinarian dying is still pretty traumatic." Just that fast, her memory whipped her back to a hospital hallway with her sister, finding out her father didn't make it, the smell of disinfectant still in her nose. She closed her eyes and took a deep breath of the smell in Carmen's office, including the light scent of vanilla hand cream sitting on her desk. She rubbed her temples. "And also, I don't feel right gaining something I want because...we lost a colleague."

"No one would think of it that way. Riverbend is our newest partner. It'd be a feather in our cap to show donors what we can do and how far we can stretch a dollar. The more dollars we stretch, the more animals we help."

Elise finished Carmen's thought with the organization's motto. "And 'every animal counts.' I'll go. If you're sure it's okay."

"Can I level with you, Elise?" Carmen's bright eyes bored into her. "No one else here is begging me to let them go to rural Indiana. The line to go release animals back into their native habitats halfway across the world is quite a bit longer. Honestly, you'd be doing all of us a favor." She looked back at her computer. "I think we can have you out there for three months since you're willing to pitch in a bit remotely. Does that work?"

Because of the unfortunate circumstances, Elise managed to keep from jumping out of her chair to pack. "Yeah, okay. I think I could manage that."

"And hey, with any luck Heath is right and there's no reason for us to be worried. Then, it'll be a pleasant trip to do some PR and visit your sister, and you can come back a little early."

"That's a nice thought, Carmen. And if we aren't that lucky, I'll help Riverbend get back on their feet."

CHAPTER 3

Finn Cooper woke up in an unfamiliar bed with a familiar nose in his face. "Morning, pretty girl." Sedona thwacked her tail against a wooden nightstand. She was small for a Labrador retriever and remarkably nimble while navigating the jungle foliage so unlike her native habitat. Which, if Sedona was to be believed, was on Finn's bed. Since he didn't believe her, and she was a bit of a bed hog, she always slept on a mat not far from his hand. That way, she could push her head into it for easier petting when he woke up. He rolled over to check the time on his phone. After some clumsy self-administered field first aid, a bush plane ride to a tiny airport, hobbling through two more stopover airports to a hospital, and crossing through more countries than he could count, he was in the U.S. Not in a jungle with a tent above his head. More specifically, he was now in rural Indiana. He'd been lucky the metal trap had been faulty, or the damage would have been much worse. Instead of a broken leg, he was only recovering from jagged muscle injuries. They'd been thoroughly treated and stitched up but still needed to be babied for a little longer to fully heal.

Finn sat up and blinked. Sedona stretched, wagging her thick tail in the air. His rented, furnished apartment in Riverbend, Indiana was an upgrade compared to the cheap furniture and sparse décor in his own place in D.C. His "permanent" apartment mostly just held his stuff. Neat piles of supplies by job type and go-bags outnumbered actual furniture. He'd gotten used to packing light when he was camping and didn't have much use for throw pillows and wall art when he was travelling so much. Generally, the FBI left wildlife trafficking to the U.S. Fish and Wildlife Service, but he and Sedona helped whenever the crimes turned transnational. And unfortunately, Finn and Sedona had plenty of work to keep them busy. There was always more work than there were humans and their dogs, but they did what they could with what they had. He rubbed a hand down his face, catching the scent of teeth that desperately needed to be brushed.

After a quick stop in the bathroom to brush his teeth, Finn padded out to the bright kitchen with white cabinets and a teal subway tile backsplash. His rented one-bedroom apartment was packed with luxuries he hadn't had while camping, like climate control, running water, and coffee he didn't have to brew himself; the River Bean coffee shop was only a short walk downstairs. Sedona did a dance and made a noise that told him it was time to go outside, whether he'd had his coffee or not. Finn pulled on a shirt and took her for a quick walk. Then he popped back into his apartment to get ready for work. Getting ready wasn't a complicated process for him — the only thing that stood between him and his coffee was the time it took to bask in the warm, fresh water coming out of the shower and get a quick shave in with his electric razor. Before the morning crowd had cleared out, he too was in line downstairs to get his morning brew from the proprietor, and his landlord, Marlene Francis. She had short, white hair with light lavender tips, and her flowing dress moved with her when she walked. She operated the coffee shop with the kind of efficiency his old Navy buddies would admire.

"Good morning, honey." Marlene gave him a wave as he entered. She poured steamed milk into a mostly full, white to-go cup and slid it across the bar to a waiting patron. She looked past the patron at Finn. "You settle in okay?"

Finn nodded. "I'm a little tired but I slept like a baby. Can I get a large black coffee, splash of cream?"

"Of course. First one's on the house." Marlene filled up a cup and gave it to him in the ceramic mug used for customers who planned on staying with their drink instead of darting out the door. Finn almost snickered at the very deliberate choice she made for him. Okay, the Navy would appreciate both her efficiency and interrogation skills. Marlene gestured to one of the large glass jars where she kept her teas, but this one was filled with dog treats. "Can I give your pup a treat?"

Sedona looked up at Marlene as if yes, she had never had a dog treat before and Marlene was the very first person in the world to realize it. Finn shook his head and rummaged in a bag at his waist. Sedona sat perfectly, maintaining eye contact with the bag as if it was a staring contest. Finn grinned. "I'd normally say yes, but Sedona is on a limited diet. You can come around and give her a piece of her kibble though."

Marlene glided around the counter and took the food, holding her palm out. Sedona gently removed the food and swished her tail. "Good girl." Marlene put her hands on her hips. "You'll be working with Alexis then?"

Finn choked on his coffee. "Sorry. Alexis who?"

"Honey, it's a small town. And you all have a look. And the treats — her dogs always have rules about what they can take from whom." Finn took a gulp of too-hot coffee, wincing at the burn on the way down. Marlene waved away his unspoken panic. "Don't fret. I'm just saying what everyone is thinking. Croissant?"

Finn looked into his coffee cup. "I don't think that's as reassuring as you think it is."

"There isn't anything secretive about being an instructor, anyway. It's obvious you aren't a student. You clearly know what you're doing and they put the new students up in the apartments close to the K-9 Academy. You didn't answer — did you want a croissant with that coffee?"

Finn blinked twice, then nodded. "Sure. A croissant would be great." Perhaps letting Marlene think she'd gotten one up on him was a better idea than laying low and not talking about what he did, hoping no one in Riverbend would notice one extra person. Obviously, he'd underestimated the little town. Not exactly reassuring for his first twenty-four hours on site. He really was going to be an instructor, after all. However, even the head of the school, Alexis Thompson, hadn't been fully briefed on all of his plans in Riverbend. Before he could think of how to embellish his backstory, Marlene slid a chocolate croissant across the countertop on a bright yellow plate. "Thank you, ma'am."

"Of course. Since she's a working dog, Sedona is welcome here anytime. And if you have good manners, you are too." Marlene started wiping down a counter and Finn bit into the flakey, buttery pastry with a rich, dark chocolate stripe running down the center. He savored the treat and watched to see if anyone besides his landlord was curious about him. Everyone else seemed absorbed in their own issues, books, and cell phones. Finn finished the coffee, wiped his crumbs onto his plate, and walked to the door. His leg was doing better now that he'd cleared a fairly aggressive infection, but his nerves still went on the fritz with shocks of pain when he sat still for too long. He probably should have given it another week before getting back to work, but his patience couldn't take it anymore. The FBI didn't have anyone else available to chase down his lead. Riverbend would be as good a place as any to recover.

And it was the perfect place to figure out why, when his team had traced the calls and emails sent to the animal trafficking ring responsible for his injury, they had come from Riverbend, Indiana.

CHAPTER 4

"*Z*oey, you aren't going to believe this, but I managed to get a long business trip to Riverbend!" Elise put her phone on speaker so she could multitask packing with sharing the news with her sister. Before Zoey could respond, Elise continued, "Not a vacation, an actual job. It's only for a few months, but they're in desperate need of some help at the Riverbend Animal Conservation Center. The World Wildlife Trust asked if I could pitch in." Elise twirled a length of her brown, wavy hair as the words spilled out of her mouth.

"Wow, Elise. That's great news." Zoey's tone was more subdued than Elise expected. Zoey ran a little on the nervous side, but her high energy and love for her family were genuine. Her hesitation stopped Elise short.

Elise froze, holding a folded shirt in midair above her suitcase. "Zo, what aren't you telling me?"

There was a long pause. "Did they tell you why you're going?"

"Oh, that's it? Wait. Do you know already? Heath said he was only telling people who worked at the Center until we have more information." Elise dropped the shirt into the open suitcase on her bed. "Never mind. I forgot the Riverbend K-9 Academy employees were helping with the search. Of course, you know."

"Oh yeah. Dr. Oliver's disappearance is an open secret here. They couldn't have communicated it more effectively if they'd put a billboard on the highway on the way into town. Especially since it's supposed to be a secret. You'll have a lot to deal with while you're here."

"Oh yeah. I assumed that'd be the case. I'm coming to help."

"Oh, okay." Zoey blew out a breath. "One second." The line went silent and Elise waited as the seconds ticked by. Zoey unmuted her line. "I'm back."

"Is everything alright?"

"Yeah. No. Yeah. I had to chase Tasha. She found a…squirrel." Tasha was Zoey's extremely well-trained partner/explosives detection dog.

Elise stopped digging through her shirt drawer and put her hand on her hip. "Okay, that's a load of nonsense and we both know it. What aren't you telling me?"

"Just one minute." The line went silent again, then clicked back on. "Okay, Mr. Procedures said I can share since I'm not going to let it go. And he's right," Zoey said, Elise suspected, for the benefit of Liam, her boyfriend and instructor at the Riverbend K-9 Academy. "Liam helped with the search and he felt like it was a little odd. Based on the marks on the ground, the sheriff, who Mr. Procedures would like me to mention has jurisdiction, concluded that Dr. Oliver had some kind of heart attack or medical issue and fell in a hard-to-access area. I know Heath is hopeful, but the sheriff doesn't think Dr. Oliver made it."

"Carmen didn't have all of those details, but we both got the sense there was a healthy helping of denial at the Center."

"Sounds like it." Zoey sighed. "Listen, I'm not going to beat around the bush. The sheriff and the rescue team didn't find any signs of someone living with the thermal cameras. And it's so hard to reach that they don't think it's worth the risk to recover his body. So, I don't know if you should come right after something like that. Someone dying that traumatically on a run doesn't sit right with me. What if it wasn't an accident?"

Elise sat down on her bed next to the open suitcase. "Zo. I love you. You know that, right?"

"I don't think that's an actual question, sis. I think you're one step before saying, 'no offense, but...'" Zoey said in a cheeky tone. Their mom had bristled whenever one of them had started a sentence in high school with "No offense," contending that if the preface was necessary, something offensive was sure to follow. She hadn't been wrong.

"Okay, fine. No offense, but don't you think that we, in particular, might want to find a reason not to believe that someone died of a sudden medical issue?" The words tasted sour in her mouth, but the memory of their father's death hadn't quite slipped away yet. It had taken her years to accept that sometimes, events in life were just horrible with no further explanation.

There was a long pause on the phone. "Yeah. I suppose you're right." Zoey snorted. "That, or I've been spending too much time with FBI agents. Their crazy stories will make you think every bad situation has a nefarious backstory. I just want to make sure you know what you're getting into."

"Thank you, Zo. That's really sweet." Elise stood and started folding another shirt. "But I'm coming because something bad happened. I can't exactly cancel because I found out that something bad happened."

"Okay, then. Do you want me to clear the guest bedroom for you?"

Elise burst out laughing. "Thank you, but no thank you. I love you, sis, but I'm not staying in your new love nest with Liam."

"For the record, it's a three-bedroom. We aren't animals in your zoo who can't control themselves."

"Regardless, dear sister, I have spent a lot of time with zoo animals who have just found their mate." Elise zipped her suitcase shut. "Plus, I may end up keeping some odd hours, so the World Wildlife Trust is going to pay for a place for me downtown. As soon as the Riverbend Conservation Center employees realize I have a background in wildlife biology, I'm sure to be helping with the animals whenever I can. It is probably one of those places where the zookeeper is also the ticket taker and tour guide."

"It's bigger than you think. And their gardens are really pretty. People even take wedding pictures there sometimes. Even more people have been visiting the Center since my little sister got involved. From what I'm hearing at Bridges, you've finally convinced Heath to expand visiting hours beyond 10–12 every other Thursday."

Elise chuckled. "It wasn't quite that bad. He was focused on the right things, Zo, but ticket sales help feed animals. And the more animals we help…"

"I know, I know. I get it, numbers girl-slash-wildlife biologist. Now get packing so you can get here already. I'll take you to Bridges the minute you get here. Oh! I can't wait for you to meet the mountain biking crew. You'll love them. Actually, you'll probably know some of them from the Center. Full disclosure, the Venn diagram of work and play here in Riverbend has a lot of overlap. It's really more of a circle." Zoey had already told Elise all about her new friends, sending selfies of them in Bridges, the pub Zoey now considered her own. Zoey had also sent Elise pictures of her especially gnarly bruises. Zoey was so eager to impress Elise with her bravery that she hadn't realized it might not be the best advertisement for her sister to join her in her new favorite activity.

"Okay. I promise to try it at least once. And I'll limit my interactions with your FBI friends to the weekly mountain biking events, okay? I don't anticipate going anywhere near an FBI investigation during my visit."

~

ZOEY HUNG up the phone with her sister and shot a look at Liam. The man she loved was wincing at her obvious annoyance. "Really, Liam? I can't tell my own sister that your old friend, Finn, who *happens* to fight wildlife trafficking *happened* to show up to help you teach classes?"

Tasha, Zoey's fluffy rescue dog and K-9 partner, trotted over to deposit what remained of a fox toy that had promised near-indestructibility on Zoey's lap. The fox had put up a respectable fight, but Tasha didn't back down from a challenge. The ears, tail, and rope insides were long gone, but the now-unstuffed shell had survived, and Tasha offered it up to her humans whenever they were upset. Tank, Liam's K-9 partner, plopped in front of Liam and lay his head on his knee. Liam patted him. "There is absolutely no evidence that Finn's presence has anything to do with the Conservation Center. He told me and Alexis that he's here to do some light duty. He'll help train new recruits while his leg heals."

Zoey snorted and Tasha picked up the fox toy and nudged it into Zoey's hand. "You told me you thought Finn was here investigating something. That he was asking a lot of questions about the town in general, and the Center specifically."

Liam rubbed his face with his hands. "I answered his questions. Then, he stopped asking them."

"Oh, so you actually believe Dr. Oliver died of a heart attack on a night run on a trail and fell down in a place where he couldn't be rescued? You don't think he found something he shouldn't and was thrown off a cliff where the sheriff conveniently can't reach him?"

"That's what the sheriff said. No signs of struggle on the path." Liam cleared his throat. "I may have gone out there with a couple of other agents to double-check. We didn't find any trace either, and the dogs didn't pick up on a scent we could chase down. At this point, I don't have enough evidence to argue with the sheriff's conclusion."

Zoey huffed out a breath. "I need to warn her."

"You did. Your sister is smart. She heard what you said and what you didn't say." Liam put his arms around Zoey's waist. "I'd feel better if she stayed away until everything settles down too, but you tried to warn her off. It sounds like she's as stubborn as the woman I love."

Zoey leaned her head against his shoulder. "Well, this stubborn woman is going to keep an eye out for her sister. I don't like the idea of her walking into a zoo where someone just died under mysterious circumstances."

CHAPTER 5

Finn entered the Riverbend K-9 Academy with Sedona at his side, slightly more comfortable than he had been on his first day. Sedona had adjusted easily to her new surroundings, and her friendly tail wags helped smooth introductions. Even though she'd been trained at another facility, the agents and trainers at the K-9 Academy had been more welcoming to a newcomer than he'd expected. While he got the distinct impression that many were holding him at arm's length until he proved himself, the feeling was mutual. Caution was typical in their business and once he felt a little more comfortable, he'd start finding out more about what the agents knew about animal trafficking in Riverbend. The dogs at RKA were trained to find explosives, drugs, accelerants, and people, but none of them had experience in animal trafficking. It was possible the Riverbend K-9 Academy trainers had missed the signs entirely, and in that case, he'd tread carefully. In the meantime, his old friend Liam had vouched for him with the director, Alexis Thompson.

Finn made his way out to the yard, putting on his sunglasses to manage the bright mid-morning light. He'd heard that Director

Thompson was back from her business trip and he spotted her showing their latest recruits the basics with the help of Waffle, her red Labrador retriever. He had expected her to be holed up in her office, however, word around the facility was that she was extremely hands-on. It'd probably be another half hour or so before she was available for a chat. He'd been meaning to give her a heads up about Marlene, the coffee shop owner, catching on so quickly when he'd arrived, but Alexis had been away on an unspecified FBI project. It was an open secret that her old team in Chicago asked her for help on occasion, and she and Waffle sometimes left to provide K-9 field support. Finn walked Sedona over to the agility course. Before they even reached it, her tail was wagging and her tongue was out in a doggy smile. He gave her a pat. "You ready?"

Sedona's tail thwacked into his leg by way of reply and she navigated all the obstacles at top speed. Tunnels, ramps, and platforms were all thoroughly explored, but Finn hadn't left any scent containers for her to find. They had to practice not finding things too. Sedona was skilled at detecting the scent of several of the most commonly trafficked species. She'd been specifically trained on tigers, pangolins, rhinos, and elephants, but with some additional work, she could probably pick up more. While there was potential for confusion with multiple species, generally, she wasn't required to differentiate. Sedona only needed to be trained on any species they might find at a dock, airport, or anywhere else an endangered animal might be. Once Sedona found the source of the scent, Liam could do his part. After a few times through the agility course, Sedona started to slow down. However, Alexis was finishing up her lesson, and it'd be a good time for them both to take a quick break. Finn clipped on Sedona's leash and walked over to where the new recruits were resting, pushing his sunglasses up on his head.

Alexis held out a hand. "Good morning. You must be Agent Cooper. Nice to meet you in person."

"Morning, Director Thompson." Finn shook her hand firmly.

Alexis waved away the title. "Just Alex, please. Director Thompson is a mouthful."

"Okay, then. Just Finn." Finn gave her a respectful nod.

"Okay, just Finn. How are you settling in?"

He nodded. "Just fine, ma'am."

"Okay, then. Just Finn who is just fine, it is." Alexis grinned, then gave him a knowing look. "What's on your mind?" She was perfectly friendly but her tone conveyed authority and backbone. He had a feeling that getting dressed down by Alexis wouldn't be a fun experience.

Finn lifted his chin. "I wanted to talk to you about my landlady."

"Ah, Marlene figured out you work with us already?" Alexis raised her eyebrows.

"Yes, ma'am. She actually figured it out the first day I was here. I thought she'd let it go, but she asks how we are doing every single day I see her. Is that a problem?"

Alexis snorted. "Maybe for your privacy. She misses nothing and knows about everything. I have a theory that she's actually secretly wealthy and just runs the coffee shop to keep her finger on the pulse of the town gossip. She's also the town treasurer. I suspect for the same reason."

"Do I need to be concerned?"

"With Marlene? I don't think so. Go ahead and chat with her. You don't need to give her confidential details. Focus on what kinds of dogs are around and anything they do that is related to play, not work. That should satisfy her curiosity."

Finn blew out a breath. "Oh good. I wasn't sure if I'd blown it when she found out I worked here, particularly if she wasn't going to let it go."

"It's a small enough town that anyone who really wanted to know could figure it out by following your car. I don't think it's a state secret. Unless you're working on something else on the side I should know about?" Alexis eyed him.

Finn straightened. "Is that a theoretical question or an actual one?"

Alexis stared at him as if she could see right through him. She put her hands on her hips and gave him a few moments to get good and uncomfortable. "Are you going to make me play games, Agent Cooper? If so, I can only pretend I believe that you only wanted to pop into Riverbend to work with my dogs for another couple of days. I've talked to Liam, and the reasons you've given him are flimsy. Your team vouches for you, so it's not a safety issue. Which means it's something I haven't thought of yet. I'd prefer if you don't make me guess."

Finn fidgeted. "It's only a theory."

Alexis tipped her head. "Come into my office. Much like your landlord, I like to know what's going on in our little town. Even if it's only a theory." She waved another instructor over, got him set up with the newbies, and then led Finn into the building for a more thorough interrogation.

Finn followed her into the former airplane hangar, renovated to hold offices for the Riverbend K-9 Academy personnel. He spotted Liam and his girlfriend, Zoey, on the way in and waved. Liam shot him a curious look and touched Zoey on the elbow. Soon, he was flanked by them both on the way into Alexis's office. There were larger offices in the building, but Alexis's office had a great view of the training yard and just enough space for the small crew to squeeze inside with all of their respective K-9 partners. Fortunately, the dogs were all pretty mature in their training. If any one of them got the zoomies, as Sedona used to when she was a puppy, someone would likely rupture an ACL.

Alexis sat behind her desk and crossed her arms. "Alright. Out with it, just Finn. Liam, you too."

"I've already told you everything Finn told me," Liam answered, diplomatically.

Finn looked between his old friend and the no-nonsense director and felt twice as cornered as when Marlene called him out. Well, if Liam vouched for the team in Riverbend, that was as good as he was going to get. "The FBI did approve of me being here to recover and do something useful. That is entirely true." Alexis lifted a single eyebrow. "And it's possible that I was working on an investigation with a lead that pointed to Riverbend."

Alexis straightened. "Here? At the Academy?" She exchanged a look with Liam.

Finn frowned. "I honestly don't know. I was working with a group of locals in Nepal, trying to find a solution for them to feed their families that didn't involve poaching and trapping endangered species to be sold globally, including in the U.S. My team here in the States was helping me trace contact information for the buyers and traffickers located in the U.S. All of the contacts were dead ends except a burner phone from Riverbend, Indiana. The team wasn't able to fully trace the signal but they know some calls were placed nearby, and a few emails have been sent from burner accounts using public WiFi networks downtown. My team didn't think we had enough information to justify a full-blown investigation, but since I was injured and have friends here, I might have offered to multitask."

Zoey crinkled her nose. "Do you really think someone working with an animal trafficking ring would be based in rural Indiana, of all places?"

Finn gave her a sad smile. "Wouldn't it be pretty easy to find a spot out in the country where people don't ask too many questions?"

Liam rubbed his neck. "And you didn't tell me this because...?"

Finn winced. "It's a long shot. And I don't have anything to work with beyond some communications that came from here. Somewhere. It sounds like a dead end. Even to me."

Alexis pointed a finger at Finn. "In the future, loop me in. Long shot or not. You'd be surprised what this team has dealt with." Alexis picked up a pencil and began tapping it on her desk. "We've had a dirty agent come through the K-9 Academy before, but I don't know what a poacher would gain from being here. After a few days in Riverbend, do you think there is anything to your theory?"

"No idea." Finn shook his head. "Honestly, my goal was to get some work done here, get to know the town, and try and see if anyone is hiding anything. However, it sounds like I should have started with Marlene. Heck, maybe it *is* Marlene."

Zoey snickered. "If it's Marlene, I'll eat my hat. *After* one of the dogs licked it."

Liam scratched his chin. "Although you have to admit, she has her finger on the pulse of what's going on in town. Or Thurston — he's the mayor and on the board of the Riverbend Animal Conservation Center."

"If you're going to arrest all of the well-connected people in town, you'll fill up the jail pretty quickly, babe." Zoey shot him a look of challenge. "There is a whole corner booth in Bridges that gathers on Saturdays just to gossip."

Alexis stilled her tapping. "Okay. Here's what we're going to do. I have puppies that'll be ready to start their training soon. Let's have you start developing a training program to detect wildlife, like Sedona was trained to do. We'll keep it quiet. That'll guarantee people will start whispering about it. Maybe we can get our rabbit to run out of its burrow; help you out a little."

Finn smiled. "I like the way you think. Thank you, Alex."

"You don't mind being bait?" Zoey eyed Finn incredulously.

"I'm pretty good at watching out for traps. Usually." He rubbed his leg absently. "You'd start a new program just to help me out?"

"A small one." Alexis shrugged. "I've been wanting to branch out, but we've never had any experts in wildlife detection on staff. If I can shamelessly leverage your expertise while you're here, it'll help both of us. Two birds with one stone and all of that." She gestured to his leg. "Your injury still bothering you?"

Finn narrowed his eyes. "It is. How could you tell?"

"Slight limp. You tried to hide it this morning but didn't remember until you made it to the agility course. Left calf would be my guess, especially since you just touched it. What'd you do?"

Finn sighed. "A trap. I got lucky. It could have been a lot worse. As it was, it was pretty deep and then got infected, so the muscle's been tender. It's fine now."

"Okay. Even though it's fine, don't push yourself too hard. Let us know how we can help." Alexis was all business, making a note in the notebook on her desk. "I've got three dogs coming in within about six weeks. They're all currently being fostered by some volunteers, but if you have any instructions our foster families can start implementing, I'll send them along, okay?"

Finn nodded. "Yes, ma'am."

"Thanks, Alex." Liam gave her a small salute.

"Anytime. And, gentlemen?" Liam and Finn turned in sync to face Alexis, who had folded her hands on her desk. "Next time, don't make me ask."

Finn felt a flush of embarrassment. "Yes, ma'am."

CHAPTER 6

By the end of the week, Elise had wrapped up her most urgent World Wildlife Trust work, cleaned out her fridge, and packed her matching suitcases for the trip to Indiana. The sturdy cloth luggage set with a playful sloth pattern had been a gift from her parents when she enrolled in the wildlife biology program in college. The bags had begun to show their age and miles, but they were still usable and easy to spot in the baggage claim. After one last walk-through of her apartment to make sure she hadn't forgotten anything, Elise loaded her last suitcase into her trunk and fired up the first of her audiobooks to listen to on the journey. She crossed the state line from eastern Colorado to western Kansas in high spirits, noting that if not for the sign, she might not have known she was in a different state. Several years prior, she'd read an article that compared Kansas to a standard restaurant pancake to demonstrate that the topography of the midwestern state was, indeed, mathematically flatter than a pancake. This stretch of Kansas highway had likely been the inspiration for their semi-serious research.

While Elise would miss the awe-inspiring beauty of the mountains, she often felt cooped up in a big city. The big Kansas sky and waving grass were the first signs that she would have the space to stretch her metaphorical wings as she travelled. It was a lovely feeling...for the first few hours. Then as the time ticked by, she was grateful for one excellent barbeque restaurant, some unexpected rolling hills, and the compelling voice of the narrator reading one of her favorite author's books.

After an overnight stop and another long day of counting miles and drinking almost entirely coffee, Elise finally reached the outskirts of Riverbend later than she'd hoped to arrive. Of course, stopping at a couple of state parks to stretch her legs had taken longer than she expected, and really, was she expected to skip the boyhood home of Mark Twain? Then, she might have been delayed when she was studying a table covered in scratches with excellent potential in an antique shop that, if her car hadn't already been packed to the brim, would have become her next project. Her very practical sister would likely tease her for taking the extra detours, but without Elise's sense of adventure, her apartment would be much duller. And her fridge wouldn't be filled with magnets from all of the places she visited, from the quirky to the awe-inspiring.

Riverbend itself was as small as Zoey had described and as far from a tourist destination as Elise could imagine. While she hadn't expected traffic in Riverbend, she did find herself unexpectedly delayed by ten minutes waiting at a railroad crossing for a long, slow-moving train to pass. The housing near the historic downtown lacked some of the shiny modern housing designs she'd seen in new developments in the Colorado suburbs, but most of the homes were well maintained. After passing through about five of the ten stoplights in town, Elise finally arrived at her temporary home. She was pleasantly surprised to find it was in a turn-of-the-century building with large windows. The building was made from what looked to be limestone, accented with a brightly colored awning covered in decorative paint splatter. Over the top of the paint splatter was black lettering indicating she'd reached the River Bean coffee shop. Elise found a free parking spot under a bright street light nearby that she would have paid a small fortune for in downtown Denver. While something told her crime rates would likely be slightly lower in Riverbend compared to Denver, old habits died hard. She hefted her bags out of her trunk and walked towards the door. A woman with short white hair with light purple tips and dangling earrings shaped like coffee mugs paused with one hand on the open/closed sign. The woman flipped the sign to closed but opened the door. There was a cheerful jangle of bells. "Well, hi there. Are you Zoey's sister?"

Elise parked her roller bag in the upright position. "Guilty as charged."

The woman waved her in, then held up a finger. She soon returned with a croissant drizzled with chocolate on a purple plate in one hand and a big white ceramic mug with the River Bean logo stamped on it in the other. "I'm Marlene, your landlord. Sorry I couldn't give you a proper welcome. I sold out of my famous chicken salad, but I'll whip up a fresh batch tomorrow."

Elise grinned. "Well if this is an improper welcome, I'm not sure I could handle the proper one." She brought her bags inside and accepted the plate and what turned out to be a surprisingly cold mug. She looked inside and found it was filled with plain cold milk.

Marlene flicked the lock behind her. "You'll want it for the croissant, and most folks don't like coffee so late at night after driving all day. Lucky for you, we had one treat left. It was bound to go to waste if you didn't arrive tonight. I'll just finish up here and then I can show you upstairs."

Marlene went to work, wiping down equipment and tables, and Elise collapsed onto a brightly painted chair. This one was pink and yellow to match the flowers painted on the table. One bite of Marlene's chocolate croissant and all of Zoey's reverence for Marlene's baked goods made sense. Soon, it and the cold milk were gone. Elise wiped her crumbs onto her plate and brought her dishes back, feeling slightly more human than when she'd arrived. "You are a magician, Marlene."

Marlene waved a hand. "I've always had a sweet tooth." Marlene whisked her dishes into a dishwasher, pushed a couple of buttons, and wiped Elise's table. She surveyed her surroundings and gave them an approving nod. "Okay. Are you ready to see your new home?"

Elise could have happily collapsed on the floor of the coffee shop using her suitcase for a pillow. A real bed sounded like pure luxury. "So ready."

"Follow me." Marlene unlocked the door and led Elise out of the eclectic café into the cool outside air. She flicked the lights off and pulled a key out of her pocket to lock the front door behind them. She walked to another outside door, which she unlocked using the same key. Just inside the door was a set of stairs. Elise lifted an eyebrow. "You trust me with a key to the café?"

Marlene studied her. "Do you plan on stealing my espresso machine?"

Elise snorted. "No."

"Well, then, between your lack of need for an espresso machine and the building security cameras, I think you can be trusted with a shared key. Here is a key for the outside door and a key for your apartment." Marlene gave her two keys on a key ring with a plastic coffee mug dangling from it. The mug almost matched Marlene's earrings. Her new landlady definitely had an aesthetic. Inside, there was a hallway separating the top floor of the River Bean coffee shop into two small apartments. The hallway was brightly decorated with wall-to-wall art.

Marlene opened the door to the apartment on the left and Elise found herself in a surprisingly updated space. More art was scattered along the walls and the apartment was furnished with a funky red couch and live edge furniture. Elise barely resisted the urge to run her hand over the beautifully made pieces and instead put her hands on her hips. "This is phenomenal. And, if I'm honest, quite a bit nicer than my own place in Denver."

"Well, Riverbend needed a touch of fun. The tables were hand-made by my nephew and the art is local. Stop by the coffee shop tomorrow morning and you can really get a good look at all of the artists we're featuring this month. The theme is 'summer in Indi-ana' and all of the color perks the shop right up. I've had my eye on one of the watercolors for the hallway." Elise had only gotten a glimpse of the hallway upstairs, but based on her first glance, Marlene could only fall in love with a few more paintings before she ran out of space.

Elise spoke through her yawn. "That sounds great."

"Well, I won't keep you, honey. Do let me know if you need help unloading anything. I know you're new in town so I'd be happy to introduce you to your neighbor." Marlene's eyebrows waggled. "He's single and about your age. Very handsome. Steady job. Works outside a lot."

Elise felt her eyes go round and only just managed to hold back her laugh. While she'd always assumed her sister's stories about the community in Riverbend had been exaggerated for effect, she began to wonder if Zoey had actually been holding back. She bit her lip. "Thank you, Marlene. I'll keep that in mind." She yawned again. "Well, I have to be up bright and early for work tomorrow. No rest for the weary. Thanks so much for helping me get settled. And for the treat."

After making Elise promise she'd stop by for a coffee in the morning, Marlene said goodbye and shuffled out of Elise's new apartment. Elise had a feeling Riverbend was going to be full of surprises.

CHAPTER 7

*E*lise's alarm clock went off and she blinked awake slowly, imagining she could smell coffee. It took her brain a couple of seconds to catch up. She was smelling real coffee from River Bean, not dreaming about it after two exhausting days of driving. At that realization, she threw off her covers. Elise had never been overly fussy about her appearance, and today, it meant she'd get her morning boost that much quicker. She sent a quick text to her sister and pulled her unruly brown hair back into a ponytail. Zoey claimed Elise's waves always looked beachy and fun, but she'd never understood where her sister got that idea. Her locks had a way of getting tangled when she had work to do, and Elise planned to start her new gig at the Riverbend Animal Conservation Center with a healthy dose of hard work. She'd been in finance long enough to know the reputation she and her colleagues had as keyboard jockeys, and Elise didn't have any desire to come into the Conservation Center providing any fuel for that assumption. Kai's positive impression of her would only go so far if she was afraid to get dirt under her fingernails.

Elise put on a pair of khaki shorts, a World Wildlife Trust

khaki button-down shirt, and her bright red sneakers. She stuffed her phone and keys in her back pocket and left her new apartment. Just as she was locking the door behind her, Elise heard her neighbor's door opening. She turned and found a tall, tanned man with an excellent backside. At his side was a yellow Labrador retriever who was watching her with open curiosity. The dog's tail wagged furiously but she didn't lunge or pull her owner towards Elise. Her neighbor turned around and met her eyes. His dark blond hair was short with a slight curl to the ends and like her, he was dressed for a day of activity. Although, instead of khakis, he was wearing athletic shorts and a quick-dry t-shirt. He tipped his head in question and her cheeks heated when she realized she was studying him as if he were a zoo animal. She gave him an awkward wave. "Morning, neighbor."

"Good morning." The man smiled and walked towards her and the exit to the street, his gray-blue eyes crinkling at the edges. True to Marlene's claim, he was fit and easy on the eyes. He made no move to introduce himself, in contrast to Marlene's warm welcome. She wanted to pet his dog, as was her tendency whenever she met a friendly animal, but neither the man nor the dog gave any indication it would be okay. Before he could pass her and amplify the awkwardness of their greeting, she gave him a quick head bob. Elise needed to get downstairs if her sister was running on time, which she almost certainly was. Zoey had an uncanny ability to hold a conversation, plan for ten different contingencies, and watch the clock at the same time.

A few minutes later, Elise spotted Zoey pulling into one of the diagonal spots in front of the River Bean. It took mere seconds for Zoey to park, leap out of the car, and pull Elise in for a tight hug. "You're here! Do you know how hard it was to let you rest yesterday instead of driving over? It was totally unfair that Marlene got to see you first." Zoey took a few steps back to open the back door of her car so that her furry partner, Tasha, could join them.

Tasha was a medium-sized dog with a fluffy mostly white coat with a few darker spots on her face. She always looked like she was smiling and wagged her tail almost vertically in the air. Elise leaned down to give her a good scratch behind the ears and was rewarded with a sneaky lick to her nose. "And good morning to you too, Miss Tasha."

"Do you have much time to catch up before you have to go to work?"

Elise checked her watch. "Half an hour. I should get there early, but I think they'll understand if I start my day off right with my favorite sister. I mean, my only sister, but winning by default is still winning."

Zoey rolled her eyes. "I'm going to ignore that. I should tell you, Marlene makes the best coffee in town. And her baked goods are a work of art. If you go once, you'll go twice. And if you go twice, well, make sure you budget for coffee every day."

"Way ahead of you on that. I agree on the baked goods and I am not surprised by the coffee." Elise patted her stomach. "She gave me a chocolate croissant and cold milk when I arrived last night. It was really sweet. And unexpected. She didn't fit my idea of a grumpy landlord who ignored you when you complained about maintenance."

"If you wanted a grumpy landlord, you shouldn't have picked the apartment on top of the River Bean." Zoey chuckled. "Marlene will have you confessing your life story over a warm scone before you even know it's happening. And since I've talked about you, she already has a tactical advantage. She has a heart of gold, though, so it's some amount of comfort when you realize she's barreled through your defenses without you noticing. Come on, let's get you your first cup of coffee and your second croissant."

"Deal." Elise looked around the small downtown, slowly

coming to life. "It's so good to see you. I feel like I've missed so much." Tasha brushed against Elise's shorts, leaving more than a little white fluff behind as she sashayed into the coffee shop next to her human.

Zoey paused to rummage in her purse and pulled out a lint roller that she held out to Elise. "Work-related hazard. She's in the middle of her summer blowout. Shedding seems too tame of a word."

Elise waved away the lint roller. "What's a little dog hair between friends?"

"I'm glad you're friends." Zoey leaned over and lint rolled Elise's shorts for her. "But, you've got to make a positive impression your first day. Are you ready to meet everyone?"

"Oh, yes. Although, I already know a few people. I've been working with them remotely since they joined the World Wildlife Trust. They're not the biggest partner we have, but their breeding programs have a great reputation. Hopefully, they know I come in peace. It's not always reassuring to have someone come from the mothership and offer to help. Particularly if said person helps with the numbers and the center is struggling."

Zoey frowned. "I thought they were doing better? Kai occasionally rides with us and he seemed less stressed lately. I mean, after the cubs were born anyway."

Marlene spotted them and shouted over the short line, "Morning, Butler sisters!" Zoey and Elise both gave Marlene a wave. Marlene wrote someone's name on a cardboard cup with a Sharpie, handed it to the barista, and then leaned in to chat with her next customer. The college-aged barista had a colorful phoenix tattoo on her arm and teal hair. She also had the classic "what do I care?" body posture. However, a careful study showed that she had some serious skills and easily kept pace with Marlene and her efficient way of taking orders while getting a sentence or two of the latest gossip.

Zoey turned to face Elise. "So anyway, we've only seen Kai when he can squeeze us in. I need details. How adorable are the cubs? I mean, having two at once has to be exciting, right?"

A wave of sadness hit Elise. "It is. Was. We — they — lost one. They're waiting on a vet from Indy to come up and check on the other cub. She's been doing some international travel, but should be getting back any day now."

"Aw. I'm sorry, sis."

Elise nodded unconvincingly. "It's part of the job. Normally, we'd lean on Dr. Oliver for answers, but, we'll manage."

Zoey studied her. "You do realize I've known you for years, right? I'm not quite that easy to fool."

Elise shrugged. "I know. But what can you say? And it seems insensitive to focus on the cub when we just lost our veterinarian, you know? And nature isn't always kind. Loss is a part of our jobs. A part we all dread, but a part nonetheless. We'll do what we always do — find a way to keep going. And honestly, I'm glad Kai wanted me to help. When I first got involved with them, RACC only wanted to be part of our breeding program collaboration. It was like pulling teeth to do the due diligence to make sure they were financially solvent, but they finally agreed to let us help."

"Wow. I'm surprised Kai was that defensive."

Elise looked around but it was obvious the town gossips were listening. She kept it simple. "It wasn't Kai. We got there. That's what matters."

Zoey looked behind her and then back at her sister. She whispered, "Freya?"

Elise made a motion like she was zipping her mouth shut. "You can't interrogate me without my attorney present. Or something like that."

Zoey snorted. "Everyone is a little afraid of Freya at first. Heath may be the director but she really keeps the wheels on the bus at the Conservation Center." Zoey leaned in. "And I'm not even sure she even likes Heath all that much. She's a tough nut to crack, but if anyone can do it, it's you."

Before Elise could thank her sister for the vote of confidence, she found herself at the front of a surprisingly fast-moving line. She greeted Marlene and reassured her that all had gone well during her first night in the new apartment, and soon, they both had their coffees and breakfast. After a few more minutes of chatting, they headed their separate ways — Zoey and Tasha to the K-9 Academy and Elise to the Conservation Center — with a promise to meet up as soon as their schedules allowed.

By the time Elise reached the large wrought iron gates of the Riverbend Animal Conservation Center, she had nearly finished her large coffee from the River Bean. She found a place to park in the employee lot and took in the sight of the zoo in person. It nearly took her breath away. The landscaping, most of it native, was contained in curving sections. It gently guided visitors to the front entrance with a wild yet welcoming appearance. The structural elements were in good condition and the landscaping was well maintained. She'd seen pictures online, but no facility could be fully captured by pictures alone. The history of the Riverbend Conservation Center was unusual, and there were hints of its founder's wealth in the quality of the buildings. After the founder made his fortune in oil, he bought a huge plot of land near his birthplace in Indiana and retired. Shortly thereafter, in a time when rules around such things were much less strict, he'd curated a personal collection of exotic animals. When his grandchildren had balked at the excess instead of sharing his enthusiasm, the story went that the wealthy owner had a change of heart. He worked with an experienced team to turn his collection into a zoo focused on animal conservation, even naming it the Riverbend Animal Conservation Center to really drive home the point. According to the inspirational quote at the entrance, his goal was to put some goodness back into the world. The move had placated his grandchildren as well as, Elise suspected, a town that you didn't really want to get on the wrong side of. Whether he did it for the reasons he claimed or so the city council wouldn't drive him out of town, Elise would never truly know. Regardless of what brought about the change, the effect had been positive. The private property had been turned into an olive branch to Riverbend. Now, animals that had been rescued and animals bred to help maintain a genetically diverse captive population could live out their days with plenty of room to stretch their legs, wings, or whatever appendages, if any, they had.

The structural changes that had happened once the owner had hired a knowledgeable zookeeper had gone largely unnoticed by the public but were immediately obvious to Elise. Thanks to the low cost of real estate in rural Indiana and the generous budget of the Center's benefactor, the animals had ample space to roam within habitats that had been designed for each animal's needs. There were private areas to allow the animals to choose if they wanted to be seen as well as large enriching spaces that could be easily viewed by the public. Arboreal animals had trees to climb and some of the herbivores' browse was growing in the fields outside the facility in attractive and practical groupings. The only unfortunate side effect of the designs had been a winding zoo without as much rhyme or reason as one might expect. Still, the resulting twists and turns in the pathways were charming (and well-labeled) enough that most people probably didn't notice.

Elise ran a hand over a railing that could use a fresh coat of paint. The Riverbend Animal Conservation Center had started off with a sufficient rainy-day fund. However, in recent years, they'd taken on more expenses than they could handle. Not least of which was because the well-meaning zoo director, Heath Green, on the advice of the accountant that was no longer with them, had cut the number of hours they were open so they could cut staff. Predictably, revenue dropped at a much greater rate than their cost savings, and out of desperation, they'd partnered with the World Wildlife Trust to placate the Center's board members. After some gentle, but firm, guidance from Elise and Carmen, they had expanded hours and people were getting in the habit of coming to the Conservation Center on weekends again. Revenue from admissions and concessions was slowly building the Center's balance sheet back to healthier levels, but they weren't out of the woods yet. They still needed to get spending under control or get revenue and donations to catch up to their spending.

On the way to the administrative building near the zoo entrance, Elise spotted someone familiar. He was wearing a River-bend Animal Conservation Center hat and khakis, leaning over to pick up some loose trash. He was also holding a sky-blue travel coffee mug with most of an old RACC logo on it. She grinned. Kai deposited the trash in the trash can and eyed her curiously. "Hey there, can I help you?" He checked his watch. "We don't open for another hour or so."

Elise took off her sunglasses. She didn't blame Kai for not recognizing her — she was usually dressed business casual, not safari ready, and she had second-guessed who he was until he spoke. She wasn't used to seeing him outside of her screen either. "Yes, actually. And no. I'm looking for Kai — you know him?"

"Elise!" Kai waited for her to approach and pulled her into a hug. "Wow, it's so great to see you in person!"

"You too." Elise snorted. "Although you look way too young to be in charge of all of the zookeepers. For a second, I wondered if you were a volunteer."

His eyebrows rose. "You are too experienced at the WWT to talk about my age."

Elise slapped a hand over her mouth. "Oh my gosh. You're right. I'm so sorry. I'm supposed to be setting a good example, not creating an HR situation. I just..."

"Thought I was a high school kid?" Kai gave her a mischievous look and she suddenly realized he was giving her a hard time, the universal sign of friendship in the Midwest.

"Kai Torres, I didn't think you'd give me as much trouble in person as you did on the phone," Elise teased, looking down at her empty coffee cup for dramatic effect. "I'm going to need more coffee."

"Thank you." He tipped his ballcap to her and placed his sunglasses atop it. "I'll take the compliment and treat the fact you thought I was a high-school volunteer as a compliment as well."

"Blame it on the travel fatigue." Elise sighed. "I'm used to flying, not driving through multiple states. Marlene's coffee can only do so much."

Kai and Elise walked into the Center's employee entrance together. Kai beeped his badge on the reader and held the door open for her. "Although, even on one cup of coffee after two days of driving, I bet you could still tell me how many puffins I would need to trade for a radiated tortoise without even having to think about it."

Elise tapped her chin with her pointer finger. "To be honest, I'd have to convert through a stingray, a sugar glider or two, and a Komodo dragon to get an accurate number." The practice of purchasing animals had long been outlawed in the United States. Some zoos and aquariums only donated or loaned animals and others used an elaborate system of trading in order to distribute the genetics of populations while avoiding actually selling their exotic animals. Which was how Elise found herself unexpectedly becoming an expert in how many blacktip reef sharks a zoo could trade for a hyena. Managing the complex logistics of genetic diversity in captive populations wasn't exactly what she thought she'd do with her life when she was sitting inside of the beige walls of her old accounting firm, but she was surprisingly good at it. And she'd connected with more Species Survival Plan coordinators than she could count through her work facilitating animal trades for the WWT, getting to learn about a plethora of animals from people passionate about conservation.

Kai stuffed his hands in his pockets. "Well, since you just got here, I'll let it slide. And we don't have any puffins right now, so it's purely theoretical. Once you're more rested, I'll make you convert through some Madagascar hissing cockroaches so you don't think I'm taking it easy on you."

"That's extremely generous of you." Elise studied the forked path past the entrance — she'd memorized the map of the facility before she left, and the clouded leopard enclosure wasn't far from here. "So, now that I know you're you and you know I'm me, how are you, really?"

Kai pursed his lips and stared off into the direction of the clouded leopard enclosure. "I'm okay. I didn't go out for drinks with Olly on a regular basis or anything, but I worked with the guy at least once a week. It's hard not to have someone up and disappearing affect you."

"I heard Heath thinks there is still hope."

Kai gave her a sympathetic look. "I understand why he wants to think that. It's sweet, really. A part of me keeps thinking Dr. Oliver is going to come back too, but it's hard not to give up hope when the sheriff stops by and explains that it's just a formality to come up with a death certificate. He said it's an access issue." He shook his head. "Can you imagine calling the disappearance of a friend an 'access issue?' Man, I know they see a lot, but it's a little insensitive."

Elise winced. "No, I can't imagine it. Carmen said Dr. Perry volunteered to come help this week. Has she been here yet?"

"Not yet, but I'll keep an eye out for her. She travels a lot — last I heard she was headed somewhere in Southeast Asia. I'm sure she'll get here as soon as she can. In the meantime, I've been keeping a close eye on the cloudeds. With Dr. Oliver gone, I've been getting other keepers trained up to help with Tej, the cub who is still with us. He doesn't need as much of our time as he did, but he's still so young. Want to come with me when I check in on them this morning?"

"Will I freak them out? I've heard they can be sensitive to change."

Kai smiled. "Believe it or not, our cloudeds have figured out if you have a khaki uniform on, you're liable to have something good to eat with you. So as long as you're wearing khaki, they actually do pretty well."

"Good to know. Since I unintentionally came dressed for the occasion, I'd love to see them." Elise tossed her empty paper cup in a nearby trash can and made a mental note to bring her travel mug to the River Bean next time. Talking about habitats and animals all day made her feel a little self-conscious about the trash she generated.

Kai led her down a lush path designated for employees. The path itself was gravel, but it should be converted to smooth concrete for accessibility. She pulled out her phone and added another item to her running list of recommended changes. The plant life at the Center required only minimal maintenance, a hat tip to Marlene's sister, a master gardener who had planted and maintained the native, and largely low maintenance, flora. The flowers were humming with pollinators and a large plant, heavy with blooming flowers, hung over the path. She paused to type another note about which species seemed to be thriving and Kai stopped on the path ahead. He placed his hands on his hips. "Why do I feel like I'm being graded by the principal?"

Elise grinned. "That sounds like a personal problem." She held up her phone. "Just making notes of what we'd like to improve."

"Ah, yes, definitely being graded."

"Ah, yes, you definitely missed the collective 'we,' my phone friend. If I didn't think the RACC was worth the effort, I'd only do my job. Largely from a comfy chair in one of the offices in the administrative building. A to-do list is the ultimate form of optimism for the future."

Kai lifted an eyebrow. "And here I thought you'd be less nerdy when you were out in the sunshine."

"Nah, I just take my nerdiness to go. I might be out here with clippers myself to trim the bushes though. No advanced technology required and instant gratification." She paused to snap a photo of a monarch butterfly flitting around the bright orange flowers of a butterfly weed. "If the local faunae don't mind, that is. Do you get a lot of monarchs?"

"In the summer, yes. We collect the eggs and make a display of their lifecycle. We even have the school kids come out and tag them right before they start migrating. We keep some of the landscaping dedicated to feeding the monarch caterpillars." Kai pointed to a larger section down the path, nearly overflowing with top-heavy milkweed plants. They weren't quite as pretty as the delicate orange flowers on the butterfly weed, but they served an important purpose. "I've been considering getting a machete to manage that particular crop — write that down while you're at it."

Elise snickered. "Wow, I feel like I should have known Riverbend did all that."

Kai studied her. "That seems like more detail than the numbers people usually care about."

"Unless your numbers person is a wildlife biologist with a lot of natural curiosity who took a turn into finance. In which case, the numbers person can't help herself." Elise shrugged. "Listen, I know your center got some tough love when you partnered with the World Wildlife Trust, but it was only because we love the animals as much as you do."

"I'm getting the feeling. Although it feels like I should have known you were secretly a wildlife biologist. You've never mentioned that. Although it certainly explains why you caught on to my explanations about the Center so quickly. Why did you go into finance if you clearly have a passion for animals?"

Elise bit her lip. "Short version? Financial security."

"I get that." Kai waited for a second, then he seemed to recognize that she was clamming up and waved an arm for her to follow him. "Come on, let's go see to the cats. No one can resist that amount of cuteness. Even the most number-oriented of accountants."

Elise followed Kai into the keeper's area of the clouded leopard enclosure. Her eyes took a moment to adjust to the perfectly bright room, dark only by comparison to the bright Indiana sunshine. Each animal had a large area to roam, climb, and explore that all came together in a central location inside a building to allow access for the zoo staff to feed and care for the animals. It also served as a place for the cloudeds to retreat if they didn't feel like being on display that day. Like the enclosures she'd seen on the way in, the clouded enclosures prioritized animal choice and control. Each door to the clouded enclosures was secured with two locks, in keeping with the best practices of managing dangerous felids. Cloudeds were adorable, but they also had teeth as large as a tiger, despite their smaller build. Two locks meant that two people would always be required to open any enclosure, a built-in safety measure for their keepers. Looking into the spacious enclosures with tall ceilings and plenty of climbing surfaces made it clear why Riverbend's breeding program had been such a success. If she were an animal, she'd thrive here too. The storage bins for the enrichments were filled to the brim with various spices and scents for them to smell, boxes to investigate, and giant toys to play with.

Elise quickly spotted a medium-sized cat, the smallest of the big cats. The approximately thirty-pound clouded leopard chuffed as it padded over to greet Kai. She immediately switched back into wildlife biologist mode, searching for signs of an unhappy felid. A well-meaning zookeeper was no guarantee of healthy animals, unfortunately.

Kai spoke to the cat instead of her. "Hello, beautiful." He turned to Elise. "This is Daxa."

Elise tipped her head. "Does she normally make that noise?"

"Yeah, we're buddies. Right, girl?" Daxa's eyes stayed fixed on her and Elise took a step back, careful not to stress the animal. Her cub appeared in the enclosure next to her, scampering in the way young animals often did, pausing to pounce on a round pumpkin. The pumpkin popped out from under him and he chased it again. Just then, Elise noticed a slightly larger cat in yet another space, keeping a close watch on them all, but from a greater distance. "And there's Dad. He's good with me, but is a little more cautious with new folks."

Soon, Kai had finished his wellness checks on the cats, fed them their breakfast of meatballs smushed through the mesh, and entered information on his tablet. "Ready for our next stop?"

Elise kept staring at the gorgeous cats. While all species were important in their own way, the clouded leopard was the perfect example of charismatic megafauna — the more scientific-sounding term for adorable animals people wanted to save. Even though she was equally concerned for the less glamorous species, like the Madagascar hissing cockroach and its less well-known insect cousins, it was impossible not to be wowed by the beauty of the shy predator. She wasn't foolish enough to pet Daxa as if she were a housecat, but she understood why some people thought they could. It would be a good idea to post pictures and videos of the cats on the Center's social media channels. Based on her cursory search, they hadn't been updated for months. It was a huge missed opportunity. If she were in Heath's position, she'd be using it as another channel to educate and connect with others passionate about protecting animals and their habitats. A live stream to the cats, perhaps, or even simple photos would be a step in the right direction. She sighed and looked around for anything more fixable in the short term. She spotted a camera facing the leopards and pointed at it. "Is that connected to anything?"

Kai nodded. "Of course. It's a real-time security system set up. We don't save the video for the sake of our ancient computer systems, but you can access a live feed whenever you want. It's too bad. It would have given us some useful information when Dr. Oliver disappeared."

Elise frowned. "Oh, man. I didn't even think about that."

Kai shook his head. "There isn't anything we can do about it now. By the time I got here the next morning, Dr. Oliver had already sent the deceased cub away for testing and left. The only person who knows what happened is the one person who can't tell us. I'm sure better cameras are on your list, but we have other things we need to buy first. I mean, you understand..."

"Yeah. I do." Feeling as if she'd stepped in something unpleasant with her observations, Elise searched the room for anything else to focus or comment on. She wasn't here to fix the past, she was here to set up the Center for a successful future. She narrowed her eyes at something in the corner. She walked over to pick up what turned out to be a lanyard with a few keys dangling from it. "Are these yours?" Elise held up the keys.

"No. Maybe those are Oliver's." Kai picked them up and turned them in his hand. "That's odd. Why did he leave without his keys to the Conservation Center?"

"Maybe he had an extra set?" Elise frowned. "Was he the forgetful type?"

"No. The opposite. Methodical to a fault. Probably the only one besides you who could rattle off the zoo's bank account information without missing a beat."

"Strange. Well, I guess they could be anyone's." Elise studied the keys, but they provided no answers. She tucked them into her pocket. "I'll get these to the office."

"I'd appreciate that. Thanks, Elise. It's good to have you here. Even with all of this in the periphery." Kai gestured vaguely in the air.

Elise gave him a knowing look. "We'll see if you still feel that way once I ask you to review the budget vis-à-vis my list of action items."

"Oh, wow. I don't think I signed up for a 'vis-à-vis' conversation. Sounds like too fancy a business term for a guy who just takes care of animals."

"Nice try, Kai, but you've made the critical error of letting me realize you can keep up with me when I start talking about the budget." She pointed at him. "That's what we call an unforced error, my friend."

Kai let out a mock sigh of annoyance. "A critical unforced error indeed. Okay, but you have to let me give you the rest of the tour before we work on one of your spreadsheets."

"Deal."

AFTER FOLLOWING Kai around for most of the day, Elise had seen both the polished visitors' side of the Conservation Center as well as the behind-the-scenes facilities necessary to keep it running smoothly. They were tidy and functional, even if there was a building or two along the way that could use some updating. She'd met the head of the mammal keepers, reptile and amphibian keepers, and got the closest look she'd ever gotten at a bald eagle at feeding time. Although she had worked with much larger mammals, she gained a healthy respect for the majestic and slightly terrifying raptor up close. True to the Conservation Center's name, a high percentage of the species on exhibit were participants in their Species Survival Plan. And after talking with the keepers, it became clear that the Riverbend keepers were well connected with other zoos and aquariums and extremely open to collaboration.

Like many conservationists she worked with, Kai found dealing with numbers to be an unpleasant necessity, instead focusing on each animal's unique behaviors and personality whenever her questions drifted into budget territory. During the tour, he subtly made the case for the important work happening and gave examples of Riverbend being good stewards of their resources. At the very end, Kai stopped in front of the new area of the zoo currently under construction. It was surrounded by temporary fencing with large letters that read: "NORTH AMERICAN CONSTRUCTION WORKER." Elise grinned. "Get that idea from the Fort Wayne Zoo team?"

"I saw it on social media and couldn't resist borrowing it." Kai led her around the fencing to show her the work in progress, but they were stopped by yellow construction tape and a sign that read *Do Not Enter*. Elise stood on her tiptoes, but couldn't see inside. "Can we take a peek or will we get in trouble?"

Kai studied the signage. There were low-pitched drill sounds coming from some distance away. "I'm not sure what they're up to today. I'd rather skip this part until we know we won't be in their way. Heath would have my head if I got hurt ignoring one of the safety signs."

"Fair enough." Elise smiled. "Speaking of Heath, I should introduce myself and say hi to Freya as well. Do you know if they're in today?"

Kai checked his watch. "Heath should be in his office soon. He's got a lot on his plate but usually keeps an hour or two in the afternoon free. Freya usually stays at her desk if he's away, so you'll definitely get one of the two of them."

Kai turned on one foot to leave but Elise didn't move, instead craning her neck for a better view of the area that was largely blocked off. "Do you know what the inside is going to look like?"

Kai's face turned red with embarrassment. "They didn't show me the price tag."

"I suspected as much. But I bet you have some pretty cool stuff in there."

Kai smiled, but it was forced. "Which we are going to figure out if we can afford?"

Elise met his eyes. "That's what I'm here to help with." She noticed the deep purple circles under Kai's eyes and decided their discussion could wait. "I'm going to head to the office and get some work done. And maybe, if I'm lucky, I can drag Heath into my vis-à-vis discussion and make him think it was his idea." Elise gave Kai a gentle nudge to cheer him up. Kai's worry mirrored her own before she'd left Colorado, but being on the ground with the people in Riverbend had caused a dramatic shift in her perspective. After seeing the work the staff put in at the Conservation Center, she'd begun to believe that underestimating this group would be a mistake. They were as plucky as they came.

Still, Elise couldn't dig RACC out of their financial mess overnight. Under the previous director, RACC had enlisted local craftspeople to help build exhibits at a reduced rate in exchange for a thank you outside of the enclosure. Now, they were locked into contracts negotiated by the cousin of a niece of a friend. Unfortunately, her "expert" negotiation skills had cost the Center money they didn't have to spend. The one exception was that she had managed to get coffee from the River Bean at wholesale prices. The Conservation Center was advertising River Bean coffee prominently at their snack stands and even offering a monthly coffee membership. Before finding her desk at the zoo offices, Elise bought herself a travel mug with RACC's logo on it. Two birds with one stone and all of that.

After hoofing it back through the zoo and waving at some of the keepers she'd met earlier in the day, Elise stopped in to visit the administrative offices. A middle-aged woman with long bright red hair was looking over her purple reading glasses to see her computer screen. She looked up at Elise, blinking slowly.

Elise straightened under her evaluation. "Good afternoon! I'm Elise Butler, from the World Wildlife Trust."

The woman shook out of whatever she was so focused on as Elise walked in. "Oh, hi, Elise. I'm Freya Griffin. It's very nice to meet you in person. Can I help you find your office?"

Elise nodded, and soon Freya was giving her a tour of the space. Freya had been an administrative assistant at the zoo since she'd graduated high school and handled most of the administrative paperwork for employees, acting both as a mini-HR department and primary issuer of checks for zoo expenses. Her enthusiasm was less than that of the zookeepers, but she seemed to be incredibly competent at her job and her tone brooked no arguments. At the end of the efficient tour of the offices, Freya returned to her desk and sat down. "May I help you with anything else? If not, I have a never-ending stack of bills to pay." She gave Elise the smallest of smiles. "At least they aren't mine, right?"

"Right. I think I'm all set, but thank you. I'd like to speak with Heath, if he's in?" Elise looked towards Heath's closed door past Freya's desk. "I suppose you two work closely together?"

Freya shrugged. "When our work overlaps, certainly." Freya turned her focus back to her computer screen.

Conversation over, Elise turned on a heel, wondering if her sister was right and Freya secretly didn't like the director who seemed nice enough so far. Or, maybe, Freya had realized she was more competent than the cousin of the niece of a friend. That would certainly annoy Elise. Well, any environment with so many financial issues wasn't likely to be stress free. One glance into the zoo director's office confirmed that Heath was buried under other administrative commitments, as Kai had indicated. Perhaps he was the classic micromanager who didn't know how to let other people help, then buckled under the weight of their self-imposed workload. Elise took a fortifying breath and tapped on Heath's door. He looked up from rubbing his temples. Instead of khakis, he wore formal trousers and a short-sleeved plaid button-down. His hair was longer than Kai's and quite a lot grayer. He had worry lines around his eyes and mouth. "Hello, can I help you?"

Elise lifted her hand in a wave. "Hi, I'm Elise Butler. We've spoken on the phone?"

Heath's eyes lit up with recognition. "Elise! Of, course, I should have known you by your voice. How are you? Did you make it here alright?"

"Very good. I've spent most of the day with Kai, learning about RACC."

"Great! We're glad to be working with you. Particularly after our last accountant left." He held his hands up. "Not due to the rest of the crew, of course."

Elise lifted an eyebrow, unsure of how honest she should be with Heath. She strongly suspected the accountant started seeking another opportunity after Elise had begun to ask her some difficult questions she couldn't answer. Not willing to be the one that undermined Heath's faith in people a minute after showing up at his door, she kept it simple. "Sorry to hear that."

Heath waved a hand. "Water under the bridge. She was highly recommended, you understand, but I think you'll do a great job. I've been doing some of the work in her absence, and Freya of course. But, we'll be glad to have your help."

"It's nice to be here. I've had a tour of the facility already and was hoping to talk through the budget and hear about the Center's fundraising activities. I have numbers on what's worked for some of our partner zoos and I'd be happy to share them with you."

Heath looked at the pile of paperwork on his desk. "Oh, yes. Of course. We've been conducting ad hoc fundraising but are always open to more ideas." Heath's phone rang and he stared at the number and frowned. "I'm so sorry, I have to take this. It's a member of the board of directors. I really would like to catch up later — does that work for you?"

"No worries at all. That sounds important. We'll talk another time."

Heath waved apologetically and answered his phone, the harried expression returning to his face. He spoke in low and urgent tones to the caller and she left feeling like she'd caught some of his stress like a cold. Containing the stress to his office, she shut his door and left. Freya was staring intently at her computer and didn't see Elise wave awkwardly goodbye. She picked up a radio from the set being charged by the door and clipped it and the holder onto her belt. The relaxation she'd felt when touring the zoo had started to slip away with the reminder that the WWT sent her because there was real work to do here. After the conversations she'd had with the keepers today, Heath was also the only one holding out hope that Doctor Oliver would come back. She couldn't imagine the tough-as-nails Freya indulging his wishful thinking. Poor guy. She hoped he was right, but if he wasn't, he was going to be in even rougher shape when reality came crashing in. Elise checked her watch. She had just enough time to do something more immediately useful.

Half an hour later, and with a greater understanding of why Kai had joked about needing a machete, Elise had cleared back some of the larger bushes and the milkweed everywhere they were hanging over the path. She heard a noise behind her and saw a woman in khakis with her curly blonde hair pulled up in a high ponytail. The woman gestured to the newly trimmed-back plants. "You're doing a lovely job, thank you!"

"It's no trouble." Elise wiped her forehead with her arm.

"I heard you were short on veterinarians. Have you seen Kai?" The woman's bright green eyes took in the pile of milkweed trimmings. She was built like an athlete, and although her khakis had the same fit as the ones Elise wore, hers had a different logo.

"Oh, of course! You must be Dr. Perry. I'm Elise Butler from the World Wildlife Trust."

"It's nice to meet you, Elise." Veronica waved her hand. "And Veronica is fine. My friends call me V. Dr. V, if you insist on a title." She looked past Elise. "I heard you needed some help with your clouded leopards."

"Yes, absolutely. They're this way, but let me get in touch with Kai. They can be a little sensitive to newcomers."

"No problem." Veronica picked up the hedge trimmers and trimmed back a few spots Elise had missed while she'd stopped to radio for Kai. Elise snapped the radio back into the holder on her waist and Veronica handed her the large trimmers. "Couldn't help myself. They do look better this way."

"It's the native flora. They grow like weeds here. I mean, some of them are technically weeds. They are beautiful but needed a haircut. They were driving me nuts."

Kai cleared his throat and stepped into the conversation. "I'm driving you nuts on your first day? And here I thought I was on my best behavior."

Elise smiled. "Nope, you're fine. It's the bushes."

Kai tipped his head to one side. "You are the first accountant I've ever met that trimmed the plants on her first day."

"I love surprising people." Elise gestured towards the visiting veterinarian. "And Veronica helped. She couldn't help herself either. You know each other, right?"

"We've worked together a few times." Kai stuck out a hand and his cheeks turned a little pink. "Nice to see you again, Dr. V. Welcome back from...?"

"Nepal. I've been working with some of our conservation partners over there, and to be honest, I'm not even sure what day it is." Veronica turned to Elise. "I'm sorry I couldn't be here sooner. I got here as soon as I could after my flight landed. Ready to go check out our cloudeds?

"Absolutely." Kai started walking towards the clouded leopard enclosure with Veronica close behind.

Elise didn't need to be told that the cats didn't want a crowd, so she gathered her supplies, cleaned up the trimmings, and put away her things. She'd stayed a bit longer than she intended, but it felt good to make progress on something at the Center.

Keys in hand, she walked through the front gate. Elise froze when she saw the bushes move near the construction zone. However, no one around her seemed to notice. She peeked into them and shrieked when a squirrel bolted out. She put a hand to her heart and laughed. Really, what kind of trouble could happen at a friendly little zoo in Riverbend?

CHAPTER 8

*E*lise spent the rest of the week at Riverbend Animal Conservation Center doing plenty of good, old-fashioned hard work. While the Center needed someone to help solve their financial troubles, they also needed extra boots on the ground working on the less glamorous tasks that kept it running. Elise graduated from trimming bushes to helping clean enclosures and feeding some of the more trusting animals. She'd studied animal behavior in college and on her internships, but the keepers weren't quite ready to let her help with anything more difficult yet. Slowly but surely, her coworkers began to see her less as a paper pusher and more as a partner they could depend on, even taking a suggestion on scents they could leave in the tiger enclosure to give them something new and interesting to investigate. Despite their initial skepticism, with Dr. V's approval, their Sumatran tiger was soon rolling in celery salt like it was catnip.

Because everyone was still reeling from Dr. Oliver's unexpected disappearance, not to mention the zoo's budget troubles, Heath hadn't started putting out feelers for a permanent replacement for their veterinarian. In the meantime, Elise helped Dr. V fill in the gaps Dr. Oliver left behind with the less glamorous, non-contact sample collection duties. Or as Zoey pointed out, Elise was the Center's dedicated pooper-scooper. If someone asked her, Elise might haughtily inform them that she was enabling important research, but Zoey wasn't wrong. Elise was just doing the more scientific version of her sister's duties at the Riverbend K-9 Academy. That said, she was sore from all of the extra exercise that came with feeding, lifting, and hauling supplies, using muscles not normally required for balancing accounts and attending remote meetings.

Despite her long-dormant muscles' fatigue, Elise didn't have the patience to take it easy on the couch when the weekend arrived. Nor did she have space to start any new projects. Instead, she accepted an invitation to spend time with Zoey and her friends. This was how she ended up leaving her apartment at the crack of dawn on a Saturday in athletic clothes, attempting to beat the summer heat. She shut the door and spotted her neighbor, similarly dressed, but this time without his dog at his side. He nodded a greeting and they both left to enjoy the day.

Elise stopped into the River Bean to pick up an extra-strong cup of coffee and Marlene gave her a side of unsolicited advice on how to mountain bike. Marlene had never mountain biked, but she'd managed to retain countless tips and tricks patrons had shared with her over the years. Elise considered the pitfalls Marlene had instructed her to avoid and downed about half of her coffee before reaching the hilly trails outside Riverbend.

Once she parked, Elise found herself in a mostly unfamiliar crowd; she only knew her sister and Liam. She wasn't shy but she also didn't possess the sort of boisterous extroversion that made friends easily. She smiled politely when everyone introduced themselves, paying a little more attention when she finally reached a familiar face. Her neighbor introduced himself as Finn, with no further detail. Well, now she had a first name.

Once introductions were done and everyone began gathering their equipment, Zoey sidled up to her and whispered, "I'll give you five dollars for every name you remember."

Elise snorted. "You are Zoey. Over there is Liam. That's ten. Oh, and Finn." Zoey cocked an eyebrow in the way she'd done when they were both in high school. Elise pointed an accusing finger at her. "None of that. He's my neighbor and hadn't introduced himself. I was curious." Zoey's mouth twitched and Elise rolled her eyes. "Remind me why I wanted to spend more quality time with you?"

Zoey smiled. "That nervous about mountain biking, huh?"

"Terrified. This is what you do for fun?" Elise winced. "I'm trying not to think about the purple bruise — scrape? — you called 'tree burn' in your text a few weeks ago. And Marlene told me a high school kid broke his arm last week?"

"It grows on you. And that was Ben. If you saw him mountain biking, you'd realize it was a miracle that was only the first time he broke his arm." Zoey gave her a helmet. "I guarantee whatever you are stressed about, you will forget about it the moment you go hurtling down one of those hills."

"Hurtling?" Elise ran a hand down her face. "You had to use the word hurtling? Couldn't have gone with zooming, steering, or even coasting?"

"Nope." Zoey leaned over, checking various settings on Elise's mountain bike. Once she was satisfied, she took a step back. "We'll start you on the easy trails, though. I even borrowed my favorite kind of mountain bike from a friend so you could start off on the right foot. Feet? Wheels."

Elise pounded what remained of her coffee and put on the helmet. "It's sweet she let you borrow it."

Zoey shrugged. "It's what people do here. And I said friend, but I should have said boss. It gets a little fuzzy sometimes."

Elise lifted an eyebrow. "Well, let's get going so I can learn before the coffee wears off. I'd rather not wreck your boss/friend's bike."

After a quick lesson on the easy trails, Elise was soon zipping up and down the hills of Indiana. While Zoey moved cautiously, picking her way carefully down and pointing out obstacles, Elise waited at the top of each hill so she could fly down once Zoey had pointed out all of the dangers. She had a healthy fear of actual risk and didn't have any desire to 'hurtle' down the hills, but Elise soon realized she could have a great time within the limits of her comfort and coordination. And she'd never been as much of an overthinker as her sister. At least where her own safety was concerned. When Zoey wanted to come work for the FBI and drop herself in the middle of an investigation, that was something else entirely. But that didn't matter now. It had turned out alright.

When the entire crew was sweaty, covered in dirt, and exhausted, they eventually all found each other again at the parking lot. There, they placed bikes on racks or disassembled them, puzzle piecing them into car trunks and guzzling water. It was late summer in Indiana and more humid than Elise was used to as the sun rose higher in the sky. She splashed a little water on her face, but it only made her wet rather than cooling her off. Zoey threw a sweaty arm around her. "Come on, girlfriend. To the humidity-controlled pub. My treat. Since I don't even have to pay for repairs when I return the bike to Alexis, I'm still ahead."

Soon, Elise found herself in a cozy pub called Bridges, surrounded by a talkative crew of mountain bikers. The walls were liberally covered with photographs taken in Riverbend and the tables were quickly filling up with the lunch crowd. However, Finn hadn't joined the crew for lunch. He'd said his goodbyes and something about icing his leg. He'd been limping a bit when he left. Hopefully, he hadn't gotten a dose of tree burn like her sister. Plenty of people came over to visit their group and soon they'd filled a line of tables they pushed together with help from staff who seemed to be expecting them. Chairs were rearranged to make room and almost as often as waters were refilled, people swapped chairs to visit. During one of the rounds of musical chairs, a woman with brown hair pulled up into a bobbing ponytail and a visor sat next to her, holding a large glass of ice water. "You must be Elise! How'd the bike do?" Elise took a moment to process the question and the woman stuck out a hand. "I'm sorry. I'm still buzzed from my run. First half marathon on the trails in ages. I'm Alex. I work at the K-9 Academy with your sister."

"Oh, of course! I've heard all about you." Elise stiffened a bit, realizing she was talking to Zoey's boss. "It's great to finally put a face to a name. Thanks for letting me borrow the bike. Oh! And for my upgraded security system." After Zoey and Elise had suffered their break-in at the hands of a criminal from Zoey's old workplace, Alexis had nudged along the effort to improve their apartment's security system. Even if Alexis had done her the favor only to convince Zoey to assist the FBI, Elise was grateful all the same.

Alexis waved away her thanks. "Not needed at all, your sister really helped us out. She's still helping us out. Well, it's great to meet you." She leaned behind Elise to catch Zoey's attention. "Hey, Zo, can I ask you a huge favor?"

Zoey nodded. "Of course."

"Sorry to bug you about it on a Saturday, but can you reach out to our current foster homes to see if anyone can take an extra puppy? Zeke, the German shepherd puppy, is a little over a month away from starting with us. His foster mom broke her leg and he's too rambunctious for her right now. It's got to be someone who can take him all day with them, though. He's super high energy." Alexis blew out a breath. "She only just got him to not chew through his crate walls."

Elise grimaced. "Is your furry jailbreaker going to be a good detection dog? Yikes."

Alexis directed her attention back to Elise. "Oh yeah. He's super smart and gets bored easily, he just needs the right partner. If he was chewing on people instead of his cage, I'd be more worried, frankly. But we need to find the right kind of home for him. One with someone who does a lot of walking."

Zoey nodded. "Deal. I could do it, but..."

"Yeah, I know. It'll pull you and Liam away from training. And Zeke needs some focused attention. I don't want to confuse him with two other dogs. Not until he's mastered the basics." Alexis rubbed a hand over her face. "We'll get it figured out. We always do."

Elise cleared her throat. "If you get desperate, I'm only going to be here for a few months, but I could take him. Zoey could teach me the basics you want him to know. If it's a foster situation, not like a permanent thing."

Alexis eyed her curiously. "That's a pretty big responsibility."

Elise shrugged. "It's only for a month. My nights are open, and I could see if the Conservation Center would mind if I brought him to work with me. I'm outside all the time. I mean, if he's friendly enough to bring around kids and visitors and stuff. And he'll have to be okay being handed off if I need to go visit an animal."

Zoey beamed. "That would be more than perfect for socializing him, Alex. Elise took a bunch of animal behavior classes in college, and she helps with animal enrichment at the Conservation Center. Heck, she's more qualified than me. You know I'm biased, but Tasha loves her, and you know how Miss Pickypants is."

Alexis rubbed her chin. "I'll need you to come by the Academy for some basic lessons. We've got specific commands and methods we'd want you to use. We're pretty careful about who works with our dogs, but if it's temporary and Tasha vouches for you..."

"Don't you mean Zoey?" Elise laughed.

"Well, yeah, her too." Alexis winked and took a drink of water. "That feels a little too easy."

"Just trying to make my older sister look good." Elise waved away Alexis's obvious gratitude. "And having a dog around would be nice."

"Okay." Alexis reached up to accept a beer in a frosty pint glass that a friendly man delivered to the table. He had a large mustache, salt and pepper hair, and a twinkle in his eyes.

The man put his hands on his hips and beamed at her. "Well, hello there, another new friend of Alexis?"

Elise looked between Alexis and Zoey. "I'm Zoey's sister."

"Then it's my pleasure to welcome you to Bridges, Zoey's sister! I'm Thurston Riley." The jovial man stuck out his hand.

Zoey gestured to Thurston's mustache. "New look, Mayor Riley?"

He paused his stroking. "Yes, I think it makes me look more dignified. And my hope is that it convinces our friends over there in the corner booth that I actually do know what I'm doing, and we really did need that tenth stoplight in town." He leaned in conspiratorially. "They bring it up at every town council meeting. It's already installed. But at least they've stopped complaining about the shifted holiday schedule for trash pick-up."

Zoey eyed the group skeptically. "I think getting them to back off is going to take more than a mustache. They tried to get me to sign a petition about the stoplight last Saturday. Your new open-faced roast beef sandwich recipe didn't do the trick?"

Thurston hung his head. "Nope." He straightened, tugging his belt up. "Well, there's always tomorrow. Ladies, it's been a pleasure, but it looks like I am needed."

A man in the corner booth started snapping his fingers in the air to get Thurston's attention and Elise's eyes widened. "Wow. That's...something."

Alexis snorted. "They're just doing their part to hit our quota of curmudgeons. Your sister thought our little town was perfect when she first came, so we're making sure you're not under the same assumptions."

"Nowhere is perfect," Zoey acquiesced, "but there is a lot of good here."

Alexis stood. "So, when do you have time to come by?"

Elise pulled out her phone. "I can give you Wednesday afternoon, if that suits? Let me check with Heath and Kai, and I'll let you know if they veto my involvement. I don't think they will. The Center attracts a lot of people who love animals, as both visitors and employees."

"Perfect. I can definitely keep Zeke happy until then. We'll have some paperwork for you to fill out, maybe a short interview. I can email you everything. Thanks again for doing us a solid."

"It's no problem." Elise slid her phone back into her pocket. "Unlike my sister, I plan to limit my help to fostering a dog. I have no intention of getting pulled into an FBI investigation."

CHAPTER 9

*A*fter a cozy family lunch with Liam and Zoey on Sunday, Elise returned to her apartment with the plan to spend Sunday afternoon curled up on the big red sofa in her living room with a new paperback. However, on her way to the door, she spotted Marlene behind the counter of the River Bean and make a quick detour to say hello. It was a little late in the day for full-strength coffee, but the quirky aesthetic and white noise of the coffee shop would be the perfect place to spend a few hours reading a book on her quiet afternoon.

Marlene leaned on the counter. "Well, hey there, stranger. How are you settling in?"

"Really well, all things considered."

"I'm sure sorry to hear about Dr. Oliver. I was hoping there was some kind of miscommunication, but the sheriff came in earlier for his afternoon coffee. He said there isn't much hope. Dr. Oliver was an unusual sort, but his heart was always in the right place. It's a darn shame." Marlene wiped the counter. "What can I get for you, Miss Elise?"

Elise tapped her finger on her mouth. "Decaf or tea. Any suggestions?"

"Tea. I make my own blends for the shop. Do you need energy or calm?"

Elise grinned. "A bit of both. Most days, actually."

"My mint blend it is, then. It'll be just the thing." Marlene turned to face her large glass canisters filled with tea leaves. A temperature and number of minutes were scrawled on the side of the glass in black marker.

A warm voice behind Elise said, "Can you make it two, Marlene?"

Marlene turned and winked. "Of course, young man. And does Sedona need anything?"

"She's all set."

Elise turned to look at the couple behind her. Her neighbor, Finn, nodded a greeting and she snickered when she had to lower her gaze to spot Sedona, Finn's cute yellow Lab. He kept a loose hold on Sedona's leash but stood protectively next to her every bit as much as she stood protectively next to him. Elise grinned. "Well, hello, neighbor. And Sedona."

Sedona swished her tail along the ground and leaned against Finn. He gave her a quick pat. "I heard you've volunteered to foster Zeke. That was awfully kind of you."

Elise quirked an eyebrow. "News travels fast. You know Alexis?"

"You could say that." He stuck out a hand. "I'm Finn. I work with Alex, Liam, and I believe your sister, Zoey, if the Riverbend gossip is to be believed." A frisson of electricity traveled up her arm when they touched, and Elise's face warmed.

Elise pulled her hand away and quickly turned around to pay for her drink. It looked like the cups of tea were ready, but Marlene didn't give them to them right away. A few minutes into watching her landlady serve others without wanting to be rude and inter-rupt, a timer went off. Marlene paused serving a customer and gave them their teas in large white ceramic mugs. "Now, Finn, I couldn't help but overhear. You've got Elise helping you out now?"

Elise put a hand over her mouth. "Oops. I should have asked. Marlene, is it okay if I have a dog in the apartment?"

Marlene waved a hand. "If it's for Alexis, that's no problem. I've had renters with worse manners than her dogs. Present company excluded, of course." She turned back to a waiting customer, effi-ciently taking orders and pulling an espresso shot.

Finn took a step toward the tables at the front of the shop and gestured for Elise to join him. She bit her lip, sneaking a glance at the book poking out of her purse. It suddenly seemed less interest-ing, and her neighbor seemed to be in a more chatty mood than the morning they first met.

Elise settled into a funky pink chair covered in blue and yellow paint splatter and Finn chose the yellow one with abstract streaks across from her, stretching out one leg. Sedona lay her head next to his foot, watching Elise carefully. Elise took a sip of her tea. "So, are you an instructor?"

Finn nodded. "Temporarily. Full disclosure, you'll be working with me to train Zeke. Alex let me know."

The frisson of energy still rushing through her system fizzled on impact with that little piece of news. Her intriguing neighbor was interrogating her, not flirting. She totally knew that. And frankly, should have expected it. Elise leaned back in her chair and wrapped both hands around her mug. "That sounds...great. Is Zeke similar to Sedona?"

"A little." Finn coughed a little to cover his laugh.

Elise narrowed her eyes. "What was that?"

"Zeke is...energetic. If you need help, just ask, okay?"

Elise eyed him skeptically. "I've worked with more species than you can imagine, from elephants to primates to tigers. I think I can handle a puppy. Especially one that's almost grown."

"Fair point." Finn raised his mug of tea in salute, but Elise could have sworn she saw him exchange a knowing look with his dog.

~

FINN STUDIED Elise and took a sip of his tea. He wasn't generally much of a tea drinker, but it was getting too late in the afternoon for coffee. And his leg had been acting up, making a good night's sleep more difficult than usual. Maybe Marlene had a tea for that too. Elise watched him carefully and he straightened under her appraisal. He didn't know her well, but Alexis had said she was clever and had kind eyes. Alexis hadn't mentioned that Elise's dark blue eyes sparkled with intelligence, or that her soft brown waves framed her face perfectly, highlighting her warm smile. He certainly hadn't expected to feel a zip of attraction when they politely shook hands. Not that it mattered. They were just working together. He should break the tension of the quiet that had fallen between them, but found himself a little lost for words.

Fortunately, Elise spoke first. She looked down at Sedona. "So, how long have you been an instructor?"

"Not too long. I've mostly been working in the field, but I had an injury and needed to take a little detour to do something less physical for a little while. Liam and I go way back, so I reached out to him, even though I'd been through a different program with Sedona. The Academy has a good one, though." Finn moved his foot to try and find a position that felt more comfortable. Once he'd stopped moving, Sedona rested her head next to his foot.

"What else do you do besides work?"

Finn hid his smile behind his mug. Her curiosity in the face of the unfamiliar was a good sign. People who asked questions generally did better in their training programs, and truth be told, he found people who didn't ask questions a bit boring. "I build furniture. Mostly wood, but I do a little welding for bases as well. My brother has a workshop he lets me use sometimes."

"Oh? Do you sell it?"

"No, usually I just take orders from friends or family looking for something custom and make it for them. I made my sister a new coffee table with a live edge for her birthday. It turned out great. If she doesn't like it, I'm taking it for my place."

Elise laughed. "I know exactly what you mean. I like to refurbish existing pieces, not create a new structure, but I've only given mine as gifts too. I'd love to learn how to make furniture though."

Finn bit his lip before he offered to teach her. They'd just met and had talked for less than an hour. He barely knew her outside of her connection with the Conservation Center. He cleared his throat and steered the conversation back to the topic at hand. "Alexis said you worked with the Conservation Center?"

"Technically, I work for the World Wildlife Trust. I'm just here to help since...everything."

"And, even with everything...it seems okay so far?" He tried to make his question sound natural, but she turned her head slightly, so he obviously hadn't quite achieved it.

"Insofar as any organization is okay when they lose one of their own. I'm only helping them out, trying to figure out how to manage expenses and raise funds." She took a sip of tea, maintaining eye contact over the brim of the mug.

"That's nice of you. Is funding a common issue for Conservation Centers?" Finn knew what the answer should be, but *someone* was making money. He wasn't particularly worried it was Elise. Alexis had likely already grilled Zoey about her sister. By the time Elise arrived to help with Zeke, the director of Riverbend K-9 Academy would have run a background check as well.

"It can be. The places we work with are all not-for-profits. And quality animal care doesn't come cheap. The previous director did some smart things, like growing some of the food for herbivores on site, but they've really struggled since he left. Heath has been trying his best to get them back on track, but he got a lot of bad advice early in his tenure that he hasn't quite recovered from."

"So, you're not seeing a lot of millionaires walking around?" Finn lifted an eyebrow, keeping his voice light.

Elise laughed, the sound doing something to his stomach. "Ah yes, all of those secretly wealthy people in the zookeeping industry. Do you know how much they pay us?"

"I don't think it's polite for me to ask that." Finn scratched Sedona behind one ear.

"Not enough to buy a private jet. We'll just say that." Mischief danced in Elise's eyes. "What did you say you did in the field?"

"Oh, this and that. Sedona has a great nose, so the FBI sends me where I'm needed." Finn looked into his mug to buy time to redirect the conversation to safer ground. "This is great." He raised his cup to Marlene in salute, who did a very poor job acting as if she wasn't eavesdropping while she cleaned a nearby table.

"Mm-hm. And how long are you in town?"

"Oh, only for a bit. My leg injury is almost recovered but I don't want to push too much, too fast. Mountain biking yesterday was probably too aggressive, but after some ice, I'm just a little sore. I'm grateful I didn't break it, or I would have missed biking entirely. And it was fun."

"Still, that sounds painful." Elise grimaced. "Well, I hope it's soon a distant memory."

Finn smiled. "Same."

"Oh, I get it. It's why you couldn't take on a second dog." Elise put a hand to her forehead. "Or you would have volunteered."

Finn nodded. "Nailed it. Zeke is too much for me to keep up with right now." He took another sip of tea and attempted to get the conversation back on track. Between the animal trafficking communications the FBI had intercepted and the suspicious death of the veterinarian, something odd had to be happening at the Conservation Center. Maybe Elise knew something but didn't realize it. "Tell me more about the Riverbend Animal Conservation Center. What do they have you working on here? Surely you're not just balancing the checkbook."

"Well, I'm an accountant by title but double majored in wildlife biology, so for a facility like Riverbend, I'm also helping take care of the animals, doing odd jobs and the like, until we can backfill Dr. Oliver."

"Sounds like a good idea. Have you met the new leopard cubs I've heard so much about?" Sedona shifted and rolled on her side. Finn reached down to scratch her stomach.

"Yes. They're adorable. I'm not allowed to handle them." Elise's face fell. "Well, him."

Finn tipped his head to the side. "Aren't there two?"

Elise grimaced, her pain obvious. She swirled the tea in her mug. "Now, there's one. A press release is coming any day now. We lost one at the same time we lost Dr. Oliver."

Finn froze with his mug in the air. "Wow, that's awful." He took a sip of his tea and kept his voice carefully casual. "What happened to the cub, if you don't mind me asking?"

"A bacterial infection. It's uncommon, but it does happen sometimes, I'm afraid. Dr. Oliver sent the cub out for an official analysis to confirm, but it's probably just a formality."

"Hmm. That's rough." Finn looked into the middle distance but no easy answer came to him. Killing a cub certainly didn't make sense if the Conservation Center was involved in animal trafficking — clouded cubs were worth far more alive. Still, it seemed like the Conservation Center was getting more than its fair share of bad luck. Elise fiddled with a string on her tea bag and he reached down to pet Sedona. "I'm really sorry, Elise. I hope your experience with the K-9 facility is less dramatic. So other than keeping it all together, any other challenges at the Center keeping you up at night?" He gave her a gentle smile.

Elise smiled back ruefully. "Fortunately, no. It's only a matter of doing the work right now."

"Well, if you're ever worried about anything, you've got a friend down the hall. Don't be afraid to reach out if you need to vent." He sat back in his chair, placing his mug on the table.

"That's nice of you to say." Elise took a drink of her tea and looked him in the eyes. "So, I get to work with the dogs, I assume?" She lifted an eyebrow. "I mean, unless we're pretending this wasn't an interview and you're just a friendly guy who never spoke to me at length until he found out I'd be working with his dogs."

Finn fully grinned. "If you didn't pass before, you would now. Plus, Marlene likes you."

Elise finished what was left of her tea and Finn stood to take their cups back. "Marlene likes everyone." Sedona rose and stretched, giving a big yawn and tap of her tail against the leg of a nearby table. Finn petted her and gave her the okay to sniff Elise. Elise gave her some pets and Sedona flopped over for a better scratch from her new friend. "You are such a good girl."

"She really is." Finn tipped his head towards the efficient owner of the River Bean, holding both mug handles in one hand. "And, yes, Marlene is sweet to everyone, but you can always tell if she really likes someone if she waits to give them their tea until it's fully steeped. She sets a timer for whatever is written on the side of the jar if she likes you. If she doesn't, she just hands it over."

Elise looked back at their landlord. "You're kidding." Finn grinned at the shocked look on her face, her jaw slightly dropped in a scandalized smile.

Finn winked. "Stick around, watch the customers, and tell me if I'm wrong. Enjoy the rest of your weekend, Ms. Butler."

～

TWO TEA REFILLS and several chapters into her book later, Elise confirmed what Finn had already noticed. Marlene set a timer and only brought her the drink once it had gone off. And she seemed to be doing this for everyone until one of the men who had been giving Thurston a hard time about the new stoplight came in. He was given his tea right away. Elise bit her lip and Marlene met her eyes, giving her a little wink. Elise chuckled and put a scrap piece of paper in her book, closing it to take it upstairs. Riverbend had provided more than adequate entertainment for the afternoon, and learning that her new neighbor was willing to interrogate her over a puppy she'd never met was pretty endearing. He was a little bit crusty around the edges, but his heart was in the right place. And that was all she'd noticed. Not his kind smile or mischievous observations. She just knew they'd make a great team. At the K-9 Academy.

CHAPTER 10

When Elise returned to work on Monday, she power walked through the front gates of the Riverbend Animal Conservation Center with a bounce in her step and a mostly full travel mug of River Bean coffee in hand. They brewed the same beans at the snack stand, but she'd gotten used to chatting with Marlene in the mornings. The teenager running the little stand inside the Conservation Center merely said a friendly good morning, while Marlene always had a juicy tidbit or two to share. Normally, Elise would declare herself above gossip, but Marlene's gossip was always the best. Without her River Bean coffee, she would have never known that the bookshop owner wasn't from around the area but seemed like a decent sort. And that a new engineer working at the Indiana Polytechnic satellite research facility had just come into town and rented an apartment from Thurston. Which, of course, was critical news for starting her day. A few steps past the aviary, she spotted Kai. She gave him a big wave, and he lowered a large steel bucket to the ground. "Good morning, Elise. Did you have a nice weekend?"

"I did! I finished unpacking and visited my sister and Liam."

"Nice! I've known Liam for a long time. He seems really happy with Zoey."

"Oh, I thought the K-9 Academy was new?"

"It is. Liam isn't." Kai grinned. "We grew up in the same small town about half an hour outside of Riverbend. To be honest with you, I had my reservations about the FBI starting a dog training facility in town when they first showed up, but they seem alright."

Elise thought back to the camaraderie of the team and Alexis's worry for a puppy who needed a home. Then, Finn's oh-so-subtle pre-interview before letting Elise come work with one of their dogs. "Yeah, I kind of got that feeling. No one in Denver will believe I spent the weekend with more than one FBI agent in a town that's barely a pinprick on the map of Indiana, but there you go."

"Sounds like you had more excitement than I did. I spent most of my time here feeding the animals."

"Don't you only do that on weekdays?" Elise narrowed her eyes. "I don't have you down for weekend overtime."

"Well, with the facility short on funds, sometimes I come in because I want to." Kai straightened. "And technically, I'm salary, so you don't have to pay me overtime. No need to write that on your spreadsheet."

"That seems like it's asking too much of you." Elise's heart lurched. "For what it's worth, I'm trying to help."

"And that's a good aspiration." Kai seemed like he wanted to say something. They'd transitioned into a weird space between friends and colleagues, so she let the silence hang for a moment. Kai cleared his throat. "And I got to take an amazing vacation to India last spring before the cubs were born, so I'm good for a bit."

"If you say so. But I insist on pictures. I know you took pictures of wildlife while you were there."

Kai grinned. "Guilty. I'll send you all of the cool insects and reptiles I saw. And I even visited a tiger reserve to connect with people out in the field. So, no feeling bad for me. This place houses a lot of animals, and the food isn't cheap. If I can be a little creative to save us a couple of bucks, I might sneak in a weekend or two. And with the leopard cub..."

"I know." Elise's stomach ached. "I'm so sorry about that."

Kai gave her a half-smile. "It's part of the job, Elise. It's hard, but it happens in nature too." Kai sighed and hefted the big silver bucket. "Speaking of, it's time to feed the cloudeds."

Elise's phone flashed with a text from Alexis. She held up a finger. "Hey, so before you go, I offered to foster a puppy from the K-9 Academy. Is that okay? I mean, if I bring him around? They want him to be a wildlife detection dog eventually and maybe it could even be a long-term partnership..."

Kai considered. "Oh wow. That's a big responsibility. You'd have to clear it with the other keepers and keep the dog outside of the animals' enclosures. And if the dog freaks the animals out, we'll have to change plans."

Elise nodded, a little too furiously. "Of course. I assumed as much."

Kai shrugged. "Well, then, it's okay with me. It sounds really interesting."

"Awesome. Thanks so much."

"Not a problem. We have to be pretty flexible around here." Kai gestured to his bucket. "However, the cloudeds aren't quite as flexible. Duty calls."

Elise soon found herself standing on the path next to the entrance by herself. She read the text from Alexis and chuckled: it was a request for animal scat for training purposes. Fortunately, it was easy enough for her to collect, since it was part of her job. It was odd but doable. She'd get it done right before she went in to help them. Thus far, her efforts to help the Conservation Center felt like trying to chop down a tree with a butter knife. By contrast, helping the K-9 Academy by fostering a puppy was a concrete, accomplishable goal. With Kai's blessing in hand, she just had to convince Heath it was a good idea.

Elise turned on a heel and headed towards the administrative building. Freya was coming from across the parking lot. Someone pounded on something in the construction area and Freya jumped. She clutched her purse closer and walked with her head down in Elise's direction. Elise cleared her throat. "Morning, Freya. How are you?"

Freya looked at her for a few seconds, as if just registering that Elise was there. "Oh, good morning. I'm so sorry, I've forgotten your name."

"Elise. Elise Butler."

"Oh, yes, of course. Hi, Elise." Freya pulled her badge out of her purse, and Elise noticed Freya's hands were shaking slightly. They badged in, and the door to the administrative building unlocked with a loud click. Freya mumbled something about an important phone call. She picked up her laptop off her desk and went into an empty conference room, shutting the door before Elise had time to ask if she was alright.

Elise peeked into Heath's office, where he was squinting into his phone and texting. She knocked on the open door and he looked up. "Oh! Hello, Elise. What brings you in today?"

Elise smiled nervously. "Morning. Sorry to bother you, but I offered to help my sister foster a dog — she works at the K-9 Academy and they need some help. I was wondering if you would mind if I helped them out?"

Heath looked down at his phone, and then up at her. He blinked a few times. "Oh, um, I'm not sure why it would affect me?"

"The dog would come with me to work."

"Oh." He blinked again. "Okay. What are you training him to do?"

"Me personally?" Elise put a hand to her chest. "Sit? Don't

chew shoes? I'm not sure. He doesn't start formal training for the FBI for another month or so."

Heath furrowed his brow and looked at his phone again. "I don't really have time to take on additional work."

Elise shook her head. "I won't need you to do anything. If he takes up more of my time than I expect, I'll make it up."

"And if any of the zookeepers have a problem..."

"Already talked to Kai. Kai and I agree that the animals come first. I'll clear it with the keepers and make sure he doesn't disturb the animals. We're trying to get the puppy acclimated to a lot of background noise and smells, and the Conservation Center is a great place to do it."

"I guess I can't think of any reason to tell you no then." Heath nodded but didn't smile.

Elise looked awkwardly at Heath's desk, wondering if he was actually going to tell her yes. When he just stared at her, she nodded slowly. "Okay...I'll let them know I can bring the dog to work."

"Okay then. Do you need anything else from me?"

Elise tapped a finger against her mouth. "I'll need to run through the finances with you at some point. I've started going through receipts from our vendors, and I think we might be able to get them to lower their prices."

"Great. I'm glad to hear that. I haven't had the time to go in and fix everything yet. Freya has offered to help, but she's got enough on her plate. We'll go through the list, and I can reach out to the places you identify."

"Of course." Elise paused for a moment, unsure if this was the right time to bring up the next subject. However, the upcoming expenses were going to happen whether it was the right time or not. Finally, she took a breath and dove in. "I'm a little worried the construction project isn't going to get finished. They need us to pay in advance and the next phase is out of our budget."

Heath ran a hand through his hair. "That's okay. We can hold off on starting the next phase until we're in a better spot, okay?"

Elise breathed out. "Yeah. That makes sense. That'll buy us a little more time. And you're working on fundraisers, I assume?"

Heath crossed his arms, his posture a little defensive. "Yes. I know we haven't done well this year, but I'm trying to do better." He held his head high.

Elise forced a smile. "Well, I'm sure whatever you have in mind will help." She bit her tongue instead of offering to send him the list of successful fundraisers she'd seen at other zoos again. There was a lot of potential here, but progress was never instantaneous. She'd give Heath a little more time to realize she came in peace, then start working with him on joint ideas, gently nudging him towards those most likely to work.

Heath sat behind his desk. "I've been cultivating several major donors and I anticipate a donation very soon. If it doesn't come through, I'll let you know, okay?"

Elise smiled. "Of course." She left the office before Heath could change his mind. Hopefully, once she had a cute well-behaved puppy on site, he would garner more enthusiasm from the director of the Conservation Center.

CHAPTER 11

*B*y the time Wednesday arrived, Elise was truly grateful she'd committed to visiting the Riverbend K-9 Academy, if only to avoid another day of paperwork in the zoo's administrative building. Heath's schedule had finally cleared up and his increased availability meant they'd had time to go through the complicated finances of the Conservation Center together. She did get an occasional break when Heath had calls with donors, and she didn't envy him that job. He was too far away for her to fully eavesdrop, but, based on the low tones, he was sharing news about the cub. All of Riverbend knew by now, but for anyone outside the Bridges/River Bean circle, a press release would be posted on the Conservation Center website that day. On their second day of finding savings in existing contracts, Freya popped into one of their many meetings to offer coffee and help. She seemed somewhat more relaxed, but Heath gently told her that they didn't want to overburden her and she tensed up again. It was thoughtful of him to let Freya focus on the day-to-day tasks, but it meant that Elise got to spend nearly every minute of their remaining time together staring at a screen with no further offers for coffee.

However, after the occasional awkward conversation with Heath and the flexing of every accounting skill she had, Elise now knew exactly where money was being spent. She could make a plan to dig Riverbend out of their financial hole, one scoopful of metaphorical dirt at a time. But first, her brain desperately needed a break. And some time outside.

In contrast to navigating the politics, stresses, and sensitivities within the Conservation Center management chain, collecting clouded leopard scat for Alexis would be easy and to the point. Fortunately, the one person's consent she needed to go rummaging through the clouded leopard enclosure got there first thing in the morning. After a quick stop at the River Bean to refill her travel mug, Elise sent a text to Kai to warn him about her unusual request and received a swift reply. Soon, she reached the clouded leopard enclosure and rapped on the wall to let Kai know she'd arrived. "Knock, knock."

Kai finished delivering a meatball through the mesh to a very happy clouded leopard. "Good girl, Daxa." He looked up at Elise. "Mom is doing great. I called in another zookeeper with a key so we could get some of the material you wanted." Kai lifted an eyebrow. "Not a lot of demand for clouded leopard scat, believe it or not, so I had my choice."

"Bless you for taking care of it so I didn't have to disrupt them. Or admit to any of the other keepers it was my request." Elise wrinkled her nose. "It's odd, I know. I promise it's for official business. Did you get any fur as well?"

"Sure did. I picked it up with gloves like you asked. So hopefully the finest of clouded leopard poo and fur that Riverbend Conservation Center has to offer will meet your needs."

Elise opened a plastic container and Kai deposited the sample bags into it. "Thank you. I feel like I need to clarify that this request is not for 'my needs.' I am merely helping the FBI with a new training program for animal trafficking."

Kai grinned and held both palms in the air. "Listen, I'm not here to judge."

She nudged him with her hip. "Hey, I asked you for help because I thought you were nice."

He snorted a laugh. "I am nice. I got you your poop without asking a single question. What more do you want out of our friendship?"

Elise shook her head, grinning, then turned when the heavy door to the outside opened with a creak. Veronica stepped in, her khakis perfectly pressed and blonde hair pulled back into an efficient ponytail. "Oh, hey, Doc!" Elise stuffed the sealed box of clouded leopard smells into her bag and looked over at Kai, who'd flushed pink again.

Veronica entered and gave them both a warm smile. "You two making trouble in here?"

"No, ma'am. I know better." Kai put his hands in his pockets. "Our mom and dad seem to be doing well. The little one is pouncing around his enclosure as normal. No repetitive distress behaviors and they're still choosing to go out into the exhibit during the day. Those are good signs."

"They sure are. I think sometimes they're more prepared to deal with loss than we are." Veronica leaned towards the large female cat, who had come closer to say hello to her new friend. While they treated all of the clouded leopards with the respect due to a wild animal, Daxa was incredibly friendly and known for greeting the keepers. Veronica worked in concert with Kai to examine her. Kai delivered more meatballs through the mesh as the clouded leopard presented her ears and her mouth for a checkup, also allowing Dr. V to draw blood. Daxa eagerly accepted her rewards and eventually, her cub got brave enough to come over and see what the fuss was about, chirruping softly, but intently, in a way that made it clear he was not to be ignored. Eventually, Dr. V tucked her vials of samples into her bags and addressed Daxa. "You are as fit as a fiddle. What a good girl." After giving the cub and dad leopard a shorter examination, she turned to speak to the humans. "I like what I'm seeing. Let me know if you have any issues, okay?"

Kai smiled. "Will do, Doc."

After she left, Kai stared at the closed door a little too long. He shook his head and started rummaging around the area, cleaning up supplies.

Elise lifted her bag in the air. "Thanks for not ratting me out. I didn't want to get too much grief for taking samples from the zoo. I would have never heard the end of it."

"For what it's worth, I think Dr. V would be the last person to judge you." Kai shrugged. "But, if you feel like you owe me one, let me know how your training goes, okay? I'm really interested in how the FBI trains their dogs."

"Yeah, of course! I wish you could come. It'll be a good experience. But I know you're busy, so I'll try to take some pictures. And next time you see me, you'll get to meet my new K-9 buddy yourself."

WHEN ELISE REACHED the signs for Riverbend K-9 Academy, she was buzzing with nervous energy. Zoey had warned her about the guard shack at the entrance and the serious people who ran it, but experiencing it personally was something else entirely.

Elise slowed to a stop in front of the liftgate and rolled down the window to give the stern-faced security guard her ID. The guard took it and looked her up and down. "Any weapons in the car, ma'am?"

"Nope, just a little clouded leopard scat." Elise grinned, but the guard's mouth stayed almost perfectly flat.

"Pardon me, ma'am?"

"Um, I'm here to meet with Alexis Thompson? I'm from the

Riverbend Animal Conservation Center. I mean, she requested it. The poop, that is. And some fur." Elise's palms began to sweat.

The guard walked into the building, squeezed a radio on her shoulder, and spoke a number into it. She couldn't quite make out the whole conversation but heard her name and Alexis's. She kept her hands on the steering wheel and spoke under her breath. "Zoey, I swear if this gets me arrested..."

"Ma'am?" The guard was closer than she expected, and Elise jumped. The guard passed over her ID. "You're all clear. Just take that road all the way to the main building and enter through the visitors' entrance. Director Thompson will be waiting for you." The guard eyed the bag on her seat, her serious expression flickering with curiosity, just for a moment.

When Elise reached the entrance, she spotted a number of fit people in casual clothing walking into the building with dogs at their heels. She'd painted a mental picture of a huge, imposing glass building filled with agents in FBI jackets and sunglasses, but reality didn't quite match her expectations. The main building was an old airplane hangar made of solid, recently re-stained wood. In contrast to the warmth of the old hangar, the entrance had a heavy metal door and standard government signage on the front. Elise grabbed her bag and followed the signs to the visitors' lobby. Alexis was passing through a door labeled RESTRICTED ACCESS. She gave Elise a big wave. "You made it! Welcome!" Her giant red Labrador retriever, Waffle, trailed her, tail wagging.

"Hi, Alexis. I have something for you." She handed over the bags. "I wouldn't open them in polite company, but hopefully they'll serve your purpose." Waffle pointed his nose in the air to sniff the containers and Alexis gave him a pat.

Waffle sat, his brown eyes looking at Elise. She started to reach out a hand but drew it back and looked at Alexis. "May I pet Waffle? He looks like he's trying to convince me that no one ever pays attention to him. I suspect he needs as much attention as I can give him right now."

"You've got him pegged exactly right." Waffle's tail thumped and Alexis grinned. "He's off duty right now, you're good."

Elise bent down to give the dog a pet and was rewarded with another hearty tail thump. "Hello, sir. Are you a good dog?" Waffle nudged his nose into her palm to help her pet him and told her that he was, in fact, a very good dog. She looked up at Waffle's handler. "So, where do we start?"

Finn walked through the door with Sedona at his side. He had sweat on his brow and Sedona had her tongue hanging out one side of her mouth. "Hey, Alex. Sorry we're late. We were just finishing up outside."

"No worries, you're right on time." Alexis reached a hand towards Finn. "This is Finn."

Finn looked at Elise. "We've met. We ran into each other in Marlene's coffee shop. We're neighbors, actually."

Alexis narrowed her eyes. "Did you interrogate my volunteer?"

Elise barked out a laugh. "I don't think I can get away with anything here."

"Finn." Alexis put her hands on her hips. "Be nice to my new recruits."

"Don't worry, he was definitely good cop when he was interrogating me. Mint tea and conversation." Elise put a hand on Alexis's arm and looked seriously at Finn, whose amusement twinkled in the corners of his eyes. "He thought he was being subtle, and I definitely think it's important for him to feel like it worked."

Finn raised his eyes to the ceiling. "Oh boy, there's two of you now."

Alexis and Elise laughed. Alexis threw an arm around Elise. "I just knew we'd get along. Thanks again for helping us out. Zeke really needs dedicated attention. I'm afraid if we don't pair him with the right person, he's not going to make it through the program. He's too smart."

Elise tipped her head. "Too smart to make it through the program without help?"

"You've worked with primates?"

Elise shrugged. "All the time."

"And what happens if they get bored?"

"Oof. Good point. So, I should treat Zeke as smart as a primate."

"In his own way, for sure." Finn nodded seriously. "And as determined."

"Well, it won't be the first time I've worked with smart animals. I'd get bored if they were too easy." Elise leaned in conspiratorially. "I never was very good at working with insects or fish, even if they were the best behaved out of the animals. Give me a gibbon or a tiger any day over a well-behaved reef fish."

Finn exchanged a look with Alexis and Alexis gestured for Elise to follow her. "Great. Come on, let's go have some fun."

Elise peeked into the offices when they walked by, but there was no sign of Zoey inside. When she reached the large training yard, she spotted a bright white dog running an agility course with her sister close by. Once they got to the end of the course with a crowd of students watching, Zoey praised Tasha, who danced and caught a ball out of the air. Then, Zoey looked up and gave her a bright wave. Zoey did a lot of her work at a desk, but Tasha was used for demonstrations, teaching, and Elise suspected, the occasional FBI case. If the distracted wiggles of the puppies were any indication, Zoey was working with a new crop of students.

Elise scanned the yard for others and soon, Liam walked over with his black Lab, Tank, and another dog on a leash. The other dog was a large German shepherd with dark coloring. However, unlike the very serious-looking adult dogs she'd seen on the internet when she was searching for information on the breed,

Zeke still had some strong puppy characteristics. Most prominently, one ear flopped over while the other stood proud. His feet didn't quite match his body yet and he seemed to be quivering with excitement. "Morning, Elise. This is Zeke." Elise squatted down to let Zeke sniff her hand and he promptly licked her face. She laughed and sputtered, wiping her cheek with the back of her arm. Zeke's mouth hung open in a doggy smile. "I think you might be a bit of a troublemaker, Mr. Zeke." Zeke replied by throwing his backside in the air and wagging his tail.

Liam eyed the dog. "You could say that. He chewed up a leash before we picked him up from his foster family. His caretaker was recovering from an injury, and when she didn't take him for a walk, he retrieved the leash and started gnawing on it." He tossed a thick rope toy at Zeke, who easily caught it out of the air and lay down to give it a good chew.

Elise covered her mouth to hide her surprised laugh and Zeke tipped his head to study her, his floppy ear falling open and rope toy dropping out of his mouth. He swished his tail, explaining that it was really just a misunderstanding, and the leash looked an awful lot like this rope toy, did it not? He snatched up the toy and tossed it into the air but got distracted and instead pounced on a leaf blowing through the yard. "And you want me to train him to be a detection dog?"

Liam shook his head. "You're just in charge of the basics. Sit, stay, lay down, walk politely on a leash, don't eat stuff you're not supposed to. Get him used to animal smells so that they are a little less interesting when we start specializing him." He looked at Alexis. "That's all, right?"

"Yeah, we don't expect him to be an expert on anything else when he comes for his formal training, although we can teach you some skills to keep him entertained for your sake when you both are ready. Oh, and hide your shoes."

Elise snorted. "Okay. Deal. Is that all of the explanation I need?"

"It's a little more involved than that." Finn gave Elise a canvas bag filled with dog food and Zeke went into a perfect sit, eyes darting between her and Finn to figure out who was going to give him a snack first.

Elise clipped the bag on her waist and Zeke's mind was made up. He focused on her bag, swishing his tail along the ground. Finn gave her Zeke's leash. She pulled a piece of food from the bag and placed it on her palm. "I think we're going to be great friends."

Zeke took the food out of her hand frantically and wagged his tail. She gave him a pat and asked him to sit again. He looked back at Liam for a moment, then Elise. He sat, and she gave him another reward. The rest of the group went back to work, leaving Finn to train Elise. Once they were alone, Finn gave her a gentle smile. "You ready?"

Elise nodded and Zeke thumped his tail. Sedona waited patiently at Finn's heel until he gave her the okay. They started off with some leash tangles and confusion when Zeke ran a circle around Sedona, but after a few minutes, they were able to take a walk around the facility without getting tangled up again. Finn coached Elise on how to guide Zeke, focusing on the positive and ignoring the negative. Zeke began to show immediate signs of improvement, and they took a break in a spot of shade with a dog dish. Finn gave her a high five. "Nice work out there." He gave Zeke a scratch behind the ears. "You too, bud." Zeke wagged his tail and leaned over to slurp water from the dog dish. Sedona nudged her way in between Zeke and Finn. Finn grinned. "And don't worry, you're still my best girl, Sedona."

Elise smiled at the sweet interaction. There was something about such a strong competent guy being a big softy with his dog that touched her heart. Her face heated when she realized she was staring at him again. She fanned it to cover her reaction. "It's warm out today."

"Oh yeah. We'll get the dogs into the air conditioning soon."

After the dogs (and humans) had their break, Zeke started to go to Elise for instructions before she said anything. Of course, all of the food coming out of the magic bag on Elise's waist probably didn't hurt. Zeke navigated the agility course quickly but was still looking around the yard much more than Sedona, and Finn coached her to give him a treat whenever he wasn't distracted. Sedona did a good job ignoring Zeke whenever he nipped at her, exchanging a look with Finn that said something like, "Puppies, am I right?"

Elise laughed when Sedona nudged Zeke with her backside when he tried to nip at her ear. "I think Sedona is teaching Zeke as much as you're teaching me."

Finn picked up a tennis ball and tossed it to his partner, who caught it easily. "You aren't wrong. That said, it's break time for all of us. The sun is getting a little hot for Zeke's fluff."

Elise followed Finn inside to a large air-conditioned indoor space past the office areas with other trainers and their dogs. Zeke pulled at the leash a bit but came back to Elise with a little encouragement.

Zeke splatted on the cool floor and looked up at her, his perky ear swiveling a bit. He army crawled over to her and flopped over for pets. She rubbed his belly. He opened his mouth and a tennis ball fell out sideways, then rolled a few inches away. Zeke frantically twisted, throwing his head back to grab his prize before another dog could get it. Then, he moved chaotically to get back onto four paws, dropped the ball into Elise's lap, and bounced backward with his backside in the air a few times, his tail waving almost vertically. She chucked the ball and he zoomed after it, beating the other dogs who weren't actually racing him by a mile. He zoomed a few celebratory circles around their small group with his prize in his mouth. She brought him back to lay down next to her. Just like a small child who had loudly proclaimed that they weren't tired, Zeke's eyes began to droop.

"So, what do you think so far?" Finn sat next to her, rubbing Sedona on the stomach. His eyes held hers, patiently waiting for an answer.

Elise cleared her throat. "I'm starting to understand why Zeke needs a foster home with someone who walks a lot. Unless he's just excited to meet me...?"

Finn bit his lip. "You can still back out."

Elise snorted. "No chance. I like a challenge."

"Speaking of, how are things at the Conservation Center? Still going well?"

Sedona squeaked her tennis ball and Zeke's ears perked up. His eyes were still drooping, but his ears twitched with every squeak. Finally, sleep won, but only just. "It's great. I mean, they're having a tough time with the loss of Dr. Oliver. The sheriff came and talked to Heath, but I only heard that secondhand."

"What do you do for the World Wildlife Trust when you aren't in Riverbend? Do you normally just help the Conservation Center remotely?"

"Oh no, it's much broader than that. I help multiple zoos and aquariums manage their finances. Riverbend is just one of them."

Finn tilted his head. "Really?"

"I think you might be the first person here who didn't already know that. And you, living in Marlene's building, working with the FBI." Elise tsked. "I thought everyone knew everyone's business in Riverbend."

Finn gave her a rueful smile. "I haven't been here much longer than you have."

"Hm. You seemed so comfortable here, I assumed you'd been here at least a few months. Alexis said you were working on a wildlife detection training program. Are you new to that as well?"

Finn shook his head. "Lots of experience in wildlife detection. That's what Sedona is trained for. I am new to teaching though." Sedona wagged her tail at hearing her name, and Zeke took this as his cue to end his nap by pouncing on her tail. Elise let the dogs play for a moment, then reined in Zeke with some difficulty and more than one piece of kibble. Finn gave Zeke a scratch behind his floppy ear. "Speaking of being trained, it was nice of you to say yes when Alexis asked for your help, even though you haven't done anything like this before."

Elise shrugged. "I actually have some experience with animal behavior, so I volunteered. Alexis was chatting with Zoey at Bridges, and I overheard."

A bit of mischief danced in Finn's eyes. "Overheard seems a little too easy. You wouldn't have heard anything she didn't want you to."

Alexis cleared her throat behind them. "I was going to ask how things were going but I think Finn is giving away my secrets." Zeke stood to sniff at Waffle, but Elise coaxed Zeke back into a sit with a few extra pieces of kibble. "I might have been *hoping* she'd volunteer." A smile played at the corner of Alexis's mouth. "I didn't want to make her feel like she had to say yes by asking outright."

Zeke scooped up a ball and looked at Elise hopefully. She plucked it out of his mouth and threw it. Zeke and Waffle both sprinted after it. Zeke had speed and enthusiasm, but Waffle beat him with experience, using his body to edge Zeke away from the thrown ball. He found a few extras on the way back and plucked at them like a bird picking up worms. Waffle returned with three balls proudly stuffed in his mouth. Zeke trotted behind him, nudging the big Lab with his snout. When that didn't work, Zeke pounced at Waffle's face, but Waffle turned so that Zeke ran into a furry solid wall. Waffle lifted his head to get it further out of range, and if she didn't know better, she'd think Waffle was smiling at her. Zeke lay on the ground with his head on his paws and whined at Waffle, who stared at the puppy, mouth full of tennis balls and tail wagging. Elise snorted. "I think Zeke has met his match."

Alexis looked out at the other trainers and dogs in the room, pride shining in her eyes. "Thanks for helping us out. We'll have you come visit us at least once a week and Zoey can give you tips in between. And, hey, if you see anything funny at the Conservation Center that doesn't add up, let me know."

Elise's blood ran cold. Finn's questions hadn't been sitting quite right and now Alexis set off her mental alarm bells at top volume. "Anything funny?" She narrowed her eyes at Finn. "I thought training the dogs here was all for some kind of unspecified future activity."

Finn crossed his arms. "It is. We have no proof it's coming from the Conservation Center."

"There's an 'it?' So, there is something." Elise glared at Finn.

Alexis took a step closer to Elise. "But it might be coming from there. And she needs to know."

Finn stood and Sedona joined him, leaning against his leg. "Alex, it's one thing to give her a dog, but she's untrained. If she doesn't know what's going on, she's going to be perfectly safe. If she finds out—"

Elise turned on Finn. "If she finds out what? In case you forgot, *she* is right here."

Finn rubbed his forehead. "This is a bad idea. We were working with civilians in Nepal and look how that turned out."

Alexis put a hand on his shoulder. "You can't just stop letting people help because something went wrong. Elise is extraordinarily capable."

"Oh. I know. That's what worries me." Finn looked up at the ceiling for answers. "She's obviously bright and has kept up with the most stubborn dog I have ever met for the last hour without breaking a sweat — which means she's stubborn too."

Elise snorted. "Says the pot to the kettle."

"I may be stubborn, but I've been trained by the FBI. If my stubbornness gets me in trouble, I know how to handle myself."

Elise gave Zeke a pat. "Technically, both of us have been trained now."

"For less than a day." Finn swallowed. "I don't like this."

Alexis gave Finn a few seconds, letting the silence hang in the air. "I agree that we don't want her doing work for us, but she does need to be informed."

"Of what?!" Elise threw up her hands and Zeke nudged her, only sniffing the bag of kibble on her waist once before picking up a rope toy and putting it in her hand, sure that it would help.

Finn set his mouth in a line. "I've been chasing an animal trafficking ring for months. They have contacts in the U.S."

"Okay..."

"The only lead I have is a series of communications — phone calls and emails that always seem to point back to Riverbend. And someone spotted a white van, like the Conservation Center uses, on video footage near one of the trades that happened here in the States. It's all circumstantial. It's not like they're the only ones who drive white vans around."

All of the breath whooshed out of Elise's lungs. "Have you asked Kai about it?"

Alexis exchanged a look with Finn. "Listen. I like Kai too, but if anyone is responsible here in town, the most probable suspects all work at the Conservation Center."

"Does Zoey know? Never mind. Silly question. When did Zoey find out?"

"Officially, she found out shortly after you got here. And she said she'd already tried to talk you into leaving and it didn't work." Alexis looked down at Zeke. "Why do you think she was so excited to get you a large dog that has to go with you everywhere?"

Elise took a moment to absorb the information. It definitely brought a new urgency to their training. "Obviously, I'm willing to let you know if I see something illegal. Do you have anything more specific for me to watch out for when I go back to work?"

Finn said, "No," at the same time Alexis said, "Yes."

Finn shook his head in resignation. "Okay. But mark my words, this could end poorly."

"It's going to end poorly if you don't include me." Elise put her hands on her hips. "I know enough now to go digging on my own. And, if it makes you feel better, I take full responsibility." She rounded on Finn. "Finn, you're giving me some real 'I'm responsible for everything' energy, and it's wearing me out."

"Oh boy." Finn closed his eyes and pinched the bridge of his nose. He waved a hand. "Alright, Alex. Looks like we have another teammate."

Alexis nodded. "Good. Why don't you come see me once you get through this next session? Get Zeke good and worn out so he'll lay down in my office."

"You got it, boss." Finn scrunched up his face and looked over at Elise. "I can't talk you out of this?"

Elise narrowed her eyes. "How is what I'm doing any different than what the WWT asks of our partners? The danger we ask them to face when they are saving habitats from poachers, working in conflict zones, and goodness knows what else. How do I face them if I'm not willing to go to work on the extremely slim chance that someone in Riverbend might figure out that I know... something...because I talked with the FBI? Please don't insult me by asking again." Zeke started to tug at the leash, ready to go play with a group of dogs on the other side of the training area. She got him back into a sit. "Now, my very high-energy dog would like to get to work. Can we do the same?"

Finn sighed and looked down at Sedona, who looked up at him with a happy doggy grin. "Okay."

After another five minutes of working with Zeke and watching his fellow trainees around her, it became increasingly clear to

Elise that Zeke was ready for more commands than just sit and stay. A moment before she could say anything, Finn introduced the smell of clouded leopard and taught Elise how to guide Zeke while they searched for it. The smart pup caught on quickly. He got a little distracted by the canisters designed to attract untrained dogs, but he did great for his first try. Once the humans and dogs were tired, they walked into the old airplane hangar-turned-FBI training center to solve a puzzle of a different sort.

Alexis's office had a fluffy dog bed for Waffle and a few extra mats for visitors. Zeke and Sedona were soon settled on the mats. Waffle eyed the other dogs but, once he was convinced Zeke wasn't going to pounce on his head, he didn't move besides a couple of sleepy taps of his tail. Alexis folded her hands on her desk. "Okay, Elise, I'd like to ask a hypothetical question and need someone who's good at knowing how animals are managed and traded within the confines of the zoo system."

"I know all about the legal side of it, but that usually doesn't garner the attention of two FBI agents."

Finn crossed his arms. "Let's talk just about the legal side for now."

Elise's heart began to thunder. Bravado aside, getting specific meant that one of her coworkers could be involved in the very thing she worked so hard to discourage. She rubbed her forehead. "Okay. Well, the legal side is the side I'm most well-versed in anyway. I mean, the only one I'm well-versed in. I know about the other stuff because if you want to rile up a bunch of zookeepers, start talking about poaching and irresponsible animal ownership. Things will get heated in a hurry."

Alexis chuckled mirthlessly. "I bet. So, I've been doing some reading, and zoos can apparently exchange animals, but not sell them, is that right?"

"In the U.S. anyway. Yes." Elise ran a hand through her hair.

"Breeding is carefully managed according to Species Survival Plans. Zoos don't intentionally breed animals they don't have space for, and when an animal is born, they have to make a plan for that animal for its entire life. The new clouded leopards in Riverbend, for example, would need new enclosures built to expand their program. It cost a small fortune, frankly, to build so many so quickly, but the last accountant thought it would bring in more visitors and therefore pay for itself. They didn't actually think to check if they could reconfigure the existing space instead and save all of those dollars." Elise closed her eyes. "Sorry, that wasn't your question. In the case where animals are being exchanged between zoos, we occasionally set up some pretty complicated trades between them for specific species. Honestly, sometimes it's easier just to donate the animal and avoid the hassle. So, some places exclusively donate to avoid any of those headaches."

Finn crossed his arms. "So, do you think it would be possible to use one of these trade chains to hide animal trafficking?"

Elise sighed and leaned back in her chair. "Theoretically, yes, but it'd be hard with so many people in the know. And it would devastate everyone involved. Dang, what's really going on?"

Alexis shot a glance at Finn. "That's what we're trying to figure out. This has been really helpful, Elise. Thank you so much for your time."

"If the WWT's partners are involved, including the Riverbend Animal Conservation Center, I need to know." Elise rubbed a spot between her eyebrows.

"As soon as we find anything that has to do with the Center, you'll be the first to hear it. Keep your cell phone on you. At the first whiff of danger, we're pulling you out of there." Finn stood and Sedona rose from her mat to follow. "In the meantime, we'll have you focus on training Zeke. That'll be the most helpful thing you can do for us."

Elise managed to keep from growling at Finn like an angry felid. "I can do more than that."

"I'm sure you can. But, for now, let's go slow." Finn sighed with resignation. "We'll let you know if we think of anything, and keep you posted with new information."

Elise nodded. "Okay. I can go slow. And I'm assuming I can't tell anyone I work with because they're all suspects?"

Alexis winced. "We'd appreciate your restraint."

"And once this is all over, maybe we could talk about liaising with the World Wildlife Trust before it gets this bad? I think there is a lot of potential to connect the FBI with some of our trusted partners. Transparently," Elise said, pointedly.

Alexis nodded. "I'd love to do that. No question. Zoey can help too — part of her job is liaising with experts."

Elise tapped her fingers on Alexis's desk. The short-term uncertainty was a small price to pay to find out what was really going on and potentially gain a long-term partner for the WWT. It'd be a slight detour that could do some real good. The WWT would never have the funds to deploy a wildlife detection dog. Working with the specialized dogs could help them without the fees associated with running their own program. Feeling a modicum of control again, Elise blew out a breath. "Okay then. I won't ask questions yet, but what do you want me to look for when I go back to work?"

"We don't know yet. For now, if you see anything odd, let us know, okay?" Alexis slipped her a card. "This is my cell number. Call Finn or me."

"And my sister?" Elise tipped her head towards the training yard.

Alexis chuckled. "I already know she'll be your first phone call. Just make sure to loop the rest of us in, okay?"

Elise picked up the bag of Zeke's things by the door of Alexis's office and walked out with an excited puppy. Probably due to his hard work during the day, he was relatively easy to keep by her side, instead of running off to chase anything that moved. It was a good thing, too, since she got to her car without really remembering her walk through the building. She had sometimes thought of all the things that could go wrong when transferring animals. But using an animal transfer to hide animal trafficking? At a scale large enough that an FBI agent would take a special interest in a little zoo in Riverbend? Pushing the long, winding train of thought from her head, she got in her car and realized she'd left without even telling Zoey goodbye. She drove home with Zeke in the back seat and tried to be grateful the FBI didn't want her more involved. She didn't need to add 'chase down a criminal' to her personal to-do list. She had enough problems to solve already.

CHAPTER 12

Shortly after Elise returned to her apartment, there was a knock on the door. Zeke barked wildly. She looked through the peephole and let her sister in. Before Zoey made it through the door, there was a soft brush of fur against Elise's thigh. She reached down to pet Tasha, but Zeke squeezed in between her and the other dog and soon, she had two dogs vying for her attention. She waved her sister inside. Zoey was lugging a metal collapsible crate. Elise slapped her forehead. "I completely forgot about his crate." Zeke nudged a tennis ball into Elise's free hand.

Zoey smiled. "I think if you throw the ball for Zeke, he'll forgive you. At least you grabbed his food. That's the most important thing."

"Speaking of important things, what do you know about someone trafficking animals in Riverbend, sis?"

Zoey placed the crate on Elise's living room floor and began to set it up. "Before I answer that, I would like to say, for the record, that I tried to keep you away. Then, you told me I was acting like I didn't want you here. And also, you're very stubborn. Did you know that?"

"No, I'm not. I'm perfectly reasonable when I have all the facts." Elise crossed her arms. "So, I would like all the facts. Alexis and Finn only gave me the basics."

Zoey shrugged. "Yeah, they don't realize that if they don't tell you everything, you'll go find out for yourself. They seem to think I'm the only high-strung one in our family. Hilarious, right?" Zoey rummaged in Elise's kitchen and poured herself a glass of water. She turned around and rested her palms on the counter. "I've been trying to help Finn and Liam with the investigation in my free time, but we haven't been able to make much headway. They're working with so little information. Finn probably wouldn't be spending so much time here if he wasn't injured. He really did need to take a break from traipsing through rough terrain. The FBI is sure that money is changing hands, but the traffickers are using methods that are difficult to track. Some teams have intercepted illegal animal sales but they're always medium players, never the big fish, and never anyone with enough information to reveal who is organizing it all. Someone is making money off of this, but who? And how are they hiding their tracks well enough that we can't trace it?"

Elise shook her head. "It can't be the Conservation Center itself. They're hardly rolling in extra cash."

"Any employees doing particularly well?"

"Not outwardly." Elise tapped her chin with her finger. "I can keep an ear to the ground."

Zoey eyed her with an expression that spoke a thousand words. "Or, now that you know the extent of what's happening, you could fake an injury and go back to Denver. Zeke can come with you, and you can bring him back when he's ready to join the program officially. We'll take it from here."

Elise gave her sister a pointed look. "Right. You and I both know that's not happening. Do you think Dr. Oliver was involved?"

Zoey sighed. "He's not our mastermind. The FBI is still tracking coded exchanges going through an IP address in Riverbend, but they're careful to use public WiFi during busy times. And it's still been happening since...everything."

"Well, at least I have a big scary-looking dog now." Zeke was currently laying on the floor, whining at Tasha to give his tennis balls back. Tasha appeared to be hoarding them between her paws, daring the larger dog to come after her. Her unwavering confidence made Zeke hesitate despite his larger size. "Even though the one ear down makes him look pretty cute."

Zoey groaned. "You don't sound like someone who is planning on leaving."

"Even I can help stake out a very sweet small Conservation Center in the middle of Indiana. There are no extra animals to traffic in the Conservation Center, Zo. Every single animal is accounted for. It's a whole thing in our electronic systems. Just ask Kai."

"I'm sure he'd say the same thing." An alarm went off on Zoey's phone and she jumped. "That's my reminder — I knew if I didn't set it, I'd keep talking to you. I need to go meet Liam at Bridges for dinner. Want to come?"

Elise grinned. "The name 'Bridges' seems a bit of a misnomer — I only saw one bridge in Riverbend."

Zoey tsked. "Well, you miscounted, then. There is both a bridge only for cars and one that has a path for pedestrians. Two bridges. Plural. Bridges can safely keep its name. And I promise not to tell Thurston you said that if you buy dessert."

"Deal."

Soon, Elise was enjoying a meal with Zoey, Liam, and all three dogs. Thurston and the other town residents seemed used to seeing dogs in restaurants and Zeke was tired enough to sleep through most of dinner. It was nice to see Zoey, who had been through more than her fair share of challenges, smiling with Liam. And Zoey managed to not make it too obvious that she was worried about her sister, very nearly succeeding a few times. They waved to several of the agents she recognized from earlier in the day and said hello to two friends of Liam's family, Delores and Rosie. Rosie was the quieter of the two, but only just. Elise thought she was also the less nosy of the two until Rosie inquired if Elise had a significant other. As Elise was blushing and before she could answer, Delores chided her friend to leave the poor girl alone. Then she whispered to Rosie that her nephew volunteered at the zoo and they'd ask him later if Elise had found her dream partner in khakis or if she needed a little extra help.

Elise nearly spat out her water. Once they were out of earshot, she leaned in. "Are they always like that?"

Liam winced. "Yes. They're a little on the curious side."

Delores shouted from her booth, "I'm old, but I'm not deaf, sweetie!"

Elise burst out laughing, wiping away tears. "I can see why you love it here." Just past Zoey's shoulder, a large television at the bar showing the local news flashed a picture of a clouded leopard. Elise looked around Zoey to read the chyron; another small facility near Indianapolis had just announced the death of their clouded leopard. "Oh no. They lost a clouded too? That seems odd."

Zoey twisted around in her seat. "Aw, that's so sad. What are the odds?"

"Not that high, considering how few there are in the country. This one was older than ours." Elise ran a hand through her hair. "Kai is going to be so upset. I know for a fact that cub originally came from our — I mean Riverbend's — breeding program." Elise pinched the bridge of her nose. She hadn't forgotten all of her college coursework — there could be a genetics problem at play and the Conservation Center didn't even know it. Hopefully, no one's cousin's boyfriend's brother was responsible for genetic testing, or their records would be as screwed as their finances.

Elise ordered dessert as promised, and sighed, even though there was a giant delicious slice of chocolate cake to share with the table. "I'll have to tell Kai tomorrow. I hate to do it. He's had enough on his plate with the cub's death."

Zoey whipped her head around. "How are you getting along with Kai?"

Elise narrowed her eyes. "Easy there, killer. I know what you're asking. And yes, he happens to work at the Riverbend Animal Conservation Center. We're coworkers. And friends. Insofar as a friendship can develop via remote meetings."

"I mean, people have been sending letters for ages and online dating is a thing, so..." Zoey took a sip of her water. Her smile tilted mischievously.

"Look, he's sweet and smart, but there's no spark." Elise shrugged. "And not to mention, it'd be weird to date someone that you work with." Zoey snorted and choked on her water. Elise shot a glance at Liam, who suddenly became interested in his own glass of water. "Not for you. For me." She barely managed to keep from hiding under her chair, remembering Liam and Zoey's story a moment past when she should have.

"What about your new K-9 instructor who lives across the hall? Since you're just doing the FBI a favor, you don't really work for him."

Elise blushed. "Zoey. You are out of control. Liam, can you help me?"

Liam shook his head. "She's out of my league too. Oh, look, there's Thurston. I need to go talk to him about...stoplights." Liam was gone so fast it was amazing he didn't leave the smoke of tires burning out on the way.

Zoey gave her a knowing look. "Finn's a good guy. Liam thinks the world of him."

Elise wrinkled her nose. "Paid or not, I work with him."

"With him, not for him. Temporarily." Elise put a hand to her forehead and eyed her sister incredulously. Zoey smiled. "But hey, now you aren't worried about the cubs. You're welcome."

Elise sighed. "Remind me why I missed having you as a roommate?"

Zoey laughed. "Because you love me so much. So no to Finn too?"

Elise lifted an eyebrow. "I was so busy taking care of Zeke and learning about everything, I didn't really have much time to think about the implications of a potential relationship with my not-a-coworker. Had I had time to squeeze it in, I would say there are probably...reasons."

Zoey took another sip of her water, looking over the rim of the glass. "Okay, I'll back off. Keep me posted on your not-a-coworker who lives down the hall. And for whom there are reasons."

Elise's neck heated. "I have a feeling there won't be much news there. I have more than enough to think about without worrying about something like that."

After dinner, Elise brought Zeke back home. He wagged his tail and explored the parts of the apartment that he'd been too tired to sniff earlier in the day. However, in the time it took for her to drop her purse off in her bedroom, Zeke found her only nice pair of black pumps and was happily chewing on the leather. She snatched one from him and he let it go easily, tail wagging. She put a hand on her hip and shook the shoe at him. "No, Zeke. Friends don't eat their friend's shoes."

Zeke went down into a play bow, eying the shoe with every bit as much focus as he had when she'd thrown tennis balls for him earlier in the day. On pure instinct, she dropped the shoe so he wouldn't get confused, and before it hit the ground, she realized her mistake. Zeke's prey drive kicked in and he pounced on it, snatching it up and giving it a good shake to show it who was boss before she could get it back, sporting a new set of puppy teeth punctures. She rummaged through his tote bag for a more dog-friendly toy, giving it a quick toss. Zeke scampered after the red plastic toy, which bounced in unpredictable directions. He nearly knocked over Marlene's side table with a quick turn before catching the toy and victoriously showing her his prize. Elise laughed. "Oh, man. Something tells me the two of us aren't going to be bored."

CHAPTER 13

*M*oments after waking up, Elise began to teach Zeke that he should chase his toys and not her shoes. After several minutes of instruction, Zeke taught Elise that she needed to keep her shoes behind a closed door. So, one of them had been thoroughly trained that morning. On the bright side, Zeke barely noticed Marlene's stylish furniture except for when accidentally running into it while chasing anything that rolled or skittered. At least he didn't have a habit of chewing table legs. As much as she didn't want to pay for new shoes, she really didn't want to pay for a new couch or replace the artistic live-edge end table that was thankfully, much stronger than she'd expected.

Somehow, she placated Zeke with treat-dispensing toys long enough to get herself ready. Elise retrieved her red tennis shoes from the closet, clicked the treat bag around her waist, filled one pocket of her khaki shorts with disposable bags for the inevitable bathroom breaks, and managed to open the front door with Zeke only getting his mouth around one shoe that she missed. Or that he'd strategically dropped behind the couch, so she'd forget about it. When she told him to drop it, the shoe clattered to the ground and he wagged his tail, delighted to show Elise his new trick. He accepted the offered snack and immediately picked the shoe up again. He dropped it with gusto a second time at her command, tongue hanging out one side of his mouth, and eyed the bag on her waist. Elise chuckled despite the hit to her budget that seemed increasingly inevitable. She tossed the shoe into her closet and shut the door before he could get to it. Then, she gave Zeke a scratch behind the ears, and he pulled her towards the door, ready for whatever the day would bring. In light of her new FBI work, she didn't share his enthusiasm for the day ahead, but she was more than a little relieved to have him by her side. While Zeke acted like a big sweetheart, he sure looked like a German shepherd that would jump to her defense if the need arose.

Pausing to correct Zeke multiple times had quite the impact on Elise's morning schedule. It was a good thing Kai approved of her involvement. Of all people, he would understand the slow and steady process of teaching an animal a desired behavior. He had taught the leopards how to present body parts for wellness checks and how to hold still so veterinarians could take blood samples and conduct examinations without sedation, which was much more difficult than training an overly energetic K-9. The whole team's love for animals made her sure they would all love Zeke as well. Provided they didn't leave their loose footwear around.

After a thankfully uneventful car ride, Elise let her new buddy out of the back seat to smell everything. It became immediately clear that Finn's guidance had contributed to their training success the previous day. On her own, Elise fumbled it a few times before getting it right. Since Zeke had only spent one afternoon alerting on the clouded leopard scent, he alerted right outside of the zoo in the staff parking lot. He sat victoriously, pointing towards the construction site, notable for its lack of any animals inside. She corrected him, and he gave her a quizzical look, his folded ear flipping open when he tilted his head in question. She grinned and corrected him again. He gamely trotted forward, checking for more smells. She'd get more scat from Kai later to help Zeke master the skills he'd only begun to learn at Riverbend K-9 Academy.

Today was going to be a sad day for everyone at the Conservation Center, as the official memorial for Dr. Oliver would be held in a church in downtown Riverbend. The Conservation Center would be closed to facilitate the attendance of those closest to the veterinarian. She, Kai, and Veronica would hold down the fort for the morning, along with a few other zookeepers and their most experienced volunteers. Kai remained convinced that the best way to honor Doctor Oliver was by taking care of the animals he cared so much about.

Elise found herself looking for Kai or Dr. V as she walked in, but they were nowhere to be found. The sound of the wind and the distant call of sandhill cranes that frequented the wetlands near the zoo were her only company. She resigned herself to making the rounds helping the zookeepers who were there feed the herbivores with Zeke in tow. There were barriers separating the zookeepers from the animals for safety, and while Zeke was curious, he was well-trained enough not to bark at the animals. The smart pup also quickly realized that if he behaved, the keepers would make a fuss over him. Elise watched the animals carefully for signs of distress, however, Kai's team had done a great job socializing the animals, and she didn't have any trouble. With the giraffes happily munching on their hay, the meerkats working through their vegetable/bug/pellet mixture, and the binturong finishing his fresh fruit and vegetables, Elise headed back to her temporary desk.

Once back at the office with Zeke settled on the floor next to her, Elise pulled up the clouded leopard's record of transfer between Riverbend and the small zoo near Indianapolis. Through a domino of trades with another zoo, from penguins to puffins to even a wobbegong shark, eventually, Riverbend Animal Conservation Center received a red panda in exchange for the clouded leopard cub in Indy. She scrolled down the chain of animal trades, grinning at the absurdity of her job. While humans hadn't always been good stewards of other species, Elise was passionate about being the change she wanted to see in the world. She couldn't change the past, but every animal life they improved, every person they educated, every time they moved a species a step further away from extinction, they added a little bit of good to the world. Still, with a sense of dread lurking in the pit of her stomach, she scoured for clues that someone else may care more about financial gain than the animals themselves.

Elise referenced her own look-up tables to convert numbers of animals traded between species, spot-checked records, and found nothing amiss. With no hard evidence to share with the FBI, a bit of hope snuck back into her heart. Elise tried to fully cleanse her brain of the negative thoughts by looking up other animals that had been traded or gifted from Riverbend Animal Conservation Center to other zoos and aquariums. The pictures on zoo websites of the offspring of their ocelots, tigers, and clouded leopards next to happy keepers helped reassure her that there was no more bad news to be found.

However, her happy mood didn't last. A zoo in Texas where they'd transferred an ocelot cub a few months prior had posted a notice that the cat had also passed unexpectedly. It was unfortunate because it was another one of the World Wildlife Trust's partner zoos. In fact, if she remembered correctly, Dr. Oliver had visited on one of his business trips shortly after Riverbend had joined the WWT. A few clicks later and she found his expense report. He'd definitely been there. This zoo had also been hard up on funds but had recently received a large donation to help renovate the ocelot exhibit for their newest addition. The website stated that the funds would be redirected to help improve the zoo in other areas. The Texas zoo's financial troubles reminded her that she did need to do her actual job for the WWT. Elise checked her watch. Heath should be in by now. He needed to be informed about the deaths of the cats from Riverbend. She pushed away from her desk.

A few moments later, Elise was at Heath's door. He was mid-conversation with Doctor Veronica, and she leaned against the doorway and waited for them to finish.

"Okay, so the remaining cub is still doing well?"

Veronica nodded. "Healthy as a horse."

Heath seemed to just notice Elise and looked up. "Well, good morning, Elise!" He walked around his desk to greet Zeke, who sniffed him gamely, then alerted on the clouded leopard smell that was definitely all over Dr. V, this time, getting it spot-on. Elise held up a finger, ran back to her office for Zeke's reward toy, and threw it for him. It tumbled down the hallway and he scampered and pounced on it, his big paws thundering and claws skittering on the hard floor when he hit the brakes. He trotted back to them with his toy in his mouth, his tongue peeking out from under the toy.

Veronica laughed. "Well, he's adorable. Who is this?"

Elise grinned. "This is my new pal, Zeke. He's training at Riverbend K-9 Academy where my sister works. The woman fostering him was injured. Considering the rate that I pull my shoes out of his mouth, I can understand why she felt overwhelmed. I'm only fostering him until he starts his formal training. Alexis thought it'd be good to expose him to wildlife smells and see if he has potential. He smelled the clouded leopard on you, I think."

Dr. V clapped. "Oh, that's very good. He's absolutely right. What a good dog you are, Zeke! Can we help you with anything while you're here?"

Elise nodded. "Actually, I was worried about the cats. I heard they lost another clouded at one of the zoos with a cub from Riverbend near Indy. And an ocelot down in Texas."

"I just heard about that." Veronica winced. "I'm actually here to let Heath know I'm leaving for a few days to go check things out in person. I don't love that we're losing these cats and frankly, I just put it all together myself."

"Thank you for your help." Heath frowned. "Sorry to send you when Dr. Oliver went so recently."

"It's not your fault." Veronica smiled ruefully. "Dr. Oliver was fairly certain the Riverbend cub died of a bacterial infection. I'll check for that first. He sent the cub we lost out for testing to be sure, but the lab hasn't dropped the new results into our system yet. I'll give them a call to see if they're done with the testing yet."

Heath waved his hand. "Let me take care of it since you've got your hands full."

Dr. V's eyes softened. "Thanks, Heath."

"It's nothing."

Elise looked skeptically at the pile on Heath's desk. No wonder he seemed overwhelmed all the time. He was a classic micromanager. Well, one problem at a time. She scratched Zeke behind his floppy ear. "Is there anything we can do in the meantime?"

Veronica sighed. "Not until we know the root cause. We'll make sure that we change the mating pair in the future if it was a genetic issue rather than an environmental one. But we're talking two different species now, which makes me think Oliver was right about the bacteria. And since it's bacterial, I need to be on site to review their records, take a closer look at the facility, and run some tests on the animals. If we don't find anything, we'll still recommend deep cleaning to be on the safe side."

Elise breathed out, grateful for the reminder of animal husbandry basics. Her brief time with the FBI had activated her imagination and she was starting to wonder if there was something nefarious going on that extended past even Riverbend's clouded leopards. That level of overthinking was something she usually teased Zoey about. "Thank you, Dr. V. You brought me a lot of peace of mind."

Veronica gave her a sad smile. "I'm glad I could help. I'll be back here as soon as I can."

"And I'm sorry, for the loss."

On her way out the door, Dr. V squeezed her shoulder gently. "Thank you for that."

Once Veronica was gone, Heath looked back at her. "Well, Elise, what can I help you with?"

"I was actually coming in here to talk about the cat deaths. I know it seems callous to talk about the numbers, but the plan I put together relies on the Center's breeding program helping other zoos and using those trades to solicit donations and help our, I mean the Center's, finances." She shook her head. "I'm not saying the cats are just numbers, they aren't..."

Heath gentled his expression. "I know what you mean. We have mouths to feed. Fortunately, we just received a major donation from someone who connected the same dots you did. I apologize I haven't had much time to spend with you, but I've been talking to potential donors. It looks like it paid off."

"No apologies necessary." Elise put a hand to her heart. "See, that's why I work in this business. Find me nicer people, I dare you."

Heath smiled. "It's going to keep us solvent long enough to raise funds for the rest of the construction project. Kai even suggested we earmark a portion of the donation to send to our partners in Nepal to help with clouded leopard habitat restoration, and of course, our donor agreed. I was just getting ready to send you the email. We should see the funds within a week."

"Well. That's wonderful." Tension rolled off Elise's shoulders and Zeke pushed his toy into her hand. She threw it down the empty hallway again and he chased it with the same exuberance he had the first time.

"Now, tell me about this work with the FBI! What does that involve? Something with clouded leopards, you say?" Heath sat down behind his desk and gestured for Elise to do the same. He looked out of his office door into the hallway where Zeke was triumphantly bringing back his prize. "I mean, it seems to be going well for day one. And did the animals do okay with...?"

"Zeke." At his name, Zeke went into a sit and for a moment, he looked so perfectly behaved that it didn't seem possible that he was in a one-dog war with every last pair of her shoes. "The animals — and Zeke — did really well. Although, really, I'm just in charge of teaching him the basics. He's been practicing smelling clouded leopards, but he's not terribly reliable yet. And won't be for a while."

"And how did you get involved in the program?"

Elise gave Zeke a pat and he dropped his toy at her feet. She rolled it along the floor. "My sister, Zoey, as you know, works at the K-9 Academy, and she's told me all about it. They needed a little extra help with this guy until he's ready to get assigned to a trainer." Zeke dropped the toy in her lap and wagged his tail. She gave him the command to lay down. He studied her, then lay down, his legs tensed and ready in case Elise changed her mind about throwing the toy.

"Of course. Is he going to sniff out explosives like the other dogs too? I've heard they do a good job." Heath leaned forward in his chair.

Elise perked up. "I'm glad you asked! They'd love for him to focus on biological smells, but the program is all a bit of an experiment for them right now. We started practicing on clouded leopard scent to help him try to zero in on one scent he isn't going to find anywhere else in Riverbend. And he's definitely had a couple of false alarms, so we're working on getting him to only alert where there are actually clouded leopards."

"That's understandable. Getting him to only smell the leopards near their enclosure has to be a challenge for an animal with such a sensitive nose." Heath nodded, noticeably more relaxed since the influx of donations. "Sounds like you're off to a great start. Why don't you work with Kai to develop some content around the work of wildlife detection dogs? I'd like to get pictures and an interactive display on how this will help protect wildlife. And pictures of Zeke working in the zoo of course."

Elise grinned. "You got it. Thank you for your support."

Heath nodded. "We help where we can. On a related note, I will be attending some meetings in the coming days, so I'll be in and out of the office. We'll chat again once my schedule clears up. Unless you have any concerns now?"

"With that new donation rolling in, I'm sure I won't. But I'd love to review areas that would be a good long-term investment for the Conservation Center when it's convenient."

"Fantastic. Thanks so much, Elise." Heath's phone started buzzing and he picked it up. "I better take this."

CHAPTER 14

*E*lise led Zeke out of Heath's office, feeling as if a heavy weight had been lifted off her shoulders. While one donation wouldn't solve all their problems, it would buy them time. And if working for a not-for-profit had taught her anything, it was to celebrate every win. She wrapped up the last of the tasks she had to finish, emailed a few donors, and then picked up a radio to figure out Kai's location. Soon, he met her at the entrance to the clouded leopard enclosure. He was wearing his normal khaki outfit and his shoulders seemed more relaxed than the previous day. "Hey, Elise. I see you brought your new friend with you." He looked down at Zeke, who sniffed his pants with great interest, then sat down. Elise tossed him the red rubber reward toy, which he scooped up, then rose to examine Kai's pants again with the toy still in his mouth and a bit of his tongue sticking out from under it. Once Elise gave the okay, Kai scratched Zeke behind his floppy ear. Zeke leaned against him, leaving a trail of black and brown fur on Kai's khakis. "What a good boy you are."

"Heath thought so too. When I told him Zeke was training to

sniff out wildlife, he asked me to take pictures and work with you to develop an exhibit."

Kai looked up from petting Zeke, and Zeke turned his nose fully vertical to nudge Kai's hand. "How did Heath rope you into designing an exhibit so soon?"

Elise bit her lip. "Same way I got roped into helping the FBI foster a dog. I'm not very good at saying no."

Kai nudged her. "Hey, I didn't mean that in a bad way. I'm excited we're getting you into this side of the business; you clearly love it. I waved at you when you were headed towards the giraffes this morning, but you had a bounce in your step and I swear you were whistling. And here I thought the only thing you liked doing was filling out spreadsheets."

"Kai Torres. And if I knew your middle name, I'd use it too. I'm just trying to be helpful. What if I got so good at feeding the giraffes that I took your job someday?" She narrowed her eyes at him in mock competition.

Kai paused. "I know you're kidding, but you could run this whole place if you wanted to, you know."

Elise laughed. "Aw, man. I was trying to get a rise out of you. And for what it's worth, I'd love to someday, but that seems like an unrealistic goal for this number cruncher."

"I'm not sure I agree with that." Kai gave her a serious look. "You're good at both. Most office people tense up, but you're almost as comfortable out here as I am."

Elise gave a rueful smile. "It is nice to spend time with the animals." She pulled a rope toy out of her bag and tossed it for Zeke, who pounced on it. Zeke trotted back but when Elise stared off into space, he whipped it over to Kai. Kai pulled on one end and Zeke growled playfully, his backside in the air. Elise tapped her chin. "Hey, can I ask you something?"

Kai looked up from playing tug-of-war with Zeke. "Sure, anything."

"When I was organizing the animal exchanges for the clouded leopards, there was a lot of genetic pre-testing to avoid inbreeding. Doctor Oliver had me reference some pretty complicated matrices to make sure we had a genetically diverse population. But with so many issues amongst these cats, should I be worried? I thought we were all doing the appropriate due diligence, but what if we're not?"

Kai gave Zeke a pat. "We should get some more information on the clouded leopard with the post-mortem. Heath said it's coming soon. Plus Dr. Oliver is — was — the SSP coordinator for all of the U.S. That was his job, and he was good at it. I'll check if the results on the cub we lost have shown up in the system yet. It's likely just a strange coincidence."

Elise helped Kai with some clean up tasks and lingered more than she meant to, but time spent with the animals was a lot more rewarding than she had expected it to be. Finally, Elise collected more fur and scat to help Zeke practice, and there was nothing left for her to do. She sighed as she put away the tools and trash. "Okay, I should probably go back to the office and get out of your hair."

"You don't really need to. It's nice to have extra help around." Kai held up his phone. "Plus, we have some data to look at."

"Right now?" Elise checked her watch. "Don't you have more animals to feed?"

"Already finished. It's coffee break time. Come on. I'll show you the pot with the freshest coffee, and we'll get your questions answered, okay?"

Soon, Elise was sitting in the shade under an umbrella, drinking a freshly brewed cup of River Bean's signature coffee blend. It wasn't quite the same as getting a cup from the quirky owner of the River Bean, but it was as close as she could get to the real thing without leaving the Conservation Center. Kai sat down next to her with an aging zoo laptop displaying an alphabet soup of DNA data and explanatory charts for the data in the software they used to track the animals. She snorted. "And you make fun of me for all of my computations."

"Fair point. But, I also bought you coffee."

"It's free for employees," Elise quipped.

"Okay, point for the numbers lady. And, in my defense, it's not the entirety of the genetic code, it's only the small portion of the DNA we're interested in." Elise lifted an eyebrow and Kai raised both hands. "Let's call it a truce for now." He clicked a few buttons, closing the open report and bringing up a folder labeled Riverbend Clouded Leopards. "So, we have two brothers, right?"

"Not twins, right? Just littermates."

Kai nodded. "Right. They're littermates." He frowned. "That's odd. The genetic analysis that we got for Atma months ago is showing it was saved again today. Someone must have been in here looking at it."

"That's hardly surprising." Elise winced. "Sorry, that was insensitive. But what I mean to say is that it's natural that people might be curious, and we were all looking for the new data. If I had access, I'd be poking around too." Elise gave him a sideways glance. "I've even seen some emails about it on the administrative LISTSERVS."

"Yeah, the clouded leopard LISTSERV has been buzzing since it happened. A lot of people are sending their sympathies, but they're also anxiously awaiting more information." Kai blew out a breath. "You're right, that's exactly why someone would be in here studying the data. Anyway, we have to send information to the new Species Survival Plan coordinator — Heath must have been in here doing that. I'll have to thank him later."

Elise frowned. "Are you worried you might save over something important on accident? I've personally had more documents than I can count labeled 'Final,' 'Final V2,' 'Final Final V2,' and 'Final Final V2_Go to Bed_Elise.'"

Kai laughed. "No, fortunately, these are read-only for most of us. You'd have to have the right administrative access to change data in the system, and I didn't take enough computer courses to figure out how to get around that. So, at least I know *I* didn't save over anything by accident since I haven't been in here. Good news, the post-mortem report from the lab is saved under a different name." He clicked on a file with a different icon. "I'll spare you the raw data on the DNA sections of interest and we'll skip straight to the report." Kai scrolled too quickly for her to read, but soon they were at the results section. The cubs were identified both by a name and unique number. It felt a little cold, but the finance side of Elise understood the need for the unique ID. Just like a social security number didn't make a person less of a person, their animals needed IDs. Kai breathed out a sigh of relief. "They re-ran the sample, and it matches the original. Which means there are no known genetic abnormalities that would contribute to the cub's death. So our theory about the bacterial illness is still the most likely scenario. Man, we were so careful."

"Is it possible he has something in his DNA that science doesn't know about yet?"

"Sure, it's possible." Kai kept scrolling, then his shoulders drooped. "But, not probable. Ah, here it is. The report says they found a rare strain of the bacteria in his bloodstream."

"How did we not know about that before it was too late?"

"The animals were acting perfectly normal. We wouldn't check for this unless they were sick. We don't do full bloodwork on them all the time — it's too hard on them." Kai winced. "Or Dr. Oliver figured out Atma was sick before he disappeared. That could have been why he was checking on him at night." Kai's voice hitched. "And he didn't even have a chance to tell me he was worried."

Elise put a hand on his shoulder. "I'm so sorry, Kai. I'm obsessing over the cubs, and you are mourning a friend."

"No, no. It's okay. It wasn't like we expected the two situations to overlap. It's just plain bad luck. Let's focus on the cubs."

Elise typed the bacteria strain listed in the report into her phone and sure enough, the report identified a particularly deadly strain. A search brought up a news article speculating about the death of the other cat less than a few hours away, who had the same kind of infection. Her mind started racing, trying to remember from her biology classes how long the bacteria could remain dormant. There was no way they caught it from one another. It answered one question but raised another dozen or so. Could the veterinarians be spreading it and not even realizing it? Was it being spread by something in their environment? Elise rubbed her temples. "Thanks, Kai. I'm not sure what I was hoping for."

"A more satisfying answer, if my own armchair psychology is any indication. We're already doing everything we can to prevent the bacteria from reaching the cubs. We deep cleaned everything here as a precaution already. And the cleaners we use should kill this bacteria. We'll send a note out to the LISTSERV for all felid keepers just in case." He turned back to his laptop, opening the files that described the DNA results in greater detail. "I don't want to bore you, but I do want to do some more research."

Elise stood, determined to do some research of her own. Still, it felt wrong not to extend some kind of olive branch or excuse for him to get away from the zoo for a while. "Hey, I'm not sure if you're up for it, but I'm going mountain biking with my sister and a group of her friends on Saturday. You should come along. It'll keep you from working on a Saturday again, at least."

Kai turned, incredulous. "Didn't you just get here? How are you better connected than I am?"

"Besides the fact that you spend all your time with animals instead of people? And you already know the mountain bikers."

"Animals have their perks." Kai grinned. "Is it Liam's crew?"

"The very one."

"Of course. I should have made the connection."

Elise snorted. "Well, since you already know everyone, you should at least pop down to Bridges for lunch on Saturday if you aren't brave enough to mountain bike."

"Wow, really? You're going after my pride now?"

Elise shot him a look of challenge. "I mean, it should be safer than feeding a hungry clouded leopard. You coming or not?"

Kai laughed. "Sure. I'm in."

An uncomfortable feeling settled in her stomach, like she should hold Kai at arm's length until she sorted out whatever mess the FBI had stumbled upon. But Elise had a hard time turning off her friendliness, and the question had popped out before she thought it through. At least he had volunteered information about the cub's death — that had to be a good sign, didn't it?

Elise returned to her office with Zeke by her side and searched for more information on the mystery bacteria, but struggled to find anything useful. After walking around and smelling everything this morning, her favorite shoe-chewer was exhausted enough to lay at her feet while she worked. She rubbed his back with the side of her foot absently. After all the work they'd done, it was heartbreaking to lose the cub to something so preventable. Elise began to twirl a pencil as she got deeper into the scientific literature but no closer to an easy answer. A knock on her door made her jump, then she looked up. Her brain took a full three seconds to process who was standing in the doorway. Elise gasped and her pencil clattered to her desk.

CHAPTER 15

"Doctor Oliver! Oh my goodness! You're here! You're okay!" Elise leapt up from her chair, raced across the room, and gave him a hug. Zeke rose to his feet and eyed the newcomer warily, tail wagging.

Dr. Oliver gave her an awkward pat on the back. "In a manner of speaking," he deadpanned, resting his hand on the doorframe.

"Are you okay? I mean…"

Dr. Oliver winced. "Yes. Unfortunately, I read my obituary online and I assure you, I'm extremely alive. I made quite the entrance at my memorial service today."

Elise slapped a hand over her mouth, her shock warring with laughter. That bit of news would feed the gossip mill for months, if not years. "What? How?"

Before Dr. Oliver could answer, Kai walked into her office, his mouth dropping open. "Olly! You son of a gun." He reached across the room and pulled Dr. Oliver into a huge bear hug, thumping him heartily on the back.

Dr. Oliver grimaced. "Oh, easy there, son."

"I'm so sorry." Kai's eyes went wide. "What happened? Are you okay? Where have you been?" His tone turned accusing. "We all thought you were—"

Dr. Oliver raised his palms in the air. "Whoa, there. Just because I'm not dead doesn't mean I'm not tired." He collapsed into a chair, and Elise noticed the dark circles under his eyes and partially healed scratches on his face and neck.

Heath came bursting through the door so quickly that it was Dr. Oliver's turn to jump with surprise. "Dr. Oliver!" Heath gasped. "You're here. At the zoo."

Dr. Oliver braced his arms on the chair. "Good to see you too, Heath. As I was getting ready to tell Kai and Elise, I went for a late-night run and got pretty scratched up taking the hard way down a hill. The ambulance took me to a hospital about half an hour from Riverbend. They took great care of me, but I had a pretty good knock on the head, and it took me some time to realize where I was. Glad I got back before my funeral was finished."

Elise thumped back into her chair. "Do you remember what happened?"

Dr. Oliver shook his head. "Not much beyond the feeling of falling. Although the doctors think I had some help falling down the hill. It could have been some kind of road rage incident or even a random attack. I wasn't hit by a car or anything. Whoever did it dropped me off at the hospital, claiming to be a cousin, leaving me under a fake name and everything. Then, they left." Dr. Oliver looked over at Heath, who was standing almost completely still, shaking his head, eyes wide.

"Wow. Does everyone at the Center know?" Elise glanced down at her phone, which she now saw was full of text messages. She grinned. "Never mind. We might be the last to know. Well, Dr. Oliver, your appearance is the best news I've had all day. I'm not sure who is going to be the most excited to see you, but I expect it will be a bit of a competition."

Dr. Oliver nodded, a twinkle in his eye. "Thank you for the warm welcome, Elise."

"Honestly, when I was coming here, I didn't think I'd ever get the chance to talk to you again." Elise's heart was still racing. She put a hand on her heart. "I'll take the shock of my life if it means you're safe and sound. Take care of yourself, okay? Don't be afraid to ask us for help until you get back on your feet. Actually, maybe you shouldn't be here. Should you be home resting?"

Dr. Oliver scoffed. "I've been resting enough."

Kai eyed him. "Just long enough to remember your name and address. And then you thought you should get back to work?"

Dr. Oliver looked at the ground. "It's important to me to be here. For the animals." He looked up at Heath, whose face was like that of a strict principal, ready to back up Kai and Elise. "I can't relax at home like I can here." Heath gave him the smallest of nods.

Kai smiled. "I get that." He put an arm around his friend. "Let's get you somewhere you can sit and watch the animals versus hobble around the offices. Best of both worlds, huh?"

"Of course. Let me stop into my office and then I'll take you up on the offer." Dr. Oliver patted Kai on the back and turned to leave. Elise spotted more scrapes and bruising all along the back of his neck. Some of them were pretty deep. Who would do that sort of thing to their veterinarian? At his age, he was lucky to be alive. She'd probably want to return to normal as soon as possible too, if she were in his shoes.

Shortly after Dr. Oliver left, Heath followed suit. Kai looked over at her, eyes twinkling. "Finally, some good news."

Elise smiled. "What a day, right?"

"Relief doesn't even cover it. Is there an opposite word for grief?"

"Joy?"

"Yeah. That's exactly what it is." Kai took a step closer, closing her office door. "That said, whoever went after Doc wasn't messing around. They better not show their face in Riverbend or half the town will take up pitchforks. I'd be right alongside them, for what it's worth."

"He seemed in good spirits though."

Kai nodded. "Yes. But he's barely functioning. He's not the type to admit that, so we'll have to let him help here and there. Which means we're still going to need your help. You okay to stick around for a while?"

Zeke looked up from his mat and tapped his tail. Elise gave him a pat. "Of course. And it gives me a little more time to help Alexis too. Now that Dr. Oliver is back, everything should be smooth sailing."

CHAPTER 16

*W*hen Elise arrived back at her apartment that evening, Zeke made a beeline for their door, likely salivating over the memory of her shoe rack on the other side of it. A door slammed behind her in the hallway and she whirled to see who it was. She spotted Finn in athletic clothes, covered in sweat with Sedona panting happily at his side. Sedona touched noses with Zeke, who misinterpreted her greeting for playtime. Before Zeke could yank Elise's arm out of her socket, she got him settled again. Finn smiled. "Nice work, Elise. You're working with Zeke like a pro."

Her heart pounded. Because of the excitement of the day. Not because his compliment sent her heart fluttering. That would be embarrassing. "Hey, Finn."

"Any excitement at the Conservation Center today?"

"You're joking, right?" Elise put a hand on her hip and Zeke nudged her to open the door so he could chew on his favorite toys. She coaxed him back into a sit with patience and kibble.

"No, I just got back from a long run. Did I miss something?"

"Dr. Oliver is back."

Finn furrowed his eyebrows. "I don't want to be insensitive, but what do you mean...back?"

Elise smiled. "He was injured and missing. Lost his memory, but he didn't die. Looks like the memorial service was a little premature. Everyone at the zoo has been over the moon about it. Isn't that incredible?"

Instead of celebrating with her, Finn frowned. "Don't you find that a bit odd?"

"He lost his memory and was recovering in the hospital. Thinks it was a road rage incident. I mean, it's tragic, but not odd."

"And he was injured...how?" Finn stiffened and Elise barely stifled a groan.

"No. Don't do this, Finn." Elise suspected Finn had a procedural stick up his backside when they'd first met. She could tell from the look in his eyes she wasn't wrong. She'd worked with his type before.

Finn ran a hand through his glistening hair. "I'm sorry, Elise. I'm very happy your coworker has returned. I should have started with that." Finn started fiddling with the phone in his pocket.

Elise narrowed her eyes. "What are you going to do?"

"Right now? I'm going to take a shower." He checked his watch. "Do you have dinner plans?"

Elise studied him. "What do you want?"

"Tacos from Curva del Río. Best Mexican food in town. Even if it wasn't the only Mexican restaurant in town, it'd still be pretty great. We'll work with Zeke on not begging. It'll be my treat."

Elise was torn between telling Finn that his attempts to get information out of her would be more successful if they weren't so obvious and agreeing to the free meal and practice for Zeke. Her stomach growled, settling that debate. "Fine. Leave in an hour? I'll drive."

"Sure."

Elise opened the apartment door and Zeke sprinted inside to

investigate the shoe rack. Upon finding it empty, he began to sniff loudly at the crack under the closet door. Elise pulled a canister out of her bag, freshly filled with clouded leopard smells, and told Zeke to sit. He squirmed but followed orders long enough for her to hide the canister in her closet. On the way back, she sprinkled a few shoes on the floor for the ultimate distraction. When she returned to Zeke, Elise gave him a treat and then gave him the command to find the clouded leopard smell. With a clear job to do, he switched into a mode of total focus. Zeke's perky ear was fully upright and his floppy one bounced with motion as he sniffed along the apartment hallway, barely slowing down on the way to her closet, shoes fully ignored. He sat to alert on the scent and looked at her hopefully. She threw her hands up in victory. "Good boy, Zeke! Who's the best boy? You are!" She tossed him his reward toy and he caught it out of the air, then sprinted back to the living room.

After a few more rounds of "find the clouded leopard," Elise ran out of spots in her apartment that might fool her very intelligent, and occasionally overexuberant, puppy. The minute he didn't have a job to do, he started making a beeline for her shoes. She quickly scooped them up and threw them all into the closet despite Zeke's obvious disappointment. Then, she picked up a ball out of a basket and gave it a squeak. Shoes forgotten, Zeke slapped his paws on the ground and threw his backside in the air. She rolled the ball across the hardwood floor of the apartment, the ball jumping when it hit an uneven spot in the flooring. Zeke skittered down the hallway, spinning out for a minute when his enthusiasm overtook his ability to gain traction, finally catching up to the ball a moment before it bounced off the wall. He turned hard at the last minute and tumbled with the ball in his mouth, standing to fluff out his fur and trot back to her with his prize. A few minutes of retrieving the ball later with varying levels of coordination, Zeke finally showed all the classic signs of being tired.

With Elise's puppy fully exhausted and repeating the truism that "a tired dog was a good dog," Elise was officially ready for her tête-à-tête with her neighbor. After a quiet drive to the restaurant, they found a table and got the dogs settled. Elise rested her chin on her hands. "So, dear neighbor, what do you want to know?"

Finn leaned back, still shamelessly trying to look affronted. "What kind of tacos you like."

"Horse manure."

Finn lifted an eyebrow. "Rather uncreative species choice, considering your line of work."

"Too bad I'm driving, or I'd order an extra-large margarita." Elise lifted her brows in challenge. Finn grinned and fortunately, the waitress came over to take their order and leave chips and salsa for them to nibble on before he softened her up too much. Zeke sniffed curiously and Finn waited for Elise to get him settled, staying out of her way to let her figure it out. Finally, she was able to direct her attention to her dinner companion. "Now, I have a feeling I'm the first person to break it to you, but you aren't as smooth as you think. You've obviously got something on your mind. The last time you slowed down enough to enjoy a cup of tea, I was getting interviewed to see if I was allowed to work with the dogs."

Finn held up his hands. "Okay, okay. I didn't realize that you were going to be as observant as Alexis."

"Wow." Elise nearly blushed. "I'd take the compliment if I trusted you weren't trying to charm me." She stared at him, daring him to throw more sugar-coated nonsense her way.

Finn cleared his throat. "Fair enough. I'll get straight to the point." He leaned in. "What happened with Dr. Oliver? I had some messages on my phone from Alexis and Liam, but no one seems to know what happened."

Elise shrugged. "That's it? You could have gotten that information from Marlene. We asked Dr. Oliver and he doesn't even know.

He doesn't remember anything outside of falling down a hill. They think there was a second person who 'helped' him with the falling, if you know what I mean. That person apparently regretted it enough to drop him off at the hospital but is long gone." She scooped up some salsa with a chip and savored the taste. Finn wasn't kidding; this little restaurant's food was delicious. More conversationally, she said, "You should have seen Heath. He's normally so stoic, and when he saw Dr. Oliver, it was the first time I ever saw him completely in shock."

"Seeing someone you thought had died will do that to a person." Finn made room on their table for two plates of freshly made tacos as the waitress approached. The smell was salty, spicy heaven.

"Yeah, he's not the warmest person, but he obviously cares. He sent an email out to everyone after he'd left my office saying that Dr. Oliver is not to do any work in the zoo without it going through him." Elise gave Finn a knowing look. "Dr. Oliver isn't the best at saying no where the animals are concerned." Finn lifted an eyebrow and looked down at Zeke. "Okay, none of us are. But it was kind of him to take care of Dr. Oliver, knowing that we all tend to put the animals first and ourselves second." She picked up a taco and smelled it with the same intensity that Zeke smelled her shoes. "Tell me these are as good as they smell."

"Nope. They're better." Finn took a break from his own plate, leaning back in his chair. "What do you think about me stopping by the Conservation Center and asking some questions? I'd like to see some of the animals, learn about some of their behaviors."

Elise eyed him skeptically. "So, you want me to believe you aren't going for any FBI stuff? Just to visit?"

"Sure. And if I happen to run into Dr. Oliver..."

Elise snorted. "You are a handful. You'll have to go through Heath — he's protecting Dr. Oliver's time like Zeke protects us all from squirrels."

"So...is that a yes?" Finn's eyes twinkled and he knew he had her.

"Okay. I can give you a behind-the-scenes tour, but I can't make any promises about running into Dr. Oliver. I'll ask first thing next week when things calm down a little, okay? I don't think Heath is going to let anyone hassle Dr. Oliver before that." She pointed at him. "But, for the record, I know you're up to something. And if you don't include me in whatever you find, I promise to come knock on your door at 3 a.m. every day until you tell me what you're up to. Sedona will bark, and I'll lure her out with bacon when you open the door. Then, it'll be both of us against you."

Finn chuckled. "Deal." He set down the taco he'd been eating and gave her an appraising look. "You're alright, Elise Butler. You're alright."

Several tacos later, their conversation was flowing, and the seemingly uptight Finn Cooper had even cracked a few smiles. They told stories and surprisingly, there weren't any awkward pauses. They both shared pictures of their crafts and it was clear that Finn didn't do things in half measures. It was no wonder his family commissioned furniture pieces from him. He was so opposite of her expectations, she stayed longer than she should have out of pure curiosity. Soon, they were the only ones left. Elise gathered her things, praising Zeke for his good behavior only to realize he was out cold. She laughed and nudged her partner awake.

When they returned home, Elise directed Zeke to his crate. He whined and pointed his nose at the basket of tennis balls. She raised her eyebrows. "It's bedtime, bud. You passed out at the restaurant."

Zeke harrumphed onto the floor of his crate, and a couple of minutes later, he was out cold, his feet sticking out as straight as his crate would allow. Elise sat down at her laptop, the object feeling a bit foreign after so much of her time away from a screen. However, in sharing the good news with her local friends — was that what Finn was? — she hadn't shared it with her colleagues outside of Riverbend. They probably wouldn't find it as newsworthy as the town of Riverbend, but it was still worth passing along, particularly to the LISTSERV that the clouded leopard keepers shared. Moments after she sent the email, she had several excited replies. The zoo community was small, and she suspected their excitement at Dr. Oliver's unexpected return was genuine. Finally, Elise sent a quick email to Dr. Kim and watched a lighthearted cooking competition show to settle her too-active brain.

WHEN ELISE WENT BACK to work the following day, the joyous mood of the Conservation Center was palpable, even though they still clearly needed her help. Even Freya had perked up a bit with Dr. Oliver's return, confiding in Elise that she had a lot going on at home, helping her mother recover from surgery. Trying to organize the chaos at the zoo with Dr. Oliver's absence had nearly put her over her limit of how much stress she could handle. Winning Freya over, even a little, was the icing on the cake.

Zeke would go in for an official checkpoint at the K-9 Academy in another week, but Elise had a sneaking suspicion her new partner would stand head and shoulders above his classmates. Elise finished the week with a plan, working with the individual keepers on a list of low-energy tasks for a recovering Dr. Oliver. With no more major drama at the Conservation Center, Elise allowed herself a little bit of hope that all of Finn's concerns were directed at the wrong suspects.

CHAPTER 17

When Saturday arrived, Elise was emotionally exhausted from her work at the Conservation Center and was looking forward to a little bit of weekend fun on the trails. Kai had even agreed to join them. She pulled into the parking lot, licking a bit of chocolate off her finger from a scone Marlene insisted was on the house because it was a new recipe. She was going to have to keep biking as long as she was living upstairs from the River Bean. Unless she wanted to buy new pants, of course. Elise parked and waved at her sister, who was once again holding her borrowed bike. She walked out to the trails to see if Kai had made it yet when she saw a surprise zooming down the hill. She put her hands on her hips. "Finn! You're letting yourself have fun two weeks in a row?"

He cocked an eyebrow at her and answered by biking over to meet her. His eyes twinkled. "Let the record show, Elise Butler, that when you say that I'm a handful, you started it this time."

Elise grinned. "So, yes?"

Finn smiled. "It's been a tough couple of months. And I may have had some nudging from Liam. My leg is doing a lot better, so

I'm taking it slow." Finn gestured to his exposed calf, which showed a jagged, just-healed scar.

"Get some dirt on you. It'll be good for you!" Liam shouted from the top of the hill.

Zoey wheeled the borrowed bike over to Elise and gave her a helmet. Elise clicked it into place and Zoey smacked her on top of the helmet. The helmet dampened the blow to just startling. "It's on there good enough."

Elise looked at Finn. "My sister is Liam's perfect match."

Zoey grinned. "Just caring for my little sister. Safety first." She whacked the top of the helmet again and Elise swatted at her like they were both little kids again.

"No one warned me about how, um, caring Riverbend can be. Very, intensely, caring." Finn's eyes went wide in mock alarm.

Elise snorted. "Not much of that when catching poachers?"

Finn's face fell. "Actually, there's a lot of caring but maybe not the history. Common goals leading to instant camaraderie and all of that. It's just not the long-term relationships people have here." He rubbed the back of his neck. "But all of the responsibility, you know?"

"Aw, now I feel like I've pushed it too far."

Finn shook his head. "Don't worry about it. I was in my own head a little when we first met, but I do promise I have a personality."

"I've started to suspect that." Elise met his eyes and for a moment, she could have sworn something passed between them. It was probably the sugar high from Marlene's chocolate scone. Hopefully, her sister hadn't noticed. Zoey wasn't the type to let things go.

Zoey waved a hand in the air. "You're all set, sis. I, uh, better go find Liam." Oh, Zoey had definitely noticed.

Elise cleared her throat. "Well, do you actually know how to mountain bike, or did you just borrow the bike from Liam?"

Finn shot her a look of challenge and then took off. Elise jumped on her bike and raced after him.

After an hour of zipping through trails and whooping at their friends, they both made it back to the start, laughing and covered in dirt. After racing each other through the trails and shouting equal amounts of encouragement and teasing, Elise was struggling to find a reason not to like Finn. She'd been worried at first that his intensity was some kind of red flag that shouldn't be ignored. However, with time and trust, his edges had softened, and she was starting to understand that he was cautious, not callous.

Finn and Elise were the last to return to the parking lot for their water break, and when they pedaled into the lot together, Zoey's eyebrows travelled halfway up her forehead. Elise shot her a warning look and Zoey snickered, throwing an arm around Elise's shoulder. She leaned close and whispered, "Making friends? Or are there still...reasons?"

Elise shot a death glare at Zoey, and Zoey grinned wider. "Your K-9 instructor friend is currently getting hit on by Heather."

Elise's head whipped around, but there was no Heather in sight. Finn was chatting easily with Liam, comparing bikes.

Elise pointed a finger at Zoey. "You are out of control."

Zoey laughed out loud. "I love you too. You've got to find a way to keep coming back here. It feels more like home with you here. And Finn, for what it's worth, is as good as they come, once you make it past the crusty exterior. Crunchy outside, sweet inside."

"Okay, that's weird. He is a human, not a candy bar. So, I'm going to act like you didn't say it." Elise took a drink of water. "I like it here too. When my sister is nice to me, that is. And minds her own business." Elise hip-checked Zoey.

Another hour later, Elise was covered in a second layer of mud and sweat, laughing and comparing bruises with Zoey. For the first time since she'd met him, Finn's shoulders were relaxed. He also seemed to be going out of his way to check in with her. As Elise had expected, the crew agreed to meet at Bridges after the ride, and despite Elise being half sure that Finn would excuse himself and find a reason to work, he actually agreed to meet them there.

Elise removed the front wheel and loaded her borrowed bike into Zoey's trunk. Then, for the first time, she spotted Kai bringing up the rear of the last group. "Hey, friend! You're taking an actual day off. I'm proud of you."

"Isn't the numbers person supposed to bust my chops since I'm salary and therefore free labor?" Kai pulled off his helmet and wiped the sweat out of his eyes.

"Nah, you're no good to me burned out. Gotta keep the team healthy first, *then* work you like crazy."

"Thanks for that. This was fun. Now that I don't feel responsible for everything, that is. I mean, it's not like I'm asking anything of Dr. Oliver yet, but it helps to know he's there."

"I know what you mean. He's so sweet."

"If you say so. He's always seemed a little grouchy to me."

Elise shrugged. "Maybe he likes me more."

Mirth danced in Kai's eyes. "Can't blame him."

Finn came up behind them and stuck out a hand. "Hey there, you must be Kai. I've heard so much about you from Elise."

"Guilty as charged. I'm Kai Torres. Great to meet you…?"

"Finn. I'm a friend of Liam's. Elise and I met at a family dinner. You must be the head zookeeper at RACC."

Kai smiled. "Exactly. Elise said I had to take a break and have some fun."

Finn's return smile was lighthearted. "I'm sure it's a lot of work. I'd love to hear more about it."

Elise managed to keep a straight face. "For sure." She looked at the parking lot. "Looks like everyone is headed to Bridges already. We'll see you there, Kai." She grabbed Finn's elbow. "Do you have a second, family friend?"

"Sure."

One step away from dragging Finn into the woods by his ear, she pulled at his elbow and he followed easily until they were well away from the group. "Dude. What are you doing?"

"Just introducing myself."

"And conveniently leaving out your name and occupation. Even I know Riverbend isn't that big. You're investigating him, Finn."

"Sedona is at home, and I don't see any reason to make it easy for people to find out what I do for a living. I don't wave my badge around like a flag. That's a good way to get hurt."

"By Kai?"

Finn gave her a look somewhere between exasperation and pleading for understanding. "I don't know him like you do. I've got some questions and I want to keep my options open for backstory when I come to the Center to do more research."

"On animals."

"I thought you didn't believe me when I told you that. Do I need to go back to pretending I'm not investigating? I can, I just want to make sure we're on the same page."

Elise pinched her nose. "Remind me why I'm helping you?"

"Because I'm charming and well-meaning?"

"One of those could be possibly true. Jury is still out."

"I bought you tacos?" Finn offered.

"True, but not compelling."

Finn stepped closer to her and brushed against her. The unintentional contact sent a current straight up her arm. She stepped away to put distance between them. The last thing she needed was for her judgement to be clouded. He sensed her discomfort and leaned against a tree. "How about this? Alexis vouches for me and if you don't like me asking questions of your friend while we're socializing, you can swap her out for me, okay?"

"I don't want either of you to have to investigate."

"Unfortunately, that might not be an option. I promise to be honest with you, but I can't promise someone from the FBI won't be poking around the Center or asking the head zookeeper questions. Hopefully when this is all a distant memory, maybe you'll even believe I'm decent."

Elise waved a hand. "You're clearly decent. A little uptight, but definitely decent."

Finn lifted his eyebrows. "Uptight?"

"If it quacks like a duck, walks like a duck with a stick up its backside..." Elise closed the distance between them to give him a nudge so he knew she was kidding and felt the same zing. He also didn't move, and suddenly, all of his intensity was focused on her. Her breath caught in her chest.

He looked her in the eyes, then down at her mouth. "Says the spreadsheet pot to the uptight kettle."

She swallowed. "That's entirely different." Finn grinned and she put a hand on his arm. "I'm going to get a beer at Bridges. Before you give me any more trouble." She gave him a cheeky grin, then made her escape.

WHEN ELISE REACHED THE PUB, Liam was exchanging stories with Alexis's husband, Matt, about trees they nearly hit and some they actually did hit. There was plenty of showing injuries and a few claps on the back. Alexis greeted Elise with a hug. Thanks to her preferred sport of running, she'd managed to stay upright and had no bruises to share. "Hey, it's good to see you! How has Zeke been doing?"

"Great! He hasn't tried to chew a shoe in twenty-four hours. A new record."

Alexis raised an eyebrow. "You hid your shoes, didn't you?"

"Guilty as charged." She felt a presence behind her and knew without turning around that Finn had joined them. However, before he could join in on the discussion, Kai came over to say hello.

Elise grinned. "I convinced a friend to come along today. Kai, you know Alexis. Alexis, Kai is my inside source for animal scat."

"In that case, I owe you thanks." Alexis's face fell. "And I'm sorry to hear about the clouded leopard cub."

Kai nodded and gave a grim smile. "It's okay. I'm glad we still have one. We'd like to save them all, but it isn't always possible"

"I understand that."

Kai looked off into the middle distance. "Actually, I'm really sorry, but I have to go."

Before Elise could ask if her friend was okay, he flitted away, paying his bill on the way out. Elise tried to push back her concern and enjoy the atmosphere of Bridges. A part of her wondered if it was something she said, but she tried not to overthink it. Instead, she sat back, taking in the buzzing atmosphere of the neighborhood hot spot. However, she didn't have to wonder where Kai had gone for long. An hour later, her phone vibrated. She jumped and discreetly checked the message. It was from Kai. *Can you meet me at the Center? I think it's urgent.*

There was only one other time that Kai skipped one of their meetings because of something urgent, and it was when a giraffe was giving birth. If he said it was important, it was important. She made her excuses and hugged Zoey and Liam goodbye. She made a quick stop at her apartment to pick up Zeke and spotted Finn and Sedona in the hallway on the way back out.

"Hey, everything okay?" Finn studied her and Zeke wagged his tail, waiting for his buddies to notice him. She wouldn't be surprised if she still had a leaf stuck in her hair, but no one at the zoo would be offended if she skipped a shower.

"I'm not sure. I got a text from Kai about something happening at the Conservation Center — he said it was urgent." Elise turned to leave and found Finn and Sedona trailing behind her. "What are you doing?"

"Coming with you."

"Finn, it's my workplace. Dr. Oliver is back. What are you so worried about? I thought endorphins from exercise were supposed to chill people out."

Finn chuckled. "You can make as many jokes about me being uptight as you want, but I don't feel comfortable with you going alone. Especially if it's urgent. On a weekend. If you'd rather have Zoey tag along, that's fine. I'll call her right now."

Elise groaned. "Fine. If you don't want Kai to know you're FBI, why is my family friend coming with me?"

Finn winced. "Learning more about the program. You just didn't mention that your family friend works for another not-for-profit focused on animals."

"Fine." Elise sighed. "Let's go."

CHAPTER 18

*B*efore Elise started the car, she sent Kai a message to let him know she was on her way and was bringing a friend. He agreed to meet her in the parking lot. She found a spot in the employee lot and spotted Kai pacing by the employee entrance. She hopped out of the car and fairly ran over to him with Zeke, Finn, and Sedona barely keeping up. "Hey, is everything okay?"

Elise saw a look in Kai's eyes she hadn't ever seen before. "When I showed you the database, you didn't change anything or access it later, did you?" He glanced at Finn warily, who had just caught up with Elise.

She looked down at her phone. "Is that what was so urgent? I could have told you no in a text. To be perfectly honest, I can't even log in. I don't have the credentials for it without supervision."

Kai closed his eyes. "Someone has modified the information in the system. I was studying the report and thought something was off, then I remembered the timestamp we saw. So, I started comparing the DNA reports of the cub we lost. And it's changed."

"So, it's not clouded leopard DNA?"

Finn was soon at her elbow. "Hey, Kai. I work with one of the World Wildlife Trust's partners and I couldn't help but overhear."

Kai's return look was less grateful and more horrified. "I don't want to give you the impression we don't know what we're doing. We do. Just with Dr. Oliver's injury..."

Finn waved away his concern. "I'm not here on official business. I was just there when Elise got your text. I'm here to help if I can. I have some experience with this sort of thing."

"Damaged records or wildlife?"

Finn reached down to pet Sedona, who could tell her partner was agitated and was nudging his hand with her snout. "Both. We had a bad situation at my last job that left me unfortunately qualified for this sort of thing."

Kai took a moment to regain his bearings. "Um, okay." He looked at Elise, who nodded. In for a penny, in for a pound. Kai let out a sigh of relief. "Well, our system is showing clouded leopard DNA. The lab said it's a match with the original sample. But it isn't. Our system deleted the old report, but I always keep a hard copy on my laptop. The new sample in the database is from a genetically distinct clouded leopard. Not related to our clouded leopard mom at all."

"That's impossible." Elise frowned.

Kai raised his hands. "Agreed. But here we are."

Elise rubbed her neck. "Could there have been a mix-up at the lab?" Before Kai could answer, Zeke pulled at the leash, and she followed behind. He sniffed around the parking lot, finally sitting at the edge of the new construction, alerting as if he'd smelled clouded leopard. She corrected him and he pulled harder, sniffing towards the back of a building that would eventually be part of their new addition. A chipmunk darted out from the bushes and Zeke's head whipped around to watch it. Elise put a hand to her chest and let out a relieved chuckle. Her shoe-chewer had merely spotted a varmint that needed to be chased. Elise got Zeke back into focus and led him back to her two friends. After her shoes, squirrels were Zeke's mortal enemy. Apparently, she also needed to add chipmunks to the list.

Kai waited patiently for them to return, then smiled at a zoo visitor passing their small group. Once they were out of earshot, he continued, "Maybe the lab mixed something up. But I'm not sure why they would have replaced a good sample with a bad one. Or why they would say the samples before and after the cub's death matched when they don't."

"Can you think of any logical explanation?"

Kai looked over his shoulder. "It was either an honest mistake or someone is trying to hide something. Sorry, I know that sounds paranoid."

Finn leaned in. "What could they hide by swapping out the DNA? The cause of death?"

Kai winced. "Maybe. I'll let Doctor Oliver know something weird is going on next time I see him. I don't want to stress him out. The only people who have access to our system work here. Someone may have good intentions, but we can't fix a problem if someone keeps changing the data."

Finn nodded solemnly. "I used to work in a lab. If you can send Elise a copy of whatever you found, she can get it to me. It'd at least give you another set of eyes."

"Thank you. I'd really appreciate that. Truly, it could be an honest mistake."

Finn gave him an easy smile, one Elise had never seen during his pseudo-interrogations of her. While Elise was fully aware that Finn was spewing whatever convenient nonsense was needed to get access to the files, Kai didn't seem to notice. "That's the most likely scenario. I'll do what I can to help you clear it up, okay?"

"Thank you. It was nice of you both to come out."

Elise shrugged. "That's what friends do. Text me if you find anything else, okay?" She raised an eyebrow. "Did you skip lunch?"

"I grabbed a veggie burger from the snack bar."

"Okay. Please take some downtime this weekend. I just got you to take a break and you made it less than a day before you came back to work."

"I'll try." Kai put a hand to his head in salute. "I better get going."

"Good luck. Give us a shout if you need anything."

"Will do." Kai looked at them both, then went back into the Conservation Center.

Once Kai was out of earshot, Elise faced Finn. "What do you think?"

"I think we need to look into those files."

"Do you want a tour first?" Elise gestured to the zoo. "Since we're already here?"

"I would like a tour, but I think we need to investigate this problem first. Then we'll know what we're looking for during our zoo tour. Let's get back to the apartments. Mine or yours?"

"Mine. I have chili in the slow cooker for dinner, and something tells me it's going to be a long night."

CHAPTER 19

*E*lise took care of Zeke and quickly showered off the dirt and sweat from the morning bike ride. She checked the time and assessed her fridge, pulling out toppings for her bison chili. She chopped jalapeños to add a little kick and checked the time again. She looked at the door, which remained stubbornly silent. She washed up, then tapped her fingers on the counter and looked at her phone. Maybe she should let Zoey know about her conversation with Kai. After several minutes of trying to convince herself that she was perfectly capable of waiting, she settled on a compromise. Instead of calling, she texted a quick update to Alexis and Zoey about their strange afternoon, just in case Alexis had ever seen anything like this before. Both women would stop by if they had any concerns. There. That was done.

A minute after she sent the text, Elise found herself pacing the apartment, tidying up the small space and fluffing the already fluffy pillows on the couch. She hid the clouded leopard scent canister a few times and Zeke found it easily, only once getting distracted by a carefully planted tennis shoe. After they were done, Zeke followed her curiously around the apartment with his reward toy clutched in his mouth, keeping pace with her and looking eagerly towards the door. Finally, he traded his toy for a tennis ball and kept her busy playing fetch while she did her best impression of someone capable of waiting patiently.

Elise jumped at a noise, and it took her a moment to realize where it was coming from. She found her phone, now aggressively buzzing its way off the coffee table. Elise swiped to answer the call from an unknown number. Alexis must be calling from the Academy. "Hello?"

There was a brief pause, then a woman's voice spoke. "You need to leave town."

"Sorry, who is this?" Elise's heart began to pound.

"It doesn't matter. I know you're working with the FBI."

Elise looked out the window but saw no one. "It's hardly a secret I'm helping with one of their dogs. He comes with me everywhere. What do you want?" She kept her voice stern and unconcerned, taking a screenshot of the unknown number and time of the call.

"You're putting your nose where it doesn't belong. If you don't want something to happen to you or your dog, you'll leave."

Elise checked the room for anything that might record the conversation and found a tablet. She had to keep her caller talking. Almost as an outsider to her own body, she realized she wasn't scared of the woman on the phone. The rage the threat generated narrowed her focus to a pinpoint. Elise put the call on speaker and held it up to her tablet's microphone. "I'm just helping with a dog. I'm not out to hurt anyone." There was a knock at the door. Zeke started barking and she quickly looked through the peephole while juggling devices. It was Finn.

"I'm only asking you this once. Leave. You won't get another warning." She opened the door to let Finn in, but the call ended. Her heart thudded in her chest, and she ended the recording and closed her eyes to collect herself. As the adrenaline subsided, there was finally brain space for fear, and it washed through her system, shortly replaced once again by rage. How dare someone call and threaten her? And Zeke? Who threatened a dog? Given the number of dogs she'd spotted in the River Bean, she wasn't the only one helping at the K-9 Academy. She could kick herself for not asking more questions to keep her caller talking.

Finn put a hand on her arm, and she screamed. He jumped back. "I'm so sorry. Are you okay, Elise?"

Elise nodded furiously but the words got caught in her throat. Sedona nudged her way around Finn to lick Elise's hand and Elise leaned down to pet her. Her phone rang, once again showing a call from an unknown number. Apparently, the anonymous jerk had forgotten something. She stabbed at her screen to accept the call and began recording. "Who is this? How do you know me?"

"Umm...it's Alexis. I met you through Zoey. You sent me a text?" Alexis's bewilderment was such a shock, Elise could have laughed, but instead, her brain felt like it was going to melt down. "Elise, are you alright?"

Elise ran her fingers through her hair. "No, not especially. I just had someone call and threaten me to stay away from the FBI."

"What?!" Finn whipped around from hiding his shoes in her closet while Zeke watched him intently.

"Oh. That's not all. They threatened my dog too. If I find out who—"

"Are you okay? Are you alone?" Alexis's voice was deadly calm.

"No, Finn just got here."

"What did they say, exactly?" Alexis asked.

At nearly the same time, Finn closed the distance between them. "There's a whole town full of people that pitch in with the FBI. Why do they care if you're helping?"

Elise held up a finger. She stopped recording on her tablet but kept the phone on speaker to include them all in the same conversation. "Okay, you two are going to give me a headache. Alexis, were you calling about the DNA situation?"

"Yes, I was. Although that takes a back seat to your safety. I'm getting in the car now. Waffle and I will be there in half an hour, okay? Don't let anyone else in until I get there."

Finn approached Elise carefully, not unlike she was a skittish dog. He paused to let Zeke sniff him, realizing he also needed to convince the dog he wasn't going to hurt Elise. Zeke's neck fur was raised, ready to protect Elise from whatever invisible force had her so upset, occasionally running to the window to see if something needed to be barked at. Finally, Zeke's neck fur went down a fraction and he stayed close to Elise, leaning against her leg. Finn gave Zeke a pat and looked at Elise. "Do you have any idea who might have called you?"

Elise shook her head. "The voice was female, but I didn't recognize her. Of course, they could have modified their voice to make themselves sound like anyone. Even internet pranksters have that one figured out. Finn, I've literally been helping feed giraffes and balancing the Conservation Center's checkbook. Why would they care that I'm here? I'm fostering a K-9, not bringing a weapon and playing detective. I talked to you and Alexis about a theoretical risk for minutes. And Kai for what, ten? About DNA, not animal trafficking. This is totally out of proportion to what I know."

"Or what you think you know." Finn paused to consider. "They know someone is looking at their files." He gently steered her to a shiny red stool in Marlene's '50s-inspired kitchen. "Bowls?"

Elise pointed and he dished up chili for them both, assembling cheese and sour cream on top and sliding it over to her. She took a bite. "Thank you."

Finn snorted. "For serving the dinner you made while dealing with anonymous threats? My job has been relatively easy. But you need to get some food in your system."

"Why do I feel like I'm being treated like a hangry feline?" Elise said weakly. Zeke licked her hand and Sedona leaned against her leg, tail thumping gently on the ground.

"Your job is to take care of and feed animals. You must know it's important to feed a hungry, highly intelligent biped." Finn winked and filled up two water glasses. "And it looks like the hungry biped is going to pass out if she doesn't start working on that chili. Plus, I have a feeling that the less you eat, the more stubborn you get."

Fortunately for Finn, Elise's mouth was already full, and she needed to swallow before arguing with him. Then her phone buzzed with a text from Zoey. *We're here.* Elise groaned.

"Another message?" Finn leaned in and laughed warmly when he saw the text. He crossed over to the door and opened it, letting Zoey, Tasha, Liam, Tank, Alexis, and Waffle inside, utterly filling Elise's cozy living room and spilling into the kitchen. Zeke barked at the visitors and greeted them all, human and canine, with tail wags and play bows respectively. The room felt even more crowded as Zeke careened around the room.

Elise closed her eyes and rubbed her temples before turning to greet her sister and the rest of the Riverbend crew. There was another knock at the door and Elise tensed up. "Did you invite someone else?"

Alexis looked through the peephole and grinned. Marlene entered with a carafe of coffee and a paper bag. "Oh, honey, I saw everyone coming in and I knew it couldn't be good."

Alexis waved her inside. "Marlene, someone is threatening Elise for working with us. You should know in case someone comes by."

Marlene pulled Elise into a hug and kissed her on the cheek. "You poor dear. I brought decaf and enough croissants to share. Chocolate. Your favorite."

Elise accepted the beverage and pointed it at Zoey. "Marlene brought me croissants when she ambushed me. Please take notes."

Zoey closed the distance between them and gave Elise a hug. "Oh, I'm so sorry, sis. This is my fault."

Elise turned her head to the side. "How is a death threat to me your fault? I mean, unless you called me?"

"It's obviously because you adopted Zeke, which I encouraged." Zoey pulled a flakey pastry out of the bag. "Oh, my goodness, Marlene, you are an angel sent from heaven. Your pastries are the best in the state, forget the city."

Marlene gave Zoey a wink. "So, what are we going to do about this?"

Elise eyed the crowd stuffed into her apartment. "We?"

Liam crossed his arms. "We. You've obviously stumbled across something someone doesn't want you to find. Finn's team suspected something was going on in Riverbend, but we haven't been able to prove it. This threat confirms their suspicions. And now we know the Conservation Center is at the heart of it. Let's talk about everything you've seen there. Marlene, we'll let you know what happens."

Marlene sat on the edge of the couch and patted it for Zeke. Zeke waited exactly zero seconds before flying onto the seat and splatting down, his head laying in Marlene's lap.

Elise snorted. "I've been working really hard to keep him off of your nice furniture."

Marlene shook her head. "Oh, honey, what's the point of nice things if you can't use them? And, I think this old lady deserves to know what's going on in her apartments. Both of my renters seem to be involved in chasing down illegal activity."

Alexis grinned. "You know, I told Matt that it'd be another year before you found a way on to one of our investigations. I underestimated you."

Marlene fluffed her short hair. "I always knew you married a smart one. Let me listen in, and I can spread whatever town gossip we decide needs spreading, okay, honey?"

Elise smiled through the stress. She closed her eyes and processed the information like she was balancing an account. Clarity regained, she opened them to face the surrounding crowd. "Something, and maybe even someone, is killing cubs. We thought our clouded died of natural causes, but Kai and I found out that someone has been rooting around in his DNA report, changing what was originally there. That person has got to be hiding evidence."

Zoey crossed her arms. "Okay, so we post someone outside the clouded leopard enclosure to protect Kai and the cats, and then you leave."

"Except something happened to two of our other cats at other zoos. That we know about. Whatever it is, it's coming from River-bend, and it's spreading. I've seen *something* important, but I don't know what. I can't just get a substitute because I got scared." Zoey eyed her in a silent *we'll talk about this later.* Elise lifted an eyebrow. Zoey had some strong big sister energy, but Elise had held her own in the business world for years. And it wasn't her sister's call.

Alexis pulled a mug from the cabinet and poured herself a cup of decaf. "Who all did you talk to today?"

Finn frowned. "Just Kai. He called us to the zoo to talk about the odd DNA results. Do you think it was some kind of test?" He winced and looked at the gathered crowd. Then, he walked over to the window and shut the curtains. "Good way to see if Elise is working with the FBI on a case — all you'd have to do is call in a threat and see who shows up to protect her."

Zoey rubbed her forehead. "Oh no. I didn't even think of that. I just reacted."

Finn frowned. "Too late to do anything different, honestly. And I would have come anyway."

Elise sat down next to Zeke and rubbed his floppy ear. He

thumped his foot along her thigh, letting her know that he adored her and would continue to adore her as long as she kept scratching. "Okay. What's our next move?"

"Our?" Zoey groaned.

Elise looked over at her sister. "Stubborn runs in the family, sis. It'll save you time to use your energy to figure out how to solve this."

Liam rubbed Zoey's back. "She doesn't sound that different from someone else I know, sweetheart."

Zoey sighed. "You aren't going to the zoo alone."

"I agree. Kai is just one radio call away and Finn was already planning on stopping by sometime this week." Elise looked at Finn, silently asking for backup from someone who wouldn't hover quite as much as family.

The conflict in Finn's eyes was obvious. "I have your back. But for what it's worth, I agree with Zoey. I think you should clear out."

Elise narrowed her eyes at him. "I will if you will."

Finn cleared his throat and stood a little straighter. "Fair point."

Zoey put her hands on her hips. "No offense to Finn, but why not Liam or Alexis?"

Liam looked at Zoey. "Finn knows more about wildlife crime than all of us combined. Not to mention, everyone in Riverbend knows who we are. Finn is still new enough to have some anonymity. He's kept a pretty low profile."

"When he wasn't interrogating me." Elise put her hand on her forehead and mumbled about someone giving her the strength.

Zoey eyed Marlene, who had taken over for Elise and was now scratching the world's happiest German shepherd on the belly. "I'm sleeping on your couch." Zoey stared down Elise, willing her to disagree.

"Honestly, at this rate, you'll have to fight Marlene and Zeke.

Although, with all the secrets in this town, Marlene might be a ninja." Elise deadpanned.

Marlene looked up from rubbing Zeke's belly. "First-degree black belt. I teach self-defense at the senior center three times a week."

"Oh, for heaven's sakes." Elise pinched the bridge of her nose. "Can I please sleep in an apartment by myself with my scary dog and an FBI agent just across the hall?" The scary dog looked up from his belly rub, his tongue hanging out one side of his mouth. He rolled slightly to expose more of his stomach to Elise's landlady for easier scratching.

Alexis reached into her bag and started handing Liam boxes. "In a minute. Let's set up a security system first. And, Finn, if you wouldn't mind keeping an ear out as well?"

Finn nodded. "Of course."

Elise looked at the ceiling. Suddenly, she desperately wanted to go to bed. She gathered herself. "Okay. What do we do about my caller?"

Alexis looked up from typing on her phone. "We're trying to trace the call now. In the meantime, we'll get some cameras installed around the Conservation Center. That way we can keep an eye on you. Finn will come by as often as he can without raising suspicions, and I'll send enough students around to get you full coverage, starting first thing Monday morning." She scribbled down a number. "One of us will always have this phone on us. Set it as an emergency contact. That way you'll always have one of us nearby. And it's a great training ground for the dogs, so really, it's no trouble." Alexis tapped a finger on her phone. "Is it possible you saw something in the accounts that scared someone?"

Elise slapped her forehead. "That's it. There must be something in the financial records. Alexis, you're a genius." Zoey sighed and Elise patted her on the shoulder. "This is going to be good for you. We're still working on that control freak thing."

Liam frowned. "You seem awfully calm about this."

Elise looked him in the eyes. "Liam, I would be the world's biggest hypocrite if I cleared out at the first sign of danger. Especially since I'm surrounded by the FBI. I have more support than our partners could ever dream of."

The room fell completely silent. Marlene leaned over and whispered to Elise, "Am I allowed to applaud?"

Elise snorted. "Sure, why not?"

"These stuffed shirts probably wouldn't like it. We'll work on them though, hmm?" Marlene gave her a wink.

Alexis looked at her, eyes serious. "Elise, even with our help, you aren't anywhere near safe. Make sure you're always around a crowd. Don't let yourself get cornered."

Fear welled up in her throat. She pushed it back so Zoey wouldn't talk her out of it, instead offering the bemused group dinner out of a lack of anything else to say. Finn offered to stay and finish their chat and everyone else decided to scatter with their own to-do lists.

Soon, everyone was packing up, securing windows and doors, and asking for multiple reassurances from Elise. To Elise's relief, even Zoey conceded that Finn was capable of keeping Elise safe without her help. Still, she didn't quite make it to the door without a little nudge from Liam. She thanked them all and they filed out, until the only ones left were Marlene and Finn. Elise eyed Marlene suspiciously. "Okay, Marlene, you are way too cool about this considering I may be leading someone dangerous to your front door. What have you been through?"

Marlene gave her a sad smile and put a hand on her arm. "More than most should. And I survived it. And I will do everything I can to make sure no one else feels like a victim."

Elise gave Marlene as tight a hug as she had given her sister. "Something tells me you're stronger than any of us give you credit for. Thank you, Marlene."

"It's no trouble, dear." Marlene's pleasant mask fell back into place. "Now, you just give me a ring if you have any trouble. My house is right down the street."

Marlene shut the door behind her, and Elise jumped. Finn walked around, picking up dishes and wiping down the counter. Elise stood frozen in place, more than a little shell-shocked at the turn things had taken. "Thank you."

Finn gave her a wry smile. "I didn't do much. Just cleaned up."

"And showed up."

"It's no problem." He held her gaze for a moment, then cleared his throat. "Now, let's take a look at those records."

Long after the decaf and croissants were gone, Elise and Finn had confirmed that Kai was right and the DNA had changed, but neither was an expert in genetic analysis. If someone was swapping DNA evidence to hide cub deaths, there was hardly a detectable explanation to a novice. If the date of the file hadn't changed and Kai hadn't flagged it, she'd never have known to look. Elise leaned into the laptop and sighed. "Do we call Doctor Oliver? He's in charge of the Species Survival Plan."

"Forgive me, but I don't know the system that well. What does that mean, exactly?" Finn tossed a fluffy bear toy to Sedona, who gently picked it up. Zeke rushed at her face, grabbing the other end for a game of tug-of-war. While the toy was worn, it was still in one piece. Sedona must not have the desire to remove the stuffing from every toy in her path. The bear would last approximately thirty seconds without the inside of the toy getting scattered across her living room floor if Zeke went at it unsupervised.

"He's basically in charge of the family tree for all of the clouded leopards in the U.S. He coordinates breeding pairs to prevent genetic issues and makes sure the population is as healthy as possible. It's why he sent the cub out for the genetic analysis. It'd just take a phone call…"

Finn gave her a look.

"You're kidding," Elise said. "You're suspecting the guy who had a major injury that required hospitalization? The whole town thought he had died! How could he be coordinating animal traffickers while unconscious?"

Finn studied her. "He said he was hospitalized. Did we verify that?"

"How? No hospital is going to give you that information without permission from the patient."

Finn shrugged. "It's convenient, is all. If someone wanted to disappear to get rid of a clouded leopard, don't you think that getting a major injury would be a good way for no one to ask questions?"

Elise let out a breath. "Dr. Oliver was legitimately injured. I saw the scratches myself. And he cares about the animals. So much." She pointed a finger at him. "Don't say it."

"Okay. I won't."

"Now what?" Elise leaned against Finn, forgetting for a minute that they were nearly always in the middle of challenging each other. Of course, she also found herself enjoying their intellectual debates that never seemed to turn personal. He didn't move, and the air in the room suddenly felt a little thicker.

"I'm not sure. We need to think about what Kai's motives could be as well as Dr. Oliver's. Freya's and Heath's too." Elise turned, incredulous. He pulled away and held his hands up. "Don't shoot the messenger."

"Freya is taking care of her aging mother, and Heath goes on business trips too frequently to manage a sophisticated animal trafficking ring singlehandedly. And Kai and Doctor Oliver love the animals way too much to be a part of anything like that."

"Then who's left?"

Elise sighed and Zeke looked up from chewing on an oversized rubber bone. Sedona had been chewing on her toy in the corner and took Zeke's distraction as her opportunity to try and steal his bone. When she put her mouth on it, Zeke gave her an offended bark and the scariest growl in his arsenal. Elise almost stood to break up the dog fight until Sedona barreled into him and Zeke flipped to his back and started nipping at Sedona from his less-threatening position on the floor. Soon, the chase was on. She laughed. "At least they're having fun. Did you see anything related to the FBI's investigation?" Elise picked up her laptop and scrolled through the reports again, for whatever good it would do.

"No. Whoever is trafficking animals has a strong network and they're good at it. And they're not getting too greedy. One here, one there. But what does that have to do with your cats dying? Are they spreading bacteria from an unusual location? That'd explain why they've all had the same infection." Finn shook his head. "If they're risking their jobs, why wouldn't they go all in?"

Elise rubbed her temples. The World Wildlife Trust would have kittens when they heard about this. The Riverbend Conservation Center could be shut down entirely if she couldn't figure out what was going on. She reviewed the transactions to known Riverbend suppliers, including Marlene for her coffee and a local construction firm for the new area. Nothing was free, but Marlene's coffee was profitable, and construction wasn't getting any cheaper. She growled in frustration.

Finn chuckled. "That's normally a noise I hear from Zeke."

She nudged him playfully. "Well, if you had to clean up the last finance person's mess, you'd growl too."

"What'd they do?" Finn's tone was casual, but Elise easily saw through it.

"They were incompetent. I don't think they were criminal."

"Humor me."

Elise sighed. "Their records were a mess. Don't even get Freya started — she's careful not to badmouth Heath, but I suspect she blames him for a lot of it. She's professional and tries to hide it, but she's not impressed with Heath's management of the zoo. And for Heath's part, he's lost his faith in people. He delegated responsibility to the old accountant who gave out jobs to friends and family instead of the most qualified or reasonably priced. We're locked into contracts for another few months."

"And the World Wildlife Trust was okay with that?" Elise lifted her eyebrows and waited for Finn to catch up. "Ah, that's why they sent the no-nonsense finance person to help."

"Yeah, once Doctor Oliver disappeared, that was the last straw. My boss had already laid the groundwork though. Dr. Carmen Kim doesn't pull punches when animals are involved."

"Well, it seems like your boss's intervention was effective."

"Dr. Kim is my hero."

"I think I'd like her."

"You definitely would. If I'm half as good as her someday, I'll be happy."

"Seems like you're more than on track." Finn pointed to the screen. "They aren't getting rid of Marlene's coffee, are they? She's so sweet, I'd be surprised if she gave the Conservation Center a bad deal."

"You're correct." Elise gave him an affectionate smile. "Our landlady is selling her coffee to the Center for wholesale prices. We buy a lot of it and it's more expensive than the bulk brands, so it adds up, but we make it back big time on sales. We have a lot of parents of toddlers who buy unlimited coffee pass add-ons with their memberships and honestly, we're still coming out ahead. And those parents love us so much — I've actually seen them rave about the coffee in their reviews online." Elise studied him. "You can't be that interested in coffee. Are you ever actually going to tell me the whole story of what brought you to Riverbend?"

Finn looked at his watch. "It's late. You sure you want to hear about my job after everything you've dealt with today?"

"Sure. Let me make a cup of tea for both of us and you can tell me all the sordid details about your work for the FBI. Otherwise,

I'll have to assume you don't want to tell me because you are the wildlife version of James Bond, leaving women pining for you in your wake." She shot him a cheeky grin to test the waters and Finn chuckled.

"Ha. The only females panting after me are dogs, and it's only because they use their tongue to cool off. It's hot in Indiana this time of year. But as a wildlife biologist, I think you know that already."

Elise rummaged in the kitchen for mugs and an electric kettle. Soon, she brought over big cups of chamomile tea for them both and they moved to the couch. "You can drink it whenever you deem it acceptable."

"And here I thought you might actually be starting to like me."

"Honestly, I don't know how long to brew it. I'm sure there are instructions and temperatures, but I just drink it when it tastes good. That level of precision is best left to Marlene." Elise took a sip of her tea. "Also, you're stalling."

Finn swallowed. "For my sake, I'm going to ask you not to repeat anything I tell you. For your sake, I'll scrub the details in case you slip. But I'm happy to give you the truth, insofar as I'm allowed to tell it."

Elise's pulse kicked up a bit. "Are you secretly an assassin?"

Finn studied his cup of tea, a smile playing around his lips. "It'll be a miracle if I can get this whole story out."

"I'll behave." Elise took a long sip of her tea, keeping her mouth on the glass to keep herself from interrupting her introspective new friend. He was always so steady that seeing him flustered was disarming.

"I've been working in remote areas of Southeast Asia to disrupt a sophisticated ring of animal traffickers. They're trying to capture some animals alive and sell them to wealthy individuals who are interested in keeping the most beautiful, and often dangerous, ones. We've intercepted what we believe is a very small percentage of these animals. Our criminals are working primarily in cash, and if the animals die, they often sell their skins or pelts to the same group of people. Your clouded leopards, for example, are a status animal. Their coats are beautiful, and people pay a fortune to wear them. We've found animals caught in snares that have died painful deaths and I personally have been threatened more than a few times. I was injured by a trap that I think was set deliberately to catch a person — not an animal."

"Were you working alone? It doesn't seem like you'd have jurisdiction overseas."

"You're right. But when the crime involves the U.S., my team gets involved with our local partners on the ground. However, our partners on the ground were wildly underfunded and understaffed. When I showed up, it drew the wrong kind of attention to them. My injury was a warning shot."

"Seems crazy to hurt someone over that."

"I agree with you but, unfortunately, the wildlife traffickers have a different set of priorities. And this crew has backing. They ship globally, including to U.S. cities via boat. They're skipping the airports — we've got those pretty well locked down, but they're coming in on small boats and they're not easy to catch." Finn shook his head.

"Do you really think you're going to find a connection to your poaching ring in a sleepy little town like Riverbend?" Elise put her mug down on the coffee table and pulled her knees to her chest.

"The sleepy town that just delivered a threatening phone call to my neighbor?" Finn frowned skeptically. "I'm not leaving until I figure it out. No one is getting hurt on my watch."

Elise studied him. "You're nicer than you let on, Finn Cooper."

"Don't tell anyone." Finn winked at her and she nudged him. The space between them had been shrinking without her fully realizing it.

Finn rubbed his forehead. "Did any of that scare you off?"

"You know, for an FBI super spy, you don't know much about me. And it's kind of embarrassing, really, when I've been giving you ample clues."

"I'd consider it a good thing I don't know everything yet since I'm not investigating you." Finn volleyed back. "If I'm wrong, and I need to add you to the suspect list, let me know. Should I be worried you put something in this tea?"

"Probably should have asked that question before you ate my chili." Elise snorted. "But no. Your judgement is sound. Just chamomile. It should help you relax. I can't speak for you, but I think I could use about a gallon more."

"I think I'd need about a gallon too. Little more excitement than I bargained for today. But it was nice to get to know you a little better, even though the circumstances weren't great." Their eyes met, and his were twinkling. After a moment too long of silence, Finn cleared his throat and stood. "If you need anything, I'm right across the hall, okay? Alexis has set up your security system and should have sent you a link so you can access it from your phone."

"Thank you. I should be fine." Elise swallowed hard.

Finn stood, still close, neither of them able to look away. Elise's heart started to pound with the pressure of the unasked question. Then Finn leaned down and kissed her on the cheek tenderly. "Night, Elise."

Elise froze in place for a moment before leading him to the door. Sedona rose from the floor and stretched, then trotted after her partner. Once Finn had left and she'd locked the door behind him, she leaned against it for a moment to regain her bearings. Then, she rummaged through the closet and found a baseball bat. Part of her wondered if Marlene had left it intentionally, just in case. She laid it on the coffee table and flopped down on the couch. Zeke nuzzled her face and she rested her forehead on his snout. "What are we going to do, boy?"

Zeke scooped up a tennis ball and nudged it into her face. Elise laughed. After more rounds of fetch than she could count, Zeke curled up in a ball next to her on the floor. She rested one hand on his fur and told herself she should put him in his crate. But the call had rattled her. Her mind raced and she decided moments before drifting off to sleep that her scary-looking puppy should be allowed to roam free, even if it meant risking a shoe or two.

CHAPTER 20

*E*lise woke up after a fitful night's sleep, ate breakfast, then put on her running gear. Once she reached the door with her excited German shepherd close behind, she reconsidered. Running was probably not the wisest course of action considering she'd been receiving death threats. Really, a death threat. There was only the one. She blew out a breath. Zeke started to dance by the door, following her when she turned back towards the kitchen, then back to the door again.

She reached for the knob. Then a pounding sound made her scream instinctively. From the other side of the door came a muffled voice, "Hey, Elise, it's just Finn."

Elise put a hand to her racing heart, willing it to still. She opened the door to Finn, who was holding out the largest cup of iced coffee Marlene sold. There was another in his other hand, along with Sedona's leash. He'd skipped a shave that morning, but the stubble somehow made him more handsome, not less. The memory of a kiss that seemed to stop short of what both of them wanted lingered on her cheek. She smiled gratefully and accepted the cold cup. "For coffee, I will forgive the heart attack."

Finn grinned. "Sorry. Should have texted. Sedona and I are headed out for a walk." At the word *walk*, Zeke pranced in a full circle around Elise, wrapping his leash around her legs. She quickly stepped out of it before they became a human/dog pretzel and reined him back in.

Elise took a big drink. "I hope you want company on your walk or Zeke is going to chew through the door when you leave."

"I do. Can't do much until Monday, and going outside usually clears my head. I went with iced since it's a little swampy out this morning. It's still early, but no one told the weather that."

Elise bit her lip. "Okay. That sounds good."

Soon, Elise and Finn were walking along the pedestrian path downtown. The two dogs were models of canine behavior as if rewarding their humans for figuring out they should go for a walk. The downtown was small, and the pedestrian path led over a bridge that spanned the river of Riverbend's namesake. The river itself wasn't very wide but would likely fill up with spring rains.

Across the bridge was the more industrial side of Riverbend, including a larger-than-expected research facility associated with Indiana Polytechnic. The building was rectangular and bland, without much character, in contrast to the historic buildings downtown. However, if her time with her sister was any indication, the engineers and scientists inside could be doing all kinds of groundbreaking research and she would never know it. Perhaps they even appreciated the pace of the smaller town with easy access to campus resources when they really needed them. Her hand brushed Finn's and she jerked it away. "Sorry about that."

He looked at her, puzzled. "About what?"

"Nothing." She cleared her throat.

"Did you want to hold my hand?" Finn asked her, his tone playful. Her stomach did a flip. Was he messing with her? Before she could answer, he had entwined his fingers with hers. "Because I'm good with that."

"Umm…" For someone who prided herself in her snappy retorts to any situation, Elise found herself at a loss for words.

"Um, yes?" Finn seemed suddenly uncertain. "Or, um, no?"

"Yes." Elise breathed out. "Um, yes."

Finn was soon rubbing his thumb over her hand and making it hard for her to think clearly. There could have been a giraffe walking down the sidewalk and she might not have noticed it. They finished their tour in a surprisingly innocent way, breaking their contact once they were back downtown by unspoken agreement.

When they got back to their shared hallway, it was Elise's turn to feel uncertain. "Um…"

"There's that word again."

Elise shook her head. "It was part of a sentence. I'm still thinking about the rest of it."

"I hope the other half is inviting me inside." Finn's eyes danced with intelligence and mischief.

"Um, yes."

He grinned and she pulled him inside. Once the door was closed and the dogs settled, she found herself pressed deliciously against the door, kissing the man she'd been fairly certain was going to be the death of her patience less than twenty-four hours prior. And she wasn't the least bit upset about it. Zeke, however, began to bark immediately. Sedona lay down, completely unbothered. Their impromptu make-out session quickly turned into laughter against each other's lips. Elise gave Finn a peck. "Is Zeke our conscience?"

"He's not mine." Finn kissed her neck.

Elise closed her eyes, breathing in his smell. Zeke barked again, this time pushing his snout in between them. Sedona stopped licking her paw and trotted over to see what Zeke was making such a fuss about. Elise groaned. "We have a crowd."

"Okay. Let's get lunch and maybe they'll settle."

Elise's phone beeped. She saw the text and looked up to the heavens for patience. "It's my sister. She's on her way upstairs, bringing a full spread for lunch."

Finn bit his lip. "That's nice of her." He snuck in one more deep kiss and Elise wound herself around him.

There was a knock at the door and Elise felt it in her back. "Lord, give me patience."

"I think she seems nice," Finn said into her neck.

"Elise! What's taking so long? I've got the slow cooker and I can't turn the handle."

Elise nudged Finn out of the way and prayed her sister wouldn't say anything. She opened the door and the dogs rushed to greet Zoey, Tasha, Liam, and Tank.

Zoey's eyes went wide. "Well, hello, Finn. It's nice to see you here again."

Liam gently poked a finger into Zoey's side. "And that's all we need to say about that."

"Look at her face! She has whisker burn!" Zoey said to Liam in a whisper Elise likely wasn't supposed to hear.

Considering that her face was flushed with embarrassment when her sister walked in the door, it had to have turned purple with Zoey's comment. There was nowhere else to go, really. Elise set her mouth in a line and blinked slowly. "It's really nice of you to drop by, sis."

"Well, we thought we'd bring lunch since you didn't know anyone in the area, but you obviously do know someone. I mean, not in the biblical sense."

Elise pinched the bridge of her nose. "I wanted to move here. I wanted to move here. I wanted to be close to my sister. This was a choice."

Finn reached for the slow cooker. "Let me help you with that. I was just checking in on Elise."

Zoey snorted and Liam put his arm around her, squeezing her

shoulder. Liam looked at Zoey as he spoke. "And we think that's great. And we have no further questions except for 'are you hungry?'"

Zoey looked like a balloon about to pop, but she managed to nod and walk into the kitchen to start rummaging for plates.

Finn put a hand on Elise's back and she swatted it away, then regretted the loss of emotional support immediately. However, there was a tilt to his smile that made her think he was more amused than offended.

The rest of Elise's afternoon was spent eating lunch and playing a board game Zoey and Liam brought over. Elise had literally moved to Riverbend to spend more time with her sister, so she couldn't exactly shoo her out because her face may stay permanently red for the afternoon. Or the week. Worse, Finn stayed and sat next to her, his hand sneaking over to touch hers whenever he thought their visitors weren't paying attention. Finn, however, didn't realize that Zoey always paid attention. Elise's embarrassment bank soon had a full afternoon of deposits. Despite the internal chaos, however, she found herself having a remarkably good time with her family and Finn. By the end of the afternoon, she was laughing with everyone, and her brain kept forgetting that she was only visiting Riverbend, as was Finn. Eventually, Elise even found herself grateful for the day of simple fun that distracted her from her bigger problems.

Before dinner, Finn left with Zoey and Liam, giving her some much-needed recharge time before work on Monday. Five minutes later, there was a knock on her door and Zeke barked, but it wasn't quite the same as it usually was, it was more of a "hello" bark. She grinned and opened the door to Finn. "I thought you were leaving?"

"I was. I have some work to do tonight, for real." He leaned in to kiss her. "But I had to do that. One more time."

Elise let out a breath. "Well, glad I could help. So, this wasn't a one-time lapse in judgement?" She smiled when she said it, but she wasn't the type to let questions fester. She would have made it approximately another hour before walking over and asking his intentions.

"I think was a very good decision." Finn put his hands in his pockets and swallowed hard. "I know it's complicated, but I should say, I'm not the casual type."

"I kind of got that. You're very focused."

His mouth tipped up. "We've got a lot on our plate to figure out. But I'm interested...in you."

"I'm glad to hear that, considering."

"Have I told you you're a handful?"

"Why, thank you. The feeling is mutual. But it sounds like you have work to do, and I want to work with Zeke tonight on his clouded leopard detection skills. I'm worried if I don't keep him busy, he'll figure out how to open the closet that's hiding all of my shoes. Especially since he was really calm this afternoon. He's had time to plan." Elise kissed his cheek. "I'll see you tomorrow."

"I'm just a phone call away if you need me."

"Thanks, Finn. I'm grateful your team is on this."

He winked. "Something may have been said about how stubborn the Butler girls are."

"And how competent." Elise lifted an eyebrow.

"Yes, ma'am. Just focus some of that stubborn competence on not getting hurt when you go to work tomorrow, okay?"

CHAPTER 21

*W*hen Elise returned to the Riverbend Animal Conservation Center, a shadow of worry disrupted the peace she usually felt when she entered through the large wrought iron gates. Zeke seemed to share her distracted energy and tugged her towards the construction area housing his chipmunk nemesis. Elise managed to redirect Zeke without rolling her eyes at the sight of the expensive project, but only just. It wasn't the construction workers' fault that the zoo had gotten a bad deal. They had to get paid too. Their bosses would just have slightly bigger wallets than was probably fair when it was all over. She rewarded Zeke's focus with a treat and took him to her office. She'd work with him more once she'd dug through the Center's financial records again. She'd given them a scan with Finn but she still felt like she was missing something.

On the way into the office, she waved to Freya, who was walking in from the parking lot. She had worry lines around her eyes but gave Elise a tentative smile. "Good morning, Elise. And Zeke."

Zeke wagged his tail and Elise walked in with the administrative assistant. "Good morning to you too, Freya. How is your mom doing?"

"Doing better every day." Freya exhaled. "I was pretty worried about her for a while."

"That's understandable. And is Heath keeping you busy?"

Freya stiffened. "I'm keeping up just fine."

"Oh yes, of course. I didn't mean that you weren't." At that moment, Heath came power walking out of his office, nearly bumping into Elise.

Elise tripped a bit and Heath reached out to steady her. "Pardon me, Elise! My mind was on other things."

"No problem, Heath. Can we help with anything?"

Heath shook his head. "No, I'm afraid this is something I need to handle. We have a regular donor who was asking about the cub's death. He asked to meet with me personally to discuss it on short notice. Privately and discreetly, so I'll avoid giving a name. You understand." He shook his head and almost rolled his eyes. "Not that it's worth trying to keep anything secret in Riverbend. You'll know who it is by the size of the donation."

Elise smiled. "Good luck. They sound...important."

"They are important. Particularly if you ask them." Heath gave her a wry smile. "I shouldn't say that. They're a big supporter."

"I didn't hear it, so you have nothing to worry about. Big supporters like to know where their money is being spent. I get it."

Heath breathed out. "Yes, exactly. I'll be back by this afternoon."

"Have fun!" Elise waved and Heath snorted. Freya retreated to her desk. Elise waved goodbye but she wasn't sure if Freya noticed, as Freya seemed focused on her computer.

Elise led Zeke to her office where he gave everything a good sniff, then found a stuffed toy he'd left the last time he'd been there. It didn't chew as nicely as Elise's favorite leather shoes, but he seemed satisfied enough with his prize. Elise estimated he wouldn't be able to tear it to bits for at least an hour or two since the label stated it was indestructible. Elise looked behind her before double-clicking on the software that led to the zoo's financial records. The beige wall with a large portrait of curious mongooses remained as it always had, although she did notice the picture was slightly tilted. She righted it and then got to work.

After successfully coming up with a whole lot of nothing from the Conservation Center's spending patterns, Elise copied all the donor information into a spreadsheet in the name of thoroughness. The call must have rattled her more than she realized if she thought reviewing donations would help her find a criminal. Still, money was a motive, and she needed to convince herself there wasn't some kind of financial exchange hiding in the Conservation Center's records. She formatted the data into a table, aggregating information from different sources and sorting by donation size, frequency, and amount. The large donation Heath had mentioned obviously pulled her attention, however, once she sorted the data, it became clear that it wasn't the donor's first gift to the zoo. He or she had given five-figure donations three times in the last year. The donor had indicated that they did not want public accolades but had provided the requisite contact information for the donation via initials and an address. She wrote down the limited information they had, but most importantly, copied down the address in Riverbend. Their mystery donor was a local. The address looked familiar, and she smiled when a quick search indicated that the donor lived in downtown Riverbend over Bridges. It was likely Kai's next-door neighbor. Must be an eccentric resident who preferred to live quietly. She'd definitely drop off a personalized thank you. And a zoo gift basket. Heck, for what they'd donated, she'd pull the picture of the mongooses off her office wall and drop it off too.

Zeke nudged her knee with his nose, tucking his face into her lap and making sad noises until she finally broke concentration.

"Okay, okay, buddy. We'll go for a walk." At the word *walk,* Zeke pulled away and stood at attention, tail wagging at top speed.

As she was clipping on Zeke's leash, Kai appeared at her door, his trusty sky-blue RACC travel mug in hand and a smile on his face. "Hey, math girl. Want to go on a quick field trip? The crew just finished up the new clouded leopard enclosure. Technically, they're supposed to let us know when it's done, but I've been keeping an eye on things and saw the last bit of construction trash leave this morning. Goodness knows we could use something to celebrate."

"You have no idea." Soon, Elise was following Kai to the newest part of the zoo. If she had a tail, it'd be wagging as hard as Zeke's. Despite the expense, the new area would be perfect for their felids.

"You're going to love the space they have for the clouded leopards. Our new cub is going to grow up in luxury." Kai gestured to the other side of the newly renovated area, ducking under a loose piece of plastic sheeting and stopping short when he reached a closed door. He wiggled the handle, but it was locked. Kai frowned. "That's odd. It was unlocked when I peeked in this morning."

"Do you think they were worried that the head zookeeper was checking their work?" Elise smiled. Zeke sniffed around the area, almost as curious about what was behind the door as Kai was. He sniffed and pawed at the unfamiliar smells. Elise gently corrected him: Alexis didn't want the dogs to paw at scents they found interesting, due to the safety hazards when the K-9s detected explosives. As Kai struggled, Elise couldn't help reaching out to try to push the door open herself. It remained stubbornly stuck. Zeke got more distraught, whining and looking up at Elise for help. She was the one with opposable thumbs, after all. Elise grinned and rubbed his head. "Good boy, Zeke." She turned her attention to Kai. "He probably smells something worth finding back there.

With all the construction workers in and out, who knows what it is?" Elise jumped at the sound of someone clearing their throat behind them. She turned around to see a familiar face.

Doctor Oliver held up a key ring. "Sorry, I was in here earlier checking out the cats' new digs. Give me a moment to move some boxes out of the way, okay? The last thing I need is for OSHA to write us up because we've tripped our fancy city accountant." Dr. Oliver winked at her.

There was a rummaging sound behind the door as Dr. Oliver worked and Zeke pulled at his leash, promising that he really was the best helper in the world and probably wouldn't eat any of the treats in Dr. Oliver's pockets. Unless they were offered, which would make them a gift, really. Elise got him back into a sit and tossed him a piece of kibble, which he wolfed down at record speed. Dr. Oliver popped his head back out. "Okay. It's safe now."

Elise grinned and followed Dr. Oliver inside. His eyes were more energetic, but he still seemed to be hobbling a bit. The new area for the cats was already set up and Zeke sniffed everything with great interest. The heavy metal door slammed shut behind them and Elise realized a little too late that she was outside of the bounds of the new security system set up by the FBI. Zeke sat down, pointing his nose at Dr. Oliver, who stood in front of the empty enclosure. Elise furrowed her eyebrows. "Have the cats already been here?"

Dr. Oliver gave her an incredulous look. "No, but I've been in and out of the enclosure inspecting it. Dogs' olfactory abilities are off the charts, so maybe Zeke is smelling residual smells off my pants." Dr. Oliver held up a finger, then pulled what looked like an oversized dog toy out of his pocket. It was a plastic ball covered with bite marks left by a small, enthusiastic feline. He immediately had Zeke's full attention. "Ah, I think we found the source of the smell."

Kai smiled. "That was Atma's favorite toy."

"Yeah, I tucked it in my pocket and forgot about it. It seems right to leave it here. As a tribute." He unlocked the door using two separate keys to place the toy in the empty enclosure and Zeke alerted again, this time on the pocket Dr. Oliver had pulled the toy from. Elise gave him his reward toy. Dr. Oliver held up the key ring. "When the cats are in here for real, I'll hand over the second key to you, Kai. This is more your area than it is mine."

"No rush." Kai put a firm hand on Doctor Oliver's shoulder and looked at the toy sitting in the empty enclosure. "You're a good man, Olly."

Dr. Oliver grimaced. "I don't think so, Kai. I'm middling on my best day."

Elise grinned. "Okay, and now we know you don't have a big head. Want to give us the rest of the tour?"

Dr. Oliver got a little bit more of the light back in his eyes and proceeded to show them around the brand-new facility. It had the best parts of the old facility with a few extra runs and separated areas to help manage future cubs. All the enclosures led both indoors and out so that the animals could have the choice of whether or not to interact with the public. Elise pulled out her phone and began snapping pictures. "Our partners will love this. You have implemented every single best practice in the WWT's recommendation guide."

Oliver studied her curiously. "Our finance expert knows about best practices in raising clouded leopards?"

Kai scoffed. "Don't let her fool you. She double majored in wildlife biology."

"Ooh, can she help with the animals?" Dr. Oliver stroked his chin.

Elise lifted her eyebrows. "She already has. In fact, I think the giraffes may like me more than Kai now."

Kai snorted. "Only because you weren't in charge of the exam of our most recent mama. I don't think she looks at me the same way anymore."

Dr. Oliver slapped Kai on the back. "All in a day's work, son."

Another door at the back of the facility opened, and Dr. Veronica entered with a wide smile. "Dr. Oliver! You told me you were going to be resting."

"Young lady, I will rest when I need to."

Dr. Veronica put her hands on her hips. "I am a trained veterinarian and if you call me young lady, I will start calling you old man."

Elise snorted and Dr. Oliver put his hands up in surrender. "Consider me corrected, Doctor. But I'm still not going home and taking a nap, even if you do call me an old man."

"Dr. Oliver, I have dealt with mules less stubborn than you. In fact, the worst one I ever had was called Stick-in-the-Mud. He was downright easygoing by comparison."

Oliver snorted, his affection and respect for the veterinarian twinkling in his eyes. "Well, I'll take that as a compliment. And how are our patients today, Dr. Veronica?"

"Very good. I documented everyone's status, so they'll be ready for you when you're feeling ornery enough to work. Which, if I had to guess, was five minutes ago." Dr. Veronica looked up from entering information on a tablet at Kai. "I already filled in Dr. O on my tour of the other two facilities that lost their felids. I didn't see any red flags or commonalities that had me particularly worried, but I've started spreading the word to start testing for that bacteria proactively. Maybe we'll catch it if it happens again. So, if you don't need anything else from me, I have a business meeting in Indy to attend." She gave Dr. Oliver a knowing look. "And I'll be back to check on the animals later this week. They're easier to deal with than non-compliant humans."

Dr. Oliver expression turned bashful. "Mostly compliant, at least. We are grateful for your help. Thanks for popping by."

Veronica waved her hand. "It's nothing, Doc. We all look after each other. I'll be back before you know it."

Dr. Oliver made his excuses about needing to go check the rest of the animals and shuffled off slowly. Once he was out of earshot, Elise spoke in a low voice. "On a scale of one to ten, how annoyed would he be if I told him to go home and rest? He obviously needs it."

Kai chuckled. "Maybe an eleven? And it wouldn't do you any good anyway. He didn't get this far in his career without being more than a little stubbornly independent. I think with Heath out of the office, Olly realizes that no one here outranks him enough to make him rest."

"Is there a partner in the situation who might convince him to take a break?"

"Nope. He claims he's too hard to live with to have a partner."

Elise snorted. "Well, at least he knows it. Dr. V is right. He's as stubborn as I've ever seen. And fixing *that* is way outside of my job description."

Kai shrugged. "Well, that's why I work with animals. Humans would be a lot easier if they had tails and displayed physical warnings before they snapped at you."

"I think they do. In a way. You just have to learn the signs."

Kai smiled. "Fair enough. Ready to see what else got finished?" He held the heavy door open for her. Zeke trotted through like he owned the place, sniffing everything in sight. The remaining upgrades were outdoors, and the potential of all of the new space cleared Elise's head and made her feel less trapped, even in light of the events of the last few days.

CHAPTER 22

*A*fter her workday was over, Elise parked her car in front of the River Bean with a bounce in her step. Her second day without any contact from her threatening mystery caller made her want to believe her FBI contingent had scared them off. A quick stop in the River Bean gave her some new, if not particularly useful, information: Marlene had been listening at the coffee shop, but nobody wanted Elise to leave Riverbend. In fact, aside from their small group of friends, her appearance wasn't particularly noteworthy. The town grouches had put aside their concerns about Riverbend's newest stoplight and were now focused on a proposal for a roundabout at what was currently a four-way stop near the elementary school. They had begun circulating a petition to stop its construction, even putting up a notice on the River Bean bulletin board. The arrival of a new, temporary, resident was not even on their radar. Thurston had come by to chat with, and perhaps vent to, Marlene, since they worked closely together on the town council. Elise left the coffee shop with no clues about who had threatened her, however, she now knew where to find the online petition to stop the latest update to Riverbend's roads.

A check of the security feeds on Elise's phone confirmed that the hallways, windows, and door to her apartment had remained undisturbed while she was gone. She was tempted to knock on Finn's door to say hello, but it felt awkward. So, she settled for cleaning up her apartment and checking her WWT email. Their busy day of walking had actually managed to wear out Zeke, and he curled up in a ball on his dog bed with his nose resting on his tail.

Elise popped open her work laptop and spotted an email from Dr. Carmen Kim. It felt like a lifetime ago that she'd been back in Denver. The email was a request for an update on the cats from Riverbend. She considered how much to tell her boss about the recent threats, suspicious changes to files, and her work with the FBI, but cringed at the idea. Carmen might have follow-up questions she couldn't answer. So, she kept it simple, attaching the reports about the cub and sending a picture of Zeke, conveniently forgetting to mention the death threats and odd happenings by explaining that she'd been "navigating business complexity" and "collaborating with the FBI."

Once she was at inbox-zero, Elise paced around her apartment, fussing over things that didn't need to be fussed over. Even Zeke looked up from his nap to determine if his human was doing okay. Her sister's hobby, painting, was a lot more portable than hers, refinishing furniture. She wasn't going to stay here long, though, so it didn't really matter. She checked the time and realized the coffee shop would be open for another hour. She hadn't settled down enough to make dinner, so she grabbed Zeke's leash. He sleepily stretched and wagged his tail, eager for a walk or any potential pets on the other side of the door. They walked down the stairs and into a coffee shop that wasn't as busy as the mornings, but still full of the quiet buzz of conversation. Groups of students were huddled in a set of comfy chairs at the back of the shop, and what looked like a book club was gathered around tables, books forgotten and gossip in full force. Elise sat on one of the funky stools at the coffee bar. Marlene studied her. "You look like you need a cup of herbal. My blend of chamomile, cinnamon, and lavender will be just the thing."

"That sounds perfect. And dinner, if you have it. I'll take whatever you recommend."

"Chicken salad it is."

"Marlene, you are a treasure of a human."

"It's my pleasure." Marlene began rummaging in the cooler, prepping a meal that was sure to be delicious.

A few moments after she arrived, Finn stopped in, giving her a wink. Elise bit her lip. Attraction flooded her system and warred with a bit of uncertainty. Marlene raised her eyebrows at Elise. "When did that happen?"

Elise swallowed. "What do you mean?"

Finn slid a hand around her waist and kissed her on the cheek. "Hey, you." He nodded to the owner of the establishment. "Evening, Marlene."

"Good evening, young man. Your young lady was just insulting my intelligence by acting like you two aren't an item, but she's had a hard time lately, so I'm going to let it go." Marlene fussed, filling a tea bag from a big glass jar, the smell of the tea wafting across the bar. She pulled a large ceramic mug off a wooden peg on the wall and dropped the newly filled tea bag into it. Marlene poured water over the top and set a timer, placing the tea on the bar next to Elise, who picked it up immediately, the mug warm in her palms. Marlene swatted at her hand without touching it. Wise, considering Elise was holding hot tea. "You may drink it when the timer beeps, young lady."

Elise grinned. "Yes, ma'am. Are you always this demanding to your customers?"

She looked at the timer, then back at Elise. "Two minutes. Can

I get you a dessert, too, honey? I am out of chocolate croissants, but I have a blueberry lemon scone that is to die for."

"I wouldn't want to argue with my landlady..."

Marlene reached for the scone and put it on a plate. "Let me warm it up for you."

"Oh, Marlene, that's not necessary." Marlene's eyebrows went up, and she held the plate suspended in midair. "I mean, if you recommend it, that sounds great."

Marlene patted her hand. "It's no problem at all, dear."

A ting of the bell above the door meant more customers. Zeke lifted his head off the floor and stood, wagging his tail in recognition. Elise turned around to see who it was and grinned. "Zoey! Liam! So great to see you! And Tank and Tasha, hello puppies."

Pets were given all around and Elise gave her sister a hug. "You're here late, sis."

Zoey nodded. "We had a late night of work and Marlene almost always has some chicken salad leftover from lunch. It's the best."

"Flattery will get you everywhere." Marlene beamed. "Give me one moment to fix two more plates up for you both. Would you like decaf, Zoey?"

Zoey took a sip from Elise's tea. "Ooh, I'll have what Elise is having." The timer went off and Elise shook her head, taking the second drink from her mug of tea.

Elise eyed the growing group around her. "Are you all here for the chicken salad, or does one of the cameras outside my apartment feed into FBI headquarters?"

"First of all, it's the K-9 Academy, not headquarters." Zoey took another sip of Elise's tea, and Elise tucked her mug protectively in front of her, glaring at her sister.

"So, yes?" Elise kept her mug close. She was tempted to lick it as if they were children, but if their childhood was any indication, it wouldn't stop her older sister from taking another drink.

Zoey looked at Elise's mug but didn't make another move. "No, we're here to check up on you independent of the cameras. So, the answer is C, none of the above."

Liam eyed Zoey. "The whole way here, you told me the story was we hadn't gotten dinner and I was not to, and I quote, 'tell Elise we are checking up on her because she already thinks I fuss too much.'"

Zoey shrugged. "Well, it was either that or she thinks we're spying on her. However, the answer remains the same. Not a spy camera. My kindness doesn't require technology."

Marlene turned around with three plates holding generous portions of chicken salad atop plain croissants. Elise breathed out. "Bless you, Marlene, her mouth will be full."

Zoey sent a sharp elbow into Elise's ribs and Marlene pointed a finger at Zoey as the tea sloshed a bit. "You will not spill her tea. You may have yours in two more minutes."

Elise tipped her head to the side. "Aw, Marlene likes you."

Zoey grinned. "Oh yeah, she can't get the town grouches their tea fast enough."

Marlene's expression was pure innocence. "I have no idea what you're talking about. I'm sure I've told them one time or another." Marlene suddenly got very busy cleaning an already clean countertop.

Zoey took a bite out of her sandwich and closed her eyes. "I don't care if she spits in my tea as long as I can eat her food."

Marlene froze and pointed her finger at Zoey again. "Zoey Butler, I would do no such thing. Even if I didn't like you."

"Sorry, ma'am," Zoey said, around a huge bite of chicken salad sandwich.

Elise eyed her sister. "I'm glad you had to check up on me. It's late to be starting dinner."

"Oh, we had a meeting with the higher-ups. They're fully supportive of Finn and the wildlife trafficking program, but frustrated by our lack of progress." Zoey looked around, then clearly decided not to elaborate. "So, that was fun."

Finn eyed their sandwiches. "Marlene, you don't happen to have enough for me, do you?"

Marlene smiled. "I have one more portion. You're in luck. Tea too, sweetheart?"

"Sweetheart?" Elise scoffed.

Finn looked at Elise, eyes twinkling. "I suppose she finds me charming."

"Oh, brother." Elise practically rolled her eyes. Apparently, she was the only one who struggled to know how to manage the FBI agent. She almost reached for his hand but instead took a sip of tea. "Were you at the same meeting?"

Finn nodded. "I helped explain why tracking live animals is different than explosives or drugs. This group is fairly new, so it'll take them some time to catch up."

Elise frowned. "I mean, they have a point. We haven't made a lot of progress."

Finn took a quick bite of the sandwich offered by Marlene. "Thank you, you're the best." Marlene began making a cup of tea for Finn, setting the timer as she had for Zoey and Elise. He lowered his voice. "Obviously, trafficking is everywhere. But they agreed with our assessment that something is happening at Riverbend. And, as soon as they agreed, they wanted it solved yesterday."

Elise frowned. "I've been thinking about it though. We have a pretty extensive animal care system at Riverbend. Everything is tracked electronically — we'd know if an animal went missing right away. We knew the cub died right away. If a stolen animal even came to the vet, there would be a risk they'd be identified by a DNA test." Elise froze with her cup of tea halfway to her mouth.

Zoey's eyes narrowed. "What is it?"

"The cubs. The DNA records had been modified for our cub

that died. We were searching for DNA anomalies and problems with animal trades, but what if Finn's animal trafficker and our mystery cub illness are the same?"

Zoey frowned. "Is there enough value in a cub to fake their death? That seems...dramatic."

"Absolutely. Particularly at scale." Finn set his mouth in a line. "There are collectors willing to pay for these animals quietly. You wouldn't need a lot of animals if you knew how to breed them. And if you could change DNA records."

Zoey snapped her fingers. "And that's why they threatened Elise. She was looking into the DNA records with Kai."

Elise closed her eyes and leaned her head back. "Oh, this is bad." She opened her eyes and gasped, whispering, "It's more than changing the DNA. We have a quiet donor. They've given varying amounts in the past year or so, but they're all substantial — five figures, so they don't trigger too much attention. Could they have been paying for a clouded leopard cub?"

Liam whistled. "Maybe. Any record of who it was?"

Elise swallowed. "I only have initials. But the address of the donor was an apartment above Bridges."

Liam pushed his dinner away. "Let's go check it out."

It was hard to say who moved first, but Elise quickly moved to the front of the pack. Finn put a hand on her arm. "Hey, why don't you and Zoey stay here?"

Liam snorted. "Good luck with that."

"And if it's just a generous donor who didn't want to be identified? Then there will be FBI agents banging down their door for doing something nice." Elise held up a finger. "I've got an idea. Marlene, do you have any gift baskets for sale?"

"In the back." Marlene soon brought out a smartly wrapped gift basket with an assortment of coffees and two new mugs.

Liam looked at Finn. "Never underestimate the Butler sisters."

"Exactly. I'll knock, and you can stand next to me, out of sight, okay?" Elise said, with more confidence than she felt.

Finn considered her question, then nodded. "Deal."

Marlene removed their plates. "I'll keep these for you. They'll be here when you get back."

Soon, they were walking a few blocks to Bridges. To an outsider, it would appear to be a cozy family gathering with people and their dogs, and one out-of-place gift basket. They walked up the stairs to the apartments above Bridges, which, unlike the River Bean, did not have an outside lock. Two of the apartments were clearly occupied including one with Torres written on the mailbox — that would be where Kai lived — but the one with the address from their system looked empty; no name on the mailbox, no friendly wreath on the door, no welcome mat. Elise knocked on the door, but no one answered. The door to the stairs opened behind them, and Elise whipped around. The large figure of Thurston appeared. "Hey, folks, can I help you?"

Elise swallowed and held up the basket. "Someone has been making donations to the Conservation Center and listed this apartment as their address. We were out on a walk, and I wanted to give them a gift, but I don't think anyone lives here."

Thurston smiled. "That's correct. I've been using that room for storage. I really should clean it out..."

Elise eyed him and did her best to put on a mischievous smile. "Are you the mystery donor, Thurston?"

He laughed a hearty chuckle. "Oh, Elise. I wish I had the kinds of funds that would get me a gift basket delivery, but no. I do serve on the board of directors, but that's not a job that pays particularly well. I just help them out because I like animals. If you're looking for a multi-millionaire, you probably should look elsewhere."

Elise fought to hide her disappointment, and instead, smiled. "Well, I guess that's what I'll have to do. Thank you, Mayor Riley." Elise's heart raced during the quiet walk away from Bridges.

Finally, after a block of silence, she finally said, "Okay, I think we found the money part of this. But the funds for the cub would be paid to a not-for-profit. Who benefits from that?"

"Did you see any outgoing transactions to anyone you didn't recognize?" Finn said.

Elise shook her head. "I've checked everything. Our employees are frugal with their expense reports, and there are invoices for everything."

Soon, they were back at the River Bean, eating their dinners in relative silence. Marlene gave Elise a quizzical look and she shook her head. She nudged the gift basket back across the counter. "Thanks for trying. Truly, it was above and beyond." Elise looked at Zoey. "Do you know Marlene sells her coffee to us for wholesale prices? That's how nice she is."

Marlene froze. "No, I don't."

"Sorry?" Elise put down her half-eaten sandwich.

"I've been providing the coffee for free — I heard the Conservation Center was down on its luck from Thurston." She waved her hand. "It's nothing, really. I get a tax write-off."

"We've been paying you, Marlene." Elise's heart began to race. "I've seen invoices."

"Who were the checks written out to?" Marlene narrowed her eyes.

"They were wire transfers, not checks." Elise's heart began to pound. Zeke stood, pushing his head into her palm, and she scratched behind his floppy ear.

Marlene frowned. "I'd look into that, honey. I haven't accepted any money from the Conservation Center. Certainly not from a wire transfer."

Zoey put a hand on Elise's arm. "We'll have the FBI check it. Want me to come to work with you tomorrow? I'll bring Tasha."

Finn shook his head before Elise could answer. "No way. Now

we know why Elise was getting death threats. I don't want her there without someone who can go armed. I'll go."

Elise put her head in her hands. "How do I sleep until then?"

Zoey pointed to the now-cold tea. "Chamomile, lavender, and patience, sis."

"I don't think Marlene sells that blend." The joke fell flat, and Elise fiddled with the string on her tea bag. "Do we tell Kai? Heath? Freya? What about Doctor Oliver?"

The FBI team exchanged looks, but it was Zoey who finally spoke. "Elise, you've just listed all our suspects."

CHAPTER 23

After a fitful night's sleep, Elise woke up to a concerned snout in her face. She blinked twice and felt a lick on her nose. "Did I not lock the kennel door?"

Zeke didn't answer. He did wag his tail, dip his head, and drop a ball on the bed. A shoe that hadn't been hidden in the closet was a little worse for the wear, but it hadn't been completely demolished. So, that was progress. The ball rolled toward her hand, and she laughed. Zeke licked her frantically and she swatted him away. He bent down into a play bow. She tossed the ball outside her door and pulled the covers up over her head. She'd assess the rest of the damage from the free-roaming mischief-maker in a minute. A moment later, she felt something rolling towards her again and she peeked out to see the world's cutest German shepherd cocking his head to the side, his perky ear ready to play and his floppy ear falling open, just a bit. "Oh fine."

Elise threw the ball one more time, then got out of bed before Zeke could return. She could hardly maintain her sour mood in the face of so much doggy joy. So she quickly put on her River-bend Animal Conservation Center khaki uniform and stopped in to get some treats from the River Bean before going to work. Perhaps Marlene's baked goods would distract from the fact her FBI friend — boyfriend? Complicated pseudo-coworker? — would be joining her at work today.

While the employees at Riverbend Animal Conservation Center had always made her feel welcome, bringing a sharing-sized portion of Marlene's chocolate croissants made her down-right popular. Kai gave her a smile, but the dark circles under his eyes meant that he hadn't been sleeping well. Of course, he could have spotted their crew in his apartment hallway and connected the dots that they were on to him. She shivered. He polished off his croissant and raised his well-worn blue RACC travel mug in a toast. "Thank you for the treat. I needed it."

Although Elise desperately wanted to confide in Kai to get more information, Zoey's words still rang in her ears. She studied her exhausted coworker/friend and wondered if he, of all people, would be guilty of animal trafficking.

Before Elise could spiral too much, she spotted Finn and Sedona coming in through the front entrance. She didn't quite realize how happy she was to see them until she jumped up and walked over to greet them, giving Finn a tight hug and Sedona a pat without letting go of Finn. Sedona touched noses with Zeke, who wagged his tail happily at the sight of his friends.

Finn ran a hand down her back. "You must be really freaked out," he said quietly into her ear. "I didn't even think you wanted me here."

Elise met his eyes. "I had mixed feelings, but after thinking about it, I'm glad you're here."

Finn's mouth quirked. "Well, I'm glad you thought about it then." He looked at the gathered crowd. "Did I miss a meeting?"

"Guilt croissants."

"I'm sorry?"

"It's just, with…everything, I felt like we all deserved a treat. So, guilt croissants."

Finn studied her and Elise realized they were still standing close. She pulled his hand into hers for a brief moment and gave it a squeeze for courage. "I think we should start with Kai."

"It's a risk, but you already know that." Finn considered. "What makes it worth it?"

"I need to know he's innocent." Elise ran a hand through her hair, and it got caught in a tangle. "I'm not built for this, Finn."

Finn got Sedona into a sit and waited for Elise to do the same with Zeke. Although it was an obvious stall, she humored him. Finn was more introverted than she and needed some time to process his thoughts before sharing them. "Why don't we see if he can give me a tour? Then, we can ask questions as we think of them. Carefully."

"And you are…"

"Liaising with the Riverbend K-9 program as part of my work with WWT's partner. Just testing to see how Zeke does when he's here." He gave her a mischievous grin. "And I might have a little crush on you and am looking for excuses to spend time with you."

Elise nodded quickly, too stressed to flirt back. "Okay. Good. Yes. I can handle that." Elise straightened, put on her metaphorical big girl pants, and made a beeline for her friend/coworker/suspect in the FBI's investigation. And she'd thought her biggest challenge in Riverbend would be helping the zoo organize its financial mess.

Elise looked around to make sure no one was in earshot and approached Kai. It was going to be difficult enough for her to let Finn take the lead on questions without a crowd. "So, this definitely won't help your schedule, but Finn has asked me to give him a tour with Zeke in tow. He's been helping out with the K-9 Academy through his work with the WWT and has been helping me teach Zeke some new skills." She leaned in conspiratorially. "And I kind of want Zeke to impress my teacher. Would you mind giving the tour so I can keep my overgrown shoe-chewer in line?" She gave Zeke an adoring look and he swished his fluffy tail on the ground as if to agree with his partner.

Kai winced and looked at his watch. "Sure, I'll help you out." He took a long drink of coffee from his mug. Elise didn't like adding to his stress, but the alternative was worse.

"You are a star. Thank you." Elise waved Finn over as if the whole conversation hadn't been premeditated and he greeted Kai, then carefully watched Zeke, in keeping with their charade.

"Hello again, Finn. Where would you like to start?" Kai made a wide gesture, coffee mug still in hand like a security blanket. "Herbivores, snakes, big cats, something else?"

"Dealer's choice."

Kai gestured to the area under construction. A small group of workers was working on a fence but the rest of it was empty of people and animals. "Let's start with an area without animals to get Zeke settled, then you can shadow us as we walk through the enclosure areas. I can give you an hour or so before I have to feed the cloudeds. Two dogs and three humans are probably too many for them."

"That should be more than plenty of time. Thanks, Kai." Finn followed Kai to the construction area with Elise close behind. Zeke followed along happily, nose snuffling the air and sidewalk. Sedona did the same.

As they approached the construction site, Zeke tugged on the leash. Elise peeked around the signs still warning people not to enter but didn't see anyone, human or animal, inside.

Kai gamely unlocked the outer door and led Elise, Finn, Sedona, and Zeke into the new space that would hold future clouded leopard cubs. The clouded leopard cub's toy was still in the empty enclosure where they'd left it, and a muffled noise came from behind a door. Kai froze and they heard the noise again. He fumbled with the keys until he found the one that opened the door, which led to a smaller enclosure.

Elise looked around Kai and gasped. Zeke sat, nose pointed at a pair of whiskers coming out to investigate their presence. "How did the cub get in here? You weren't supposed to move him yet, Kai! There's way too much noise in here." Her heart fell a little. She'd thought the world of Kai and surely, of all people, he knew the distress moving the cub would cause.

"I..."

Elise tried to contain her anger, but the past several days had taken their toll. And nothing upset anyone at the WWT than an animal being mistreated, including Elise. "Listen, I'm in finance, so I recognize I'm not in charge. But this is an active construction zone. At the very least, you should have checked with Doc. Or Heath." She rubbed her forehead. "Even I would have told you—"

Kai put his hand on her arm. "Elise. I didn't move the cub."

Elise snorted. "Well, Tej didn't move himself."

"He didn't move at all. This isn't Tej, Elise. This is Atma. The one we thought we'd...lost." Kai pointed to the cub. "See, his spots are darker on his tail. His brother's tail is lighter." The cub began to rub his face on the enclosure, clearly happy to see Kai. "What are you doing here, little guy? I don't know why or how he is here, but we need to get him back into the other enclosure so we can check him out, make sure he's getting proper care. And food. Right now. I'll text the team so we can get a full checkup. I need to get the carrier. He's small but he won't be very happy with me if he's hungry."

Finn put his hand on Kai's arm and Kai jerked back as if he'd been burned. "Hey, Kai, I think it'd be better if you wait."

Kai eyed Finn, and the two men stared each other down. "What is it you say you did for the WWT again?"

"I didn't say. But I know something suspicious when I see it. It certainly isn't normal that a cub who isn't actually dead reappeared after his veterinarian made a similarly miraculous reappearance. What do you think happened?" Finn crossed his arms.

Kai let out a breath in a whoosh. "I assume it was a miscommunication. At a minimum, I need to tell Dr. Oliver. Who knows what state this cub is in? Where he's been? Who's been taking care of him?"

"Maybe we shouldn't stress Doctor Oliver. Let's...let's call Dr. Veronica instead." Elise looked at Finn, who gave her a small nod.

When Kai stepped away to place the call, Finn pulled on her arm to move her closer to the exit. He whispered, "I don't like this. I'm texting Alexis."

"What if it was an honest mistake?" Elise hissed.

"This cub was supposed to have died a tragic death, but here it is, with its DNA records swapped. The cub's veterinarian similarly disappeared, reappeared, and has a case of amnesia. I'm bringing in backup."

Elise shivered. "Okay. That's fine. Good, even. Should we act like everything is normal? I mean, someone here knows something is going on. The cub isn't opening doors by himself. Do you have another one of those security cameras?"

Finn shook his head. "Not on me. I'll ask Alexis to bring one."

Kai returned to the room, running a hand through his hair. "Dr. V can't get here until this evening, but she's going to head our way as soon as she can to check Atma. I won't leave him alone for long, but I really do need to get his carrier. And to go feed the rest of his family. I'll be quick about it. Then, we need to make a plan." He shut the door gently behind him, careful not to startle the cub.

"Can I take a closer look while you're gone?" Elise stopped Kai on his way out.

"Honestly, Elise, I know you can handle it, but I don't want to upset this cub any more than he already is. He should only be near people he knows."

Finn cringed. "Okay. But can you be quick about it?"

Elise shot him a look. "Filter, Finn."

"Can you be quick about it, please?" Finn said with a winning smile. Elise slapped her forehead and Kai chuckled.

Kai gave a small salute. "I know what he means. And yes, I'll make it as fast as I can, okay? The cub has access to a small outdoor area, but it's fenced in. He's not going to escape."

Finn frowned. "How long has he been here?"

Kai looked pained, his head moving between the location of the cub and the exit. "I don't know. He could have been hiding somewhere we didn't spot him. The enclosures are designed to look like their natural habitat and their camouflage is excellent. Give me twenty minutes, okay?"

What felt like hours but was actually minutes later, Finn and Elise both received a text message from Alexis. More help was on the way. Now, it was a race to see which FBI employee got there first.

Elise's phone dinged. "Ah, plot twist. Zoey is in the parking lot. Apparently, she was headed down to Indiana Polytechnic to work with one of the professors and we were on her way. I'll go meet her."

By the time Elise reached Zoey, her sister was practically jogging to the employee entrance with Tasha in tow, similarly amped up. Elise soon found herself enveloped in a hug. "Sis! Alexis said to meet you here ASAP. Is everything okay?"

"Yes! No? I think so. We found the clouded leopard cub we thought had died. It was in the new area."

"That's wonderful!" Zoey lifted her hands in victory, then froze. "Wait. No. That doesn't make any sense. How did they mess that up?"

"We don't know. But he seems okay, like someone has been caring for him." Elise frowned.

"Oh. Oh no." Zoey's eyes darted around the parking lot. "Is Finn here?"

"Yes."

"Oh good. And Kai? Does he know?"

"He found the cub." Elise swallowed. "The cub couldn't have been there the whole time, right? Do you think he knew?" A chill ran down Elise's spine.

"And then discovered it dramatically for you and Finn's benefit? I doubt it." Zoey shook her head. "Alexis is a better judge of people than I am, but logically, it doesn't make a lot of sense. Unless it's a double bluff. Or they're trying to frame *you* for something."

"Well, that's reassuring," Elise deadpanned.

"Well, what are our other options?" Zoey asked reasonably. Tasha closed the distance between them and lay her fluffy head against Elise's leg, reasoning that her partner's sister needed some extra reassurance. She stared at Zeke, daring him to challenge her presence, and Zeke wisely stayed on the other side of Elise. "Dr. Oliver, Heath, any of the zookeepers here?"

Elise rubbed her neck. "Heath hasn't been around much the past few days, so it's hard to imagine how he could have orchestrated a cub kidnapping when he's been gone so much. Dr. Oliver just came back a few days ago. Neither one of them has been here enough to manage the cub. These animals need round-the-clock care."

"Who else knows how to take care of clouded leopards, keep them fed and healthy? The cub is healthy, right?" Zoey winced.

"Yes, he seems to be. I mean, I could take care of the cub, if I wanted to. But I don't know the ins and outs of the zoo like the other keepers do. Even Dr. Veronica would know the zoo better than I do, but she's not here much either. Freya has her hands full at home — there's no way she could be managing a cub too. Which leaves no one." Elise closed her eyes. "What do we do, Zoey?"

Zoey reached for her elbow. "We collaborate on next steps

with law enforcement. Lucky for you, Riverbend isn't a very big town." She pointed to the parking lot, where Alexis and Liam were pulling in. "Law enforcement has arrived."

At that moment, Finn joined them. "I checked all around that room and there's only one way into it for people. There is an enclosure out back I'd like to take a closer look at, but the outer gate is locked with two locks, like the existing enclosure. We'll need Kai's key ring unless you want me to pick the lock."

Elise grimaced. "Probably not the best idea. We can give Kai a little bit more time."

A few minutes later, Elise felt a little silly about how large of an FBI contingent had joined them. It seemed incongruous with the outside appearance of the sweet little Conservation Center. "You know, it's possible that Dr. Oliver moved him and doesn't remember doing it. He was pretty out of it when he got back." Elise reached for Zeke, and he licked her hand.

Zeke looked up at the person jogging towards them in the parking lot. Kai smiled sheepishly when he reached them. "Did I miss a party invite?"

Alexis waved him into their little group. "Not at all. We're just getting started. Finn said he didn't see signs that the cub was forced into the enclosure or that anything violent had happened. I'd like to go in with Zeke, see if we can figure out where the cub has been hiding all this time. Maybe then, we'll figure out why he was there." Alexis's tone was light, but she watched Kai carefully without fully explaining why a group of FBI agents just happened to be in the parking lot.

"I ran into Dr. Oliver when I went to feed the cloudeds and asked him a few questions about the night he disappeared to see if he had any memory of it." Kai rubbed his neck. "He didn't even remember writing the report about the cub's death. I don't want to make him feel bad about it, but one of us would have to approve the cub's move and it wasn't me. How would he forget something like that?"

"Drugs? Some kind of medical issue?" Liam shrugged. "Did he say anything else about that night?"

"No. Only that he doesn't remember much." Kai looked a little sheepish. "I wasn't as subtle as I thought I was being though. He asked me why I was asking him all of the questions and figured out that I found Atma. And before he even went to check on him, he was already calling Heath, not to mention sending an email to all of our employees and volunteers to let them know the cub had been found." Kai ran a hand through his hair. "Should I have told him you all were coming?"

Alexis fidgeted with Waffle's leash. "Don't sweat it, Kai." She looked around. "Well, we aren't going to figure anything else out standing here. Let's bring Zeke back to the building. I have a feeling if the whole facility knows, a bunch of people are going to be spreading the smells around pretty quickly."

Elise straightened. "Okay, let's go."

Soon, a group of FBI employees, one head zookeeper, and a finance employee-turned-animal caretaker/FBI volunteer were headed back into the Animal Conservation Center. Although he was the newest K-9 at Riverbend K-9 Academy, Zeke was the most experienced finder of clouded leopard scents. It was an odd thing to see the experienced and frankly, a little intimidating, FBI agents defer to a dog, but they coached Elise as she led Zeke through the Conservation Center. He led them to the new area again, covered in construction signs and looking as deserted as it had this morning.

"He's just in here," Elise whispered, although she wasn't sure why. It wasn't as if she was going to open the door and be attacked by mom leopard. She pushed the door open and Zeke alerted in multiple spots. Elise slowed enough to praise and reward him, but otherwise, let him tug on the leash towards the source of the smell. They arrived at the door, but when she opened it, she didn't see the cub right away. She peeked out into the relatively sparse yard, but couldn't see him. Elise pointed at the little house sitting in the large space. "He's probably in there. I just can't see from here."

Kai held up a finger and soon came jogging back with a bucket of treats they gave the leopards. He shook the container, the treats inside hitting the lid. This sound was enough to cause any of the leopards to come running, but the enclosure stayed silent. Zeke tugged on the leash towards the back door and an expletive left Alexis's mouth. A few minutes later, Kai confirmed what Alexis had already deduced. Their cub, once again, was gone.

CHAPTER 24

"That's impossible. People and animals can't keep disappearing." Elise's heart thudded and there was a rush of white noise in her brain, crowding out any possibility for rational thought. She opened both locks on the enclosure with the key ring for the construction zone. Once she confirmed that there were no signs of the cub, she led Zeke around the area, following him through the doorway into the outdoor yard. Zeke snuffled around the ground, then doubled back on the way they came.

Elise startled at a hand on her arm. She whipped around and spotted Kai, who held both hands in the air. "Whoa. Hey, you okay?"

Elise shook her head. "No, I'm really not. How did we lose the cub? That doesn't make any sense, Kai. He was here. We saw him." She patted Zeke and told him what a good dog he was, tossing a reward toy for finding the scent. Elise had no doubt that Zeke was on the right track, she just wasn't sure why the right track led to a dead end. They walked out of the front of the building and spotted Dr. Oliver coming in from the parking lot, flipping his keys in his hand. He gave Elise and Kai a hearty wave and practically jogged over to say hello. "Well, if it isn't my favorite zookeeper and favorite honorary zookeeper! How is our long-lost cub doing?"

Elise winced. "He seems to have gone missing again."

Oliver shot them an incredulous look. "Ha. Ha. Unless he's grown opposable thumbs during his time in hiding, I find that hard to believe."

Zeke sniffed Doctor Oliver's pants, then Kai's. He alerted on Dr. Oliver's pants. Elise patted his head. "I'm sure you smell clouded leopard, buddy, just not the one we're looking for."

Alexis, Finn, Zoey, and Liam soon appeared next to them, their own dogs eager but not sure what they were searching for. Zoey frowned. "Any sign of the cub?"

Elise shook her head.

Alexis held out a hand. "You must be the famous Dr. Oliver. I'm Alexis Thompson. I'm working with Elise on our training program with Zeke and she was giving me a tour."

Elise closed her eyes and tipped her head back. "Well, it was a memorable tour at least."

Alexis turned to Kai. "Can you get me access to security footage of anyone coming in or out of the area? This cub must be an escape artist."

Dr. Oliver frowned. "Our cameras don't save the footage, but maybe someone saw something. Let me head back to the office and see what I can find."

Dr. Oliver left and Elise rubbed her forehead. "Do we need to initiate the escaped animal protocols?" It was extreme and would require extensive reporting to the agencies that regulated animal care, but Elise had always been transparent when her teams had problems. Issues weren't solved by shoving them under the rug.

Kai closed his eyes. "I don't know that he even escaped. He had to have been moved."

Finn grimaced. "And he got moved again once we found him. That cub was about to be sold."

Elise groaned. "Dr. Oliver emailed the entire Conservation Center — how would we know which person panicked?"

Kai's eyebrows shot up. Before Kai could ask any questions, Alexis started pointing at her crew. "Let's split up and watch for odd behavior, anyone where they shouldn't be. Zoey and Liam, you stick together. Kai, I'd like for you to show me anywhere you think you could hide a cub. Finn and Elise, you start checking behind the scenes. Let Zeke show you what to look for. Trust your dog and help guide him. He's young, but he can smell things we can't see. Everyone keep their phones on and reach out if you need help."

Elise swallowed. "Okay." As soon as they started walking back into the Conservation Center, Zeke tugged on the leash, nose pointing deeper into the construction area. Elise followed him, leading him gently to a different path in the event they'd find another clue. However, Zeke tried to pull them towards a field adjacent to the zoo, outside the boundary of where the crew had been working.

Finn whispered, "Let him lead us."

"But how will that get us closer to the cub?" Elise looked skeptically past the construction zone. There was a large outbuilding they were using to store construction supplies and highly concentrated cleaning chemicals. It was liberally plastered with signs warning of specific, and alarming, chemical dangers.

Finn took a few steps closer to the building and Zeke followed, wagging his tail and prancing hopefully. "One way to find out."

Finn pulled a weapon from under his shirt and Elise's eyes went wide. "You shoot one of my animals, we're going to have a problem. Have you had that on you the whole time?"

"Getting attacked on the job makes a person cautious." He put a finger to his lips as they approached the building. Zeke alerted, sitting with his nose pointed at the door. Finn turned the door handle, threw the door open, and shouted, "Freeze!" before Elise could even see if there was anyone in the room.

A few moments of silence followed Finn's declaration, then he gave a low whistle. He turned back and waved Elise inside.

Elise entered the room and gasped, clasping both hands to her mouth. Enclosures filled with beautiful endangered animals greeted her. Poison frogs, a cage with a variety of exotic birds, including a macaw and a pair of African gray parrots, and one clouded leopard cub chuffing softly at their entrance, along with countless other animals. Unlike the rest of the facility, the enclosures were cramped, and there were far too many animals in too small a space. She approached Atma cautiously and he rubbed against the bars of his small cage. Tears filled Elise's eyes. "This can't be happening." Elise approached each animal, examining them carefully. Most appeared relatively healthy, but some were showing signs of repetitive behavior and one of the gray parrots was missing feathers. Living in a room this cramped was clearly stressing them out.

Finn kept his weapon drawn and scanned the room. "No one is here. Do you recognize these animals?"

Elise shook her head. "Aside from Atma, I haven't seen these animals before. However, there are some breeding pairs here. Who knows where they all came from?" She looked away from the animals, her gut clenching. Then, she spotted something impossibly worse on a small table. Elise closed her eyes to shut out the sight of it long enough to think straight. She bit her lip, trying to keep the tears from falling.

Finn took a step closer. "What is it?"

Elise pointed to a sky-blue mug with an old RACC logo with a letter worn off, just like Kai's. "I know that mug." Her gut clenched. "I thought Kai was my friend. That he was in the dark as much as I was."

"He's with Alexis. We need to get him here before he realizes we've found his animals and has a chance to run." Finn immediately started typing on his phone. "If he finds out he's cornered, he'll probably confess."

Elise felt like a deflated party balloon. She heard herself say, "Yes. That's a good idea." Elise walked over to study the mug, and she felt suddenly nauseous when she realized she shouldn't touch it because doing so would contaminate the evidence.

Finn looked up. "Alexis is bringing him here. Liam will be close for backup but will stay out of sight. Get behind me."

Elise was tempted to argue that Kai had ample opportunities to hurt her before, but the magnitude of his betrayal made her doubt her own judgement on every level. His explanations had sounded so believable, and she'd fallen all of them, hook, line, and sinker.

What seemed like a lifetime later, the sound of the door opening, then clanging shut made her pulse jump impossibly higher. Finn kept his weapon trained on the door and as soon as Kai saw him, he lifted his hands in the air, one hand holding his trusty travel mug. "Whoa, Finn, take it easy. What's going on?" He blinked a few times, taking in the sight of all of the animals in the building. "What is all of this?" A mix of betrayal and fear flashed in his eyes. "Elise? Did you and Finn take these animals?" He kept his eyes trained on Finn's weapon without moving.

Finn kept his voice even. "Kai, we know you were here."

The fear in Kai's eyes shifted to confusion. Before he could answer, relief rushed through Elise's system as her brain registered what she was seeing. "Finn," she said urgently, "look at what he's holding."

Kai looked up as if seeing the mug for the first time and grimaced with disgust. "Why do you care about a coffee mug? We've got bigger problems." His eyes fell on the mug sitting on the table and sucked in a breath. "Oh no. That's not mine. You can fingerprint it or whatever, but look, that one is missing the 'C' in

Conservation. I'm missing the 'R' for Riverbend." He kept his hands in the air but turned the mug so they could see where the letter had been worn away by his thumb.

The breath whooshed out of Elise's lungs. "So, this wasn't you?"

"No! Of course not, Elise!"

Elise closed her eyes. "That's a relief."

Desperation flashed in Kai's eyes. "No, it isn't! Where did these animals come from? Why is Atma in a tiny cage? How did he get there?"

At that moment, they heard the sound of footsteps outside. Alexis grabbed Kai by the arm. "Come with me." In seconds, they were stuffed into a small supply closet by the front door.

Finn pulled Elise behind a set of terrariums holding the poison frogs, for whatever good it would do. The door opened a few inches, then opened fully. Elise's heart sank when she realized who else had been at the zoo long enough to have the old style of coffee mug.

The door closed with a loud bang, and Finn stepped out from behind the terrariums with his gun raised. "Freeze! Put your hands in the air."

Dr. Oliver placed the silver bucket he'd been holding on the ground and raised his hands as instructed. "Please don't shoot my animals."

"What's going on, Doc?" Elise's voice came out in almost a whisper.

At this, his eyes began to well with tears. "I had no choice, Elise."

"There's always a choice." Elise's voice was hard, rage bubbling up through her system. She finally understood why a mother bear was so scary when someone tried to hurt her cubs. This room, filled with some of the most valuable animals to poachers, represented everything she fought so hard to prevent.

"See, if we breed them, they won't take more from the wild." Dr. Oliver began to look around wildly. "And it helps the Conservation Center."

"Helps the Conservation Center?! Are you kidding me right now?" Elise's anger boiled to the surface and Finn took a step closer to Dr. Oliver, who was explaining the unexplainable with his hands still in the air.

"We were losing money." Dr. Oliver averted his gaze. "And we can use the funding from working with responsible owners to pay for the animals we help. Listen, everything in life is morally complicated. The funds were helping save animals."

"Oh. So these animals are being well taken care of by your poachers, your animal traffickers?"

"I make sure the people taking them know how to care for them like their own pets."

"A clouded leopard is a wild animal, not a pet." Elise gasped. "Your accident."

"I was visiting a customer." Dr. Oliver waved his hands in explanation. "And one of their animals was more defensive than I expected."

"You were attacked?! How are these animals better off?"

Dr. Oliver lowered his hands to gesture and Finn yelled, "In the air!"

Dr. Oliver thrust them back in the air, quivering. "Heath said..." Elise bit her lip to keep from swear words flying out. Of course, the zoo director had to know. Two keys were required to get into the enclosures. And that's why animals were disappearing when no one person was around enough to be responsible — there were two of them. "To pay our bills, you understand."

"Heath is skimming. That's why we needed the money." Elise shook her head. "Marlene's invoices were fabricated — she was donating her supplies. And I'll bet the construction company isn't charging what he said they were. He's lining his pockets."

Dr. Oliver's mouth dropped open. "He what?"

"Is he giving you a cut?" Elise snarled.

"No, I'm only keeping the Conservation Center's doors open. I thought. He told me that it needed to be done or we'd shut down." Dr. Oliver waved his hands. "Can I put these down now? You can handcuff me. I deserve it."

Finn snapped handcuffs on Dr. Oliver. "Did Kai have anything to do with this? Dr. Veronica? Freya?"

Dr. Oliver scoffed. "Kai would skin me alive if he knew. Dr. V would help him. They didn't understand what was at stake. Freya seemed to know something was off, but every time she questioned Heath, he'd get defensive and take away some of her work. So, she never figured us out."

Elise closed her eyes. "What else did Heath say?"

"He said the animals would get hurt if I didn't help. Or I could get hurt, but that wasn't what mattered."

"Did you threaten me?" Elise glared.

"I would never. Heath thought you were a risk."

Elise groaned. "My caller. It was Heath. I knew someone was modifying their voice."

"I told him if he did it again, I'd stop helping him. I didn't want any part of that. He threatened the cub once I came back, thought I'd have a change of heart and tell you what was going on. But the cub was worth too much and we already had a buyer lined up."

At that, Finn perked up. "When is the deal going down?"

"Tonight. That's where Heath's been. He's been setting up the enclosure, making sure the cub would be comfortable."

"Got to keep those customers happy," Elise said, bitterly. "I wish you would have come to us, Olly."

Dr. Oliver hung his head. "I was in too deep, kid. I was just trying to protect you all."

Finn tipped his head. "Come with me. If you're willing to help us track down Heath and the rest of his network, we'll see what we can do to reduce the charges. And I have a feeling that once Heath isn't running the facility, Riverbend's financial problems will suddenly be a lot more manageable."

A hopeful look sparked in Dr. Oliver's eyes. "Okay. That'll be okay."

CHAPTER 25

Three hours from Riverbend, in a parking lot near the chain breakfast restaurant on Heath's expense reports, a crew of FBI agents waited in the back of a Riverbend Animal Conservation Center van. They were joined by the Center's remorseful veterinarian, who was now wearing surveillance equipment. Local police had been notified and confirmed that there had been more traffic than usual around the land Dr. Oliver had described as the customer's house. Locals knew the owner kept a lot of animals but didn't know much else. However, whether the owner kept any illegal animals was unproven, as they lived quietly and kept to themselves, only coming into town for groceries and supplies.

Their wait was longer than expected. Heath was running late, perhaps to minimize the amount of time he could get caught. The clouded leopard was still at the Center, being cared for by Kai and Dr. Veronica, who seemed to be spending quite a lot more time together at the Conservation Center than was strictly necessary. Once Kai had realized the extent of Dr. Oliver's deception, he'd been remarkably understanding about being accused and subsequently stuffed into a supply closet with Alexis. Elise smiled despite the circumstances. Of all people, Kai deserved a happy ending.

Heath's car pulled into the drive and Dr. Oliver left the van. He approached the small group, the FBI filmed and recorded enough evidence, and when Dr. Oliver returned to the van with the excuse of picking up Atma, the clouded leopard, Heath and his customer were duly arrested and brought in for questioning.

For the first time in their investigation, Elise managed to stay away from the active crime scene. Of course, Finn had wisely piped in the audio from Dr. Oliver's microphone to the van, realizing that including Elise was key to keeping her safe. Finn's stubborn determination came in handy while he asked Heath and the property owner questions. Elise and he had already deduced so many details about them that when Finn started asking about Heath's partners in Nepal, Heath's scheme unraveled in record time. Finn's team would be more than busy making arrests, and catching the front man for the operation would make a huge dent in the profitability and anonymity of everyone involved.

After an hour of sitting with an increasingly impatient Zeke and a quiet FBI agent who didn't introduce himself, Elise was ready to go. Alexis gave her and Zeke a ride home. The rest of the team finished their interviews, collaborated with local police, and wrote their reports. The sun had set, and by all accounts, the team would be in for a long night.

When Elise and Zeke made it back home to their rented apartment, Elise threw her shoes in the closet and flopped on the couch. Zeke soon joined her, a freshly stored shoe in his mouth. She looked at the cracked closet door with one eye open, realizing too late that she hadn't gotten it fully shut. She eyed Zeke and the shoe tumbled out of his mouth. Elise gave him a pat and he rested his furry snout on her shoulder, nuzzling her. "I love you, even if you eat my shoes. After today, you probably deserve a shoe or two."

Zeke wagged his tail by way of reply. Her phone buzzed with a text from Zoey, and she groaned, sitting up. Fortunately, Zoey was only texting to let her know that she'd gotten all the details from Liam and would catch up with her later when she'd had some time to rest. It was so considerate Elise was almost certain Liam was behind it. She texted a reply. *Tell Liam I said thanks.*

Zoey's reply was instantaneous. *He made me behave.*

Elise snorted and closed her eyes, then she startled at the feeling of wet strings on her face. She opened one eye and Zeke pranced back a few steps, tail wagging. Without sitting up, she tossed his heavy rope down the hall and he scampered after it. After a few throws, rest seemed futile, and she rose to find her laptop to update her boss back at WWT headquarters. She started to draft an email, but after a few minutes of trying to sum up the past few days, she settled on a meeting request for the following afternoon in the only gap in Carmen's calendar. How, exactly, she was going to explain everything, she wasn't sure yet, but tomorrow was another day.

Her phone dinged again, and she resisted the urge to chuck it in the corner until she saw who sent the message. *It's going to be a late night. Breakfast tomorrow? -F*

Elise bit her lip. *It's a date.* Carmen would surely want her in Riverbend a little longer. Maybe the time would give her and Finn enough of a foundation to date from a distance. Or something. Too bad Marlene's shop was closed, and she'd have to do with her own regular chamomile tea tonight. Although, she'd be back to that soon enough. Riverbend was temporary, as odd as that felt. All of her antics with her sister and the largely well-intended nosiness of the community had started to grow on her. After even such a short time, she almost felt like she belonged.

CHAPTER 26

When Finn woke up, Sedona barely opened an eye instead of sprinting to the door and looking hopefully at her leash. The night before had netted more information than months spent traipsing through the jungle. His team would be tying up loose ends on this case for a long time. The on-the-ground work near the poachers was important, but Heath had been facilitating a poaching and breeding ring at a scale Ponzi schemers would be jealous of. And, like most gamblers, he couldn't quit. Nor did he ever realize the profits. He just kept squirreling away money for when he needed to disappear. His forced partnership with the WWT had been used as another networking opportunity, poking around for unscrupulous people by seeing the reports of problematic or suspicious activity firsthand.

The FBI would be deploying teams to shut down Heath's coconspirators and freeze his assets, which had been cleverly hidden in not-for-profits intended to enrich him once he decided to cash out. If he'd done so earlier, they never would have caught him. It wasn't the first time that greed helped them catch someone, and it wouldn't be the last.

Finn showered and shaved, checking the clock to make sure he'd make his date with Elise. How he was going to manage a relationship with her, he wasn't sure yet. But if they could chase down an animal trafficking ring hiding in plain sight in Riverbend, surely, they could find a way to make it work. Fortunately, Sedona and Finn spotted Elise and Zeke as they were leaving their apartment and before they made it down to the coffee shop. He swept her up and held her to him for a long and much-needed kiss. She felt like home. When he pulled away, she was flushed. "Good morning to you too."

"Good morning. Coffee?"

Elise lifted an eyebrow. "I think it can wait."

Several minutes later, they left Elise's apartment, substantially more rumpled than they had entered it and both grinning like fools. After taking the dogs outside for a quick break, they reached the coffee shop as the morning rush was nearing its end. Marlene discreetly whispered, "I heard you got them. Doctor Oliver *and* Heath. Who would have believed it?"

Finn eyed Marlene. "Seriously, Marlene, can we hire you?"

Marlene winked. "Your usual? Since you two seem to be a little flushed this morning, I can make it iced." She fanned herself dramatically. "It's a warm morning."

"Um, yes, iced coffee sounds nice." Elise's face nearly turned purple, and Finn reached for her hand. The same sparks he'd felt the first time they'd touched shot up his hand, but this time, she gave him a knowing smile. He stood frozen to the spot until he heard the bell jingle behind them.

A moment later, Alexis and Waffle walked in. "Good morning, everyone. Do you have a second, Finn?"

Elise groaned. "Do I want to know?"

Alexis smiled. "You might." She looked past Elise. "Can I get a small matcha latte, Marlene?"

"Of course, Alex. I'll get to work on it and you can come get it when you're ready. You seem like you have important matters to discuss."

Alexis led them to a small area at the back of the shop with comfy sofas. "Sorry to interrupt your morning, but, Finn, I wanted to talk to you. And, unless I'm wrong, you might want Elise's opinion."

Elise's eyes darted and Finn squeezed her hand, settling whatever internal debate she was having. "Alright. I'm listening."

"My management thinks it's worth starting a wildlife detection program and your management said your team wants to do more work stateside. What do you think about starting a program with us? Officially? Your first student-in-training has more than demonstrated it's possible. Just imagine the impact you could have if you and Sedona kept the program going. The FBI would still send you out as needed, so you could keep working with your team, but you'd be based here."

Finn nodded. "Thank you, Alex. I'd like to think about that and let you know, okay?"

Alexis stood. "Of course. We'll see you later today then. Take your time. I know you had a long night."

Finn took a sip of iced coffee. "Okay. That sounds good."

After Alexis left, Elise looked at Finn. "Well, that's nice. What are you going to say?"

He blew out a breath. "I'm running on like three hours sleep and my brain is not fully operational."

Marlene took Alexis's seat and Elise laughed. "Well, hello, Marlene."

"Are you going to take her job offer, Finn, or do we need to sweeten the pot?" Marlene wiped a coffee ring off a table with a spare napkin.

"All the coffee I can drink?" Finn chuckled. "That's tempting."

"Not exactly." Marlene studied Elise. "Do you know that

Thurston is on the board of directors for the Conservation Center?"

Elise bit her lip. "I do."

"Hm. Well, are you planning on going there today?"

Elise leapt up. "Yes. I should have gone sooner, I was just... processing." She snuck a glance at Finn, gathered up Zeke's leash, and before Finn could talk her into staying any longer, she left. Marlene stayed put, studying Finn carefully.

"Marlene, what do you have planned?" Finn eyed her.

Marlene responded by petting an off-duty Sedona. "Oh, I'm sure I don't know what you mean."

WHEN ELISE RETURNED to the Conservation Center, she was nearly bowled over by Kai running to greet her and pulling her into a hug. "You're okay!"

Elise chuckled. "I texted you as much."

"And then didn't show up at your normal time. After everything, I wasn't sure if you'd gotten hurt or we'd scared you into taking the first flight back to Colorado."

Elise smiled. "I'll stick around a little longer." She pushed a hand through her hair. "I have to meet with Carmen this afternoon anyway. I have to see how much longer she'll let me stay."

"Miss Butler, may I take a moment of your time?" The booming voice of Thurston Riley startled her. He looked a bit out of place at the Conservation Center instead of at Bridges. He looked particularly out of place wearing a well-worn khaki shirt with the Conservation Center's old logo on it. "And you too, Mr. Torres?"

Kai checked his watch. "Sure thing. I have half an hour I can spare."

Elise followed the men wordlessly to a conference room in the administrative building. For the first time since meeting her, Freya was beaming. Elise waved at the woman who looked like the weight of the world had just been taken off her shoulders. For a moment, Elise felt a pang of guilt for not digging deeper into why their administrative assistant seemed so stressed around her boss. However, if Freya's smile was any indication, it would soon be a distant memory.

Soon, they were all settled around a conference table. Elise folded her hands on top of it. "Can I help you, Mayor Riley?"

"As you know, I'm on the board of directors for the Conservation Center." Generally, someone in her role didn't interact with the BOD unless they were in trouble, but after yesterday, it was natural he'd have some questions. "And Marlene has filled us in on your role in stopping the illegal activity here. We had an emergency meeting this morning to discuss it."

Elise swallowed hard. "I assure you, had I been sure the board wasn't involved, I would have informed you."

Thurston waved away her concerns. "Of course. I've already spoken with Alexis and she cleared the whole thing up. But you understand, we are in need of a new director for the Conservation Center."

Elise nodded. "I'm happy to support a search. The WWT has a database—"

Thurston waved away her offer. "I think we've found our candidate."

"Oh! That's wonderful, Mayor Riley. And fast. I can let Carmen know this afternoon." Her heart tripped a little at the realization she'd be going back to Colorado earlier than planned, but she kept her smile even.

Thurston grinned. "I hope you will. We'd like you to stick around Riverbend as the director of the Riverbend Animal Conservation Center. It's a big job, but you've proven yourself more than capable. And we need someone who knows the ins and outs of finance and animals to get us back on our feet." He slid a piece of paper across the table. It wasn't anywhere near what she would make at an accounting firm in Denver, but it was enough for Riverbend, Indiana.

The air whooshed out of Elise's lungs. "Wow. I. Wow. Thank you. For the offer. Are you sure about this?" She put a hand to her chest. "I just never thought I'd be considered for something like this. Do you think I have enough experience?"

Kai grinned and looked at Thurston. "That's not a no."

Thurston nodded. "I'd rather have integrity and grit than experience, Elise. You seem to have that in spades. The board has experience to spare. In fact, we might drive you nuts with all of our experience."

Elise nodded. "Let me think about it, okay? It's been a bonkers night and the FBI team should be here soon to finish cleaning everything up. Meanwhile, I've got to place all the animals from the storage shed into proper enclosures and find them permanent homes."

Thurston stroked his generous mustache. "So, you can't accept because you'll be too busy doing the actual job to think about it? I'll take that for now."

Elise shook her head and looked between the two men. "I better get back to work."

AFTER A FULL DAY at Riverbend Animal Conservation Center, answering messages, working with zookeepers, catching up with her boss back in Denver, and liaising with Finn's team, Elise didn't have time to consider her job offer until she brought Zeke back to her apartment. A knock sounded moments after she'd collapsed on the couch. She dragged herself to the door and opened it to Finn holding a Curva del Río bag. "Even if we weren't sort of dating, I would totally kiss you right now if you brought tacos."

Finn leaned in for the promised kiss. "Good to know. Alexis told me about your job offer. It's crazy, right? This town doesn't want us to leave."

Elise put the tacos down on her kitchen counter and threw a ball for Zeke. "I'm not sure if that's a bad thing or not. I like it here, it was just unexpected. And, Finn, we've barely gotten past flirting. What if we annoy each other in a week? We can't make life decisions this quickly."

Finn wrapped a hand around her back. "I can think of much dumber decisions I've made much faster."

"Carmen said she understood if I didn't want to leave." The words tumbled out of Elise's mouth. "But this wasn't in my ten-year plan."

Finn kissed her and smiled against her mouth. "What if this is even better? Don't you think it's worth taking some time to find out?"

Zeke's tail thumped and he rested his head against her leg. Sedona nudged him out of the way and pushed her nose into Elise's hand. Elise grinned. "I think it just might be."

Veronica and Kai feature in Book 3 of the Riverbend K-9 Series! **Find more small-town mischief, new mysteries to solve, and plenty of wagging tails with each book in the Riverbend K-9 Series.**

Join Alexis on her earlier crime-solving adventures with the FBI in The Calculated Series. You'll find clever women in STEM, a race to solve a crime (or two), and a dash of romance in every book!

NOTE FROM THE AUTHOR

Thank you, dear reader, for joining my characters and me on this adventure! If you enjoyed this book...

1. Leave a review on Goodreads, Bookbub, or your favorite book retailer. Even a short review is a great way to help other readers find this book!

2. Sign up for my newsletter for exclusive content and news about new releases at: https://ktleeauthor.com/

3. Follow me on social media:
   Twitter: @ktleewrites
   Instagram: @ktleeauthor
   Facebook: https://www.facebook.com/ktleewrites

4. More books are in the works! Visit https://ktleeauthor.com/ to stay updated on new releases and find all of K.T. Lee's books.

ACKNOWLEDGMENTS

Thank you so much to Bonnie and Emily at the Fort Wayne Zoo, who took the time to answer my questions about clouded leopards specifically and zookeeping in general. Getting to talk with you both was an absolute highlight of writing this book. It's clear that you are both passionate about helping animals and educating people about them. All mistakes are mine or taken as artistic liberties for the story.

Thank you, as always, to my incredibly supportive family. To my husband and kids who root for me in this crazy adventure — your support is not something I take for granted. Thank you to my mom, who helped beta read this book and as usual, offered great suggestions and feedback. Thank you also to my sister, who also provided feedback and more than a little inspiration for Zoey and Elise's sisterly banter. I am grateful I have the kind of sister I can laugh with. I promise not to lick my food to keep you from sharing it now that we're adults, unless it's absolutely necessary. Thank you also to Jenni, whose friendship and funny texts about writing are appreciated even more than I appreciate you beta reading, which is saying a lot. As always, my dear friend Emily is a huge source of support and it's been so fun reading your writing now too. Thank you to my dad, who not only roots for these books, but reads every single one and shares his knowledge with me about cop and military stuff whenever I need his help.

Last but not least, any author will tell you the difference a great editor makes to a story and I will always add my voice to that chorus. For Laura Anderson's enthusiasm and helpful feedback, I'm extremely grateful. Thank you also to Aimee Walker for her eagle eye for typos — I appreciate your work on this series!

ABOUT THE AUTHOR

K.T. Lee is a writer, mom, and engineer who grew up on a steady diet of books from a wide variety of genres. She's the author of multiple books, including those in the Riverbend K-9 Series and The Calculated Series.

Printed in Great Britain
by Amazon

87384862R10144